CUMBRIA LIBRARIES

3 8003 04128 8457

MAL

County

KT-408-114

Libr

SPECIAL MESSAGE TO READERS

THE ULVERSCROFT FOUNDATION
(registered UK charity number 264873)
was established in 1972 to provide funds for
research, diagnosis and treatment of eye diseases.
Examples of major projects funded by
the Ulverscroft Foundation are:-

- The Children's Eye Unit at Moorfields Eye Hospital, London
- The Ulverscroft Children's Eye Unit at Great Ormond Street Hospital for Sick Children
- Funding research into eye diseases and treatment at the Department of Ophthalmology, University of Leicester
- The Ulverscroft Vision Research Group, Institute of Child Health
- Twin operating theatres at the Western Ophthalmic Hospital, London
- The Chair of Ophthalmology at the Royal Australian College of Ophthalmologists

You can help further the work of the Foundation
by making a donation or leaving a legacy.
Every contribution is gratefully received. If you
would like to help support the Foundation or
require further information, please contact:

THE ULVERSCROFT FOUNDATION
The Green, Bradgate Road, Anstey
Leicester LE7 7FU, England
Tel: (0116) 236 4325

website: www.foundation.ulverscroft.com

Brian Van Reet was born in Houston and grew up there and in western Maryland. Following the September 11 attacks, he dropped out of the University of Virginia, where he was an Echols Scholar, and enlisted in the U.S. army as a tank crewman. He served in Iraq under stop-loss orders, achieved the rank of sergeant, and was awarded a Bronze Star for valour. After an honourable discharge, he studied at the University of Missouri and later at the University of Texas. His fiction has been recognised with awards and fellowships from the Michener Center for Writers, Gulf Coast, and the *Iowa Review*, with stories and essays also appearing in the *New York Times*, the *Daily Beast*, the *Washington Post*, and in various literary magazines and anthologies, including *Fire and Forget*. He has twice won the Texas Institute of Letters short story award. He lives in Austin with his wife and two children.

You can discover more about the author at https://brianvanreet.com

SPOILS

It is the spring of 2003, and coalition forces are advancing on Iraq. Images of a giant statue of Saddam Hussein crashing to the ground in Baghdad are being beamed to news channels around the world. Nineteen-year-old Specialist Cassandra Wigheard, on her first deployment since joining the U.S. army two years earlier, is primed for war. But for Abu al-Hool, a jihadist since the days of the Soviet occupation of Afghanistan, war is wearing thin. Two decades of fighting — and the new wave of super-radicalized fighters joining the ranks in the wake of the September 11 attacks — have left him questioning his commitment to the struggle. When Cassandra is taken prisoner by al-Hool's mujahideen brotherhood, both fighters will find their loyalties tested to the very limits.

BRIAN VAN REET

◆

SPOILS

Complete and Unabridged

CHARNWOOD
Leicester

First published in Great Britain in 2017 by
Jonathan Cape
an imprint of Vintage Publishing
London

First Charnwood Edition
published 2018
by arrangement with
Vintage Publishing
Penguin Random House
London

The moral right of the author has been asserted

Copyright © 2017 by Brian Van Reet
All rights reserved

A catalogue record for this book is available
from the British Library.

ISBN 978–1–4448–3649–3

Published by
F. A. Thorpe (Publishing)
Anstey, Leicestershire

Set by Words & Graphics Ltd.
Anstey, Leicestershire
Printed and bound in Great Britain by
T. J. International Ltd., Padstow, Cornwall

This book is printed on acid-free paper

For Heidi

PART I

Low lie the shattered towers whereas they fell,
And I — ah burning heart! — shall soon lie low
  as well.

— Aeschylus

1

Cassandra: Roundabout

```
Iraq (Triangletown): day of
```

She is the most dangerous thing around. The best soldiers are like her, just on the far side of childhood. Their exact reasons for fighting don't matter much. They can carry deep resentments or have been blessed with an easygoing temperament; fear and shame are the army's two great teaching tools, and they work equally well on most personality types. The main thing, what makes Cassandra good at soldiering, is simply her age. The training won't transform anyone much over thirty. No amount of drilling and shouting and rote repetition through pain and humiliation and hardship can erase the kind of wariness that comes through the accumulated calamity of years, the adult fear of death that makes taking the kind of risks you must take to personally win a ground war too unlikely a feat for anyone but a megalomaniac, a latent suicide, or a teenager.

This one is bored tonight. Rather than guard the roundabout, she would move closer to the war's hot center. Even with what she has seen so far, she wants more. She knows this is a naive and even foolhardy thing to want. Nevertheless, the desire is there, this crazy urge to strap on her rifle and leave behind the Humvee, Crump and McGinnis, to walk the dark and rainy highway to Baghdad like a modern-day *ronin*. A ridiculous thought, but lingering. The rain pelts her parka with a crackling sound, and rainwater beads on the black oily machine gun in front of her. Never would've thought it could rain so hard in Iraq. Leaning against the rim of the gunner's hatch, she wipes the fifty's action with a soggy towel and stows the towel and jams her hands into the armholes of her bulletproof vest. Wet, exposed, the skin has begun to blanch, joints stiffening, a wave of shivers, thinking off and on about Haider, his fruitless search for a doctor for his sister.

Time passes, and Sergeant McGinnis knocks on the Humvee's roof.

'Wigheard. Put the cover on the fifty and get in here.'

For half an hour the rain has been blowing diagonally into their truck through the gunner's hatch, soaking McGinnis and, to a lesser degree, Private Crump, who has the good fortune to be seated on the leeward side. Crump is asleep again. Snoring in an odd rhythm, he takes quick sharp breaths, his face smushed against the foggy driver's-side window.

She'd been on the verge of asking if she could be relieved from her post for a few minutes to sit inside the truck and warm up. But when this relief becomes an order, she resents it a little, decides to have some fun with it.

'Negative,' she says, pitching her voice too

chipper. 'Shit, Sar'nt. Send Crump's sleepy ass up here. Then I'll come down.'

'Wigheard. Shut that damn hatch and get in here.'

She can't help but grin at his kindness veiled in saltiness, ducking into the truck's cab, taking a knee on the transmission hump that doubles as the platform on which she has been standing to gun. She squats deeply, swings the hatch over her, and buttons it tight. Rain peppers the roof, and the steady staccato drum of it, like a million ghostly fingertips rapping on the truck, diffuses the throaty growl of its diesel. McGinnis and Crump have the heater running full-bore. Right away she can feel it drying the black fleece she wears under her parka and body armor, drying her skin and eyeballs. Apparently, the heater is the one thing on this ramshackle vehicle that works perfectly.

She scoots from the gunner's platform into one of the rear canvas seats. The Humvee's interior is a dun-colored exercise in sharp edges and constricted, cost-saving efficiencies. McGinnis has added the only human touches. Fuzzy dice dangle from the rearview, and on the die-cut aluminum dashboard, he has taped a novelty baseball card featuring a photo of his son in a Little League uniform, Louisville Slugger slung over his shoulder, sweaty mop of hair plastered under a red ball cap.

The photo makes Cassandra uneasy. Has from the very start, back in Kuwait, when he taped it there. She thinks it's a bad idea for it to be posted on the dash, where he can't escape the

5

kid — she is having trouble even remembering his name — always occupying his father's line of sight, continually reminding him of the stakes, what he might lose if he were to slip up. It's like McGinnis is deliberately tormenting himself.

Her eyes have grown inflamed from lack of sleep and the recycled hot air steadily blowing, and she blinks to wet them, losing focus sleepily, the kid's photo blurring into a nondescript splotch. She's lulled by the darkness and the roaring heater and the rain that pools on the gunner's hatch and drips through a leaky rubber seal. Like Chinese water torture. Like they are trapped in an unsound submarine. With the hatch closed it has grown muggy inside, hot and slimy as a locker room with all the showerheads blasting steam. Beads of condensation join in branched rivulets that dart down the windows, themselves no more than flexible sheets of vinyl. Their crew wasn't lucky enough to draw an up-armored truck. Lieutenant Choi and his bunch have received the only one allotted for the platoon. Their own is nothing but a rolling coffin. No, not even that sturdy. Oak would at least stop some shrapnel, but these vinyl doors wouldn't stop a pellet gun.

The heater, the rain, sleeplessness, bring on a rheumy-eyed stupor, fuzzy and electronic. Her pruned hands twitch involuntarily, a hypnic jerk acute enough to bring her back. She wills her eyes open. McGinnis and Crump are both nodded off in the front seats. Radio and GPS cables lie kinked around them like black umbilical cords; there's the humming sound of

6

the truck, and, half dreaming, caught in the tripping sensation of present eternity dwarfing the past, for a moment she forgets herself and might be convinced that all her days have been lived like this, in here, the truck, the only solid place in the universe.

★   ★   ★

The three of them jolt awake at the same time. Something pounding on the hood, *thunk thunk thunk*.

McGinnis just sits there rigidly, looking out from under a confusion of gear. She's never seen him like this. All through their predeployment training, the poison-gas drills in Kuwait, the first weeks of the war, he always seemed so competent, poised, always with the answers, and now it shakes her to see him lacking.

Crump stops waiting for someone to tell him what to do. He shoots forward and with his sleeve wipes the film of moisture that obscures the view out the windshield. At the same time, Cassandra dings her knee scrambling from the backseat to throw open the hatch, man her station, charge the fifty; she takes an underhanded grip on the gun's handle but before she can rack a round, she sees it is only Haider, down near the hood of the truck. The kid looks even thinner now that he has been soaked in the rain, his green nylon soccer jersey clinging to his skin.

McGinnis sees him, too, and curses in both relief and anger at the kid who has officially graduated into a pest with this second appearance at the traffic circle. 'See,' McGinnis says, projecting his voice up through the hatch, 'this is why we don't feed them. We're an army. We're not damn Save the Children.' He reaches back and unlatches the passenger's door, flinging it open, and Haider climbs into the truck, out of the rain.

Cassandra drops back into the cab.

'Special-ist, my friend.' The boy points down the highway in the direction of Triangletown. 'There. Mujahideen. Very bad Ali Baba.'

The woodcutter from *One Thousand and One Nights*, a rare point of cultural overlap between them and the locals, has in a short span of time come to be conflated with the den of thieves that he stumbles on, a kind of literary guilt by association, *Ali Baba* standing in for any bad guy.

'Ah, bullshit,' Crump says. 'You know he's just playing us for more chocolate. Watch, he's about to ask for some.'

'Long way to come in the rain just for that,' she says.

McGinnis looks Haider squarely in the face. 'Where did you see the mujahideen?'

'They go . . . *Kay fallah quooloo* . . . They go to the father to my father.'

'Your grandfather?'

'Grandfather, yes. He is sheikh. He is saying to them, *Ishta, ishta*. Mujahideen are saying . . . ' In pantomime he acts like he is driving a car that crashes. He beats his hands on an imaginary steering wheel in frustration. 'They are wanting good car. Grandfather Toyota. They take.'

8

'When — today? Tonight?'

'Today, yes.' Haider nods enthusiastically and cranes his neck like he is peering over the horizon. Then he turns back to McGinnis, his face suddenly too serious for a child's. 'Mujahideen and you are like this.' He finishes the thought by drawing the index finger of his good hand like a blade across his throat. 'My friend, go now, okay? Very bad for you here. We go soon. Sister, very bad. We are leaving to doctor. Okay? You leave now?'

'Hell no, we ain't running,' Crump says. 'Go back where you came from. Tell them dickless muja fucks to bring it on.'

'Hey,' McGinnis says. 'Quiet, all you.' He picks up the handheld mic and keys the military-radio net. He raises Lieutenant Choi, parked on the far side of the roundabout, using his on-air call sign. 'Red One, this is Three. I've got a local national here advising foreign fighters may be in our AO. Over.'

There follows a ponderous silence, a static squelch, a clearing of a throat, the lieutenant, sounding sleepy: 'Three, say again?'

McGinnis scowls at the hand mic. He breaks radio protocol by slipping into the vernacular, enunciating each word and phrase with admonishing clarity. 'LT. I've just been told by a local kid. Jihadis went through Triangletown earlier. Supposedly they're driving a Toyota. How copy? Over.'

'Roger. I'm calling it up to Higher. Wait one.'

The radio falls silent while Lieutenant Choi switches frequencies from platoon to company, where he will pass the intelligence report to the captain, who will in turn call Lieutenant Colonel Easton on the battalion frequency and deliver the news. Both of these last two officers are back at Palace Row, in the battalion's operations center. It seems so difficult for any of her junior leaders to make a critical decision on their own in the field. Though it isn't really their fault. They aren't naturally cowards or idiots. They are, for the most part, highly able and motivated, but they've been trained *not* to act independently, instead to report the situation up the chain of command, sit tight, and await further guidance. Death by micromanagement.

The lieutenant comes back over the net. 'Three, this is One. Battalion says they've called the report in to Brigade. They're saying charlie mike for now.' *Charlie mike* is alpha-phonetic shorthand for *continue the mission*. Maintain their position at the roundabout.

'I copy. Break.' McGinnis goes on to tell the other three truck crews that Haider will be passing back through their perimeter. *Hold your fire. Don't shoot the kid*. It's not a good sign he was able to sneak through their lines in the first place. No one mentions it, but Cassandra is thinking it, we fucked up, bad. Everyone sheltering from the rain, catching z's, and she's pissed at McGinnis for encouraging her — maybe not to fall asleep — but he did tell her to leave her post and take a break; he let them all fall asleep and did it himself. She stares at the back of his head as he briefs the other trucks on Haider's intel. When he finishes with the radios he sets the hand mic on the dash near the baseball card of his son, brushing his forefinger along the edge of the photo to straighten it where it has started to curl in the humidity, taking refuge for a moment in that mawkish sentiment when instead he should be arguing the case with headquarters, insisting on permission to go out and hunt the enemy. Why else are they here if not for that?

'So we're not going to collapse this thing and drive around looking for these guys? Just sit here and wait for them to hit us. Bullshit, Sar'nt.'

He turns around in his seat and ruffles Haider's thick black hair at the same time that he gives her a canny look. She gets the message: Show solidarity in front of outsiders, even if children. 'Thanks for what you did,' he tells Haider. 'That was brave of you to come out here alone. But you have to go home now. You understand ?'

★   ★   ★

She suspects she might've taken one too many. The crew has been passing around its communal bottle of diet pills, dosing themselves in the four hours since Haider left the truck. No more falling asleep on watch. The kid's warning, heeded.

Hydroxycut is the thing for staying awake, but she wishes she would've stopped while she was ahead, about two pills ago. She works her jaw muscles and scrapes her tongue over a palate gone dry with tacky cotton mouth, head aching,

11

blood vessels constricted by stimulant, her focus inexplicably stuck on a few lines of jogging cadence sung during early-morning physical training sessions at Fort Hood before they deployed.

Line a hundred Iraqis up against a wall.
Bet a hundred dollars I couldn't kill 'em all.
Shot ninety-eight till my barrel turned blue.
Then I pulled out my knife and stabbed the
other two.

Stupid stuff, she knows. Nothing more than brutal background noise, but she hasn't gotten more than a few hours' sleep at any one time in the past three days, and her mind is doing strange things. No matter how much she wants to, she can't close her eyes, and even if she did, no sleep would come. Her heart feels like it's working too hard, straining itself like a leaky pump with more air than blood rushing through fleshy valves. Time stretches thinner and thinner, shedding its one elemental quality, forward progression, like a strand of gold spun so fine, it loses its atomic color and becomes clear.

McGinnis flexes his knees to keep limber. From her vantage point inside the truck, he's a pair of disembodied legs, the rest of him extending out the hatch, pulling a shift behind the fifty, her relief. This time, when he offered to take her place up there, she didn't object, not even to joke.

Couple hours after dark, the rain stops. The wind hasn't. The latest chatter on the radio is about a sandstorm that Brigade is tracking. A shamal — as some show-off staff officer keeps calling it — blowing in on the back edge of the cold front that brought rain to central Iraq as a dry western wind rushed across the country, hitting the moist salt air coming off the gulf.

Crump listens to the traffic about the storm and sneers at the blinking radio console when he hears something he doesn't like. He squirms incessantly behind the wheel as if sitting on a tack. His right foot pumps the brake, the pedal on an imagined kick drum, and with his thumbs he taps an angry beat on the dash.

'They's fucking fools,' he declares in response to nothing, his abrasive tenor wavering under the effect of jangly stimulants and wrath. Boys that age, she thinks. The absolute worst.

He waits for her to take the bait, to ask why they — whoever they are — are fools. She expects he will soon embark on one of his asinine political tangents. His views on modern life are uncomplicated, to put it kindly. Against her better judgment, however, she decides to indulge him. Bullshitting to kill the time, besides the killing itself, is the one great and necessary art form practiced in the army. In these circumstances, to deny conversation to a willing participant is just plain mean.

'Who's a fool?' she asks, making sure he can tell she's not particularly interested.

'Who you think?' He readjusts himself in the front seat, picking at his groin, and pulls a knee up so he can face her, his long chin like a starving Appalachian's. 'Higher, duh. We could be out getting some. Or, back at the Row, where it's safe, before this sandstorm hits. I get the feeling they forgot about us.'

'No kidding.' Leave it to Crump to state the obvious.

He turns in his seat to face forward again. He worries a flap of torn rubber on the steering wheel. 'All I know is, none of this is like I thought it would be. This ain't no way to fight a war. But I'll tell you what they need to do. You ready for this — it's real fucking simple. One word. *Nukes.*'

'Jesus, Crump.'

'Hear me out. I'm serious. Forget camping by this trash heap all fucking night in the wind and rain. Forget Humvees and dirt kids and moo-juh-huh-deens and all the rest of this shit. We got to start showing these hajjis who's boss. 'Oh, you wanna blow up the World Trade?' Errrr — wrong — nuke your ass. Tell you what. There's one thing that wins a fight. Punching harder than the other guy.'

There is humor in his tirade but not a splinter of irony. He is actually advocating preemptive nuclear war. She rolls her eyes at him, even though he can't currently see her in the backseat. What is it like to be inside his head? The Crump brain, gray matter calcified, frontal lobes shrunken like dried beans to shiver and rattle inside the skull's brittle gourd. The army has distilled and eventually dissolved his every sense of nuance and tact, although she doubts he had much of either to begin with. For a person like him, military life eats away like acid at those softer,

14

finer qualities, reducing everything to the toughest, starkest of truths. War is about utterly destroying the enemy. Yes, sometimes. But we're not doing that, not even trying to. We're just sitting here, targets ourselves. Therefore, this isn't a real war. This must be some other kind of mess.

Cassandra can sympathize with his point of view. On the one hand, in the lead-up to the invasion, they were told, over and over, to the point of indoctrination, that one half of their mission was to free this country, that they would go down in history as the great liberators of the Iraqi people. On the other hand, they trained to liberate them by doing things like jogging in cadence to cute little ditties about slaughter.

> Shot ninety-eight till my barrel turned blue.
> Then I pulled out my knife and democra-
>   tized the other two.

The army's mixed messages troubled guys like Crump in the same way that sanitizing a needle before sliding it into the forearm of a death row inmate would trouble any thoughtful executioner. Guys like Crump hate fakeness more than anything, she thinks, the way the politicians cloak something as basic as war in grand ideas. Funny how, despite their misgivings, guys like him never seem to arrive at the right explanation for the big lie, for the gap between what is said and what is meant, the difference between what they know to be the army's true purpose, to kill people and destroy property, and its advertised purpose, Operation Iraqi Freedom, or, as he has taken to calling it, Operation Iraqi Fuckdown. Crump craves something rawer, 'realer' — another of his favorite words — and never quite grasps the true reason for sanitizing the poison needle.

Then again, she wonders if she could be guilty of the same flaw she has assumed in him. The sin of underestimation. She believes he has underestimated the depth of logic behind the army's scheme, and likewise, possibly, she may have misjudged his reaction to army life. It could be that he only plays the role of provocative jester, taking on the part as a protest, a way to pass the time, to hide the depths of himself, or simply as a familiar mask worn by a class clown, C+ high school student whose primary social outlet was *World of Warcraft*.

'I don't think you believe half the shit coming out your own mouth,' she says.

'Whatever. Hey. Who got the stash, anyway? Hook a brother up.'

'Your call, Sar'nt.' She peers up at McGinnis, still at his station in the hatch.

'Go ahead and give him another one,' he says. 'Maybe it'll make his brain explode.'

'We can hope.'

Cassandra passes the bottle of Hydroxycut to Crump, considers the possibility of pseudoamphetamine psychosis, and grasps her leg with fingers clawlike behind the knee, pinching herself to induce pain as a reality check.

Crump taps a horse pill into his palm. 'Wigheard. Lemme get your canteen real quick. I'm dry.'

'You would be.' She starts to pass it to him

16

when there comes to them a pinging sound like a sledgehammer striking a railway spike far away. The wind and the dark fields of trash and rubble flatten the sharp sound, and then another and another like it, which arrive in quick, steady succession — *ping, ping, ping.*

'Christ,' McGinnis says. 'What now?'

They've been in country five weeks and never under fire, or they would've known already. There is enough time for him to wonder and ask that question, hanging as the mortars complete their high invisible parabola to fall a hundred meters behind them, the rounds lighting up the black skyline like sulfur flashbulbs, cracking explosions changing the air pressure.

McGinnis drops inside the truck and swings himself into the commander's seat, fumbling for the hand mic.

'Fuck those radios!' Cassandra explodes on her sergeant in a way she never has before and moves toward the gunner's hatch to replace him — someone has to be up there on the fifty — but he reaches back to block her way.

'Stay under cover!'

'You call this cover?' She punches the flimsy fiberglass roof and looks at him in disbelief.

He concedes the point and allows her to climb up to the gun. She fights to stay loose. Every muscle in her body wants to clinch up like she's on a plane about to make a crash landing. The next barrage of mortars is already on its way, hurtling Doppler-shifted directly over-head; whoever is doing the shooting has readjusted their tube. The salvo misses the roundabout again, but not by as much, blowing geysers of earth on the far side of the concertina. Pebbles thrown by the blast skitter across asphalt. A burst of machine gun fire from Specialist Worthy, the gunner on Treanor's truck, who starts shooting — at what, Cassandra can't tell. Maybe he has spotted the mortar team or more likely is firing at an ominous-looking shadow, an unlucky farm animal mistaken for the enemy, or at nothing at all. But once the shooting starts, the other gunners follow suit, flinging tracer rounds like rays of solid red light.

The third salvo is a concussion that sucks the air out of her lungs and sprays shrapnel ringing like bird shot against the Humvee's engine block, the truck listing down and to the left as two of its tires blow. The blast raises a white cloud, mist of atomized chalk, and she too starts to shoot, firing the fifty blindly into the dark field where she thinks the mortar team might be set, based on the sound of the pings, the buzzing flight of the rounds. Maybe a thousand meters away — they would be at least that far, but then again one of them has to be much closer, spotting, using a radio to call in the targets. There's no way they could've adjusted fire so quickly and accurately without help from a forward spotter. So, spray the whole goddamn field.

The gun bucks and clatters in its mount like a centrifugal machine spinning out of control, the truck's roof juddering under the recoil. A weird feeling replaces the tension she experienced just as the attack started. This new sensation is the unnatural calm that comes after a disaster has begun. She has known a few disasters in nineteen years but none more alarming to her youthful invulnerability than this. Someone is actually trying to kill me, she has to tell herself, repeating it like a mantra to make it seem real. Which it soon does. But the strangest thing is how little hate there is in it. She doesn't hate them at all for trying. It seems only right, even essential, that it should happen this way, killing and being killed, the enemy dispassionately working a mechanical device, plotting the azimuth and elevation, aligning the tube, dropping in the shell that might flatten her skull on the asphalt. Without ever having seen her. Or she them. Sending rounds blindly downrange through the white cloud of dust and gun smoke, squeezing the trigger paddle on the fifty and holding on with all she has, forcing the barrel to the correct elevation — with each round expended it continually wants to ride up — and she gets a glimpse of her tracers and thinks they're probably too high to be effective but who can tell; she doesn't have a target to shoot at. Everything breaks down to chance. There is no getting out of this.

One minute has passed since the first mortar fell. Crump and McGinnis are still sheltering down below in the truck. Neither has let off a round. McGinnis is on the radio. Not much else they can do down there, with no heavy weapons, only their rifles at hand, no clue where to shoot, but still, they shouldn't be in the truck. Seek cover. First rule in a firefight. They're effectively on a road in the middle of a field, the nearest structure hundreds of meters away. McGinnis barks something over the net that sounds like *Drive!* but her ears are almost worthless. The only thing she can control is whether or not to keep shooting bursts, hunkering down behind the gun and not letting off the trigger as another salvo falls, a death from above as impersonal as lightning. Down below, the driver's door opens, and Crump stumbles into the street, clutching his face, yelling: black blood falls from his hands, stringy flesh draped on his cheek. The other door opens, and McGinnis looks up at her helplessly before ducking around to the back side, out of her line of fire, going for Crump, who has stumbled farther away and tripped over a roll of concertina, thus entangling himself in razor wire. Everything going to shit too fast to believe. In her periphery Sergeant Gonzales's truck billows thick smoke from its engine compartment, threatening a greater fire, its crew frantically off-loading ammo. Gonzales grabs a can in each hand and moves out full tilt for the irrigation canal across the road. He clears the concertina obstacle with a leap that would've been comical if not for the fact he's running for his life. He dashes across the last piece of open ground and goes for it again and lands like a long jumper in the canal, the lowest point around, best cover from shrapnel, and suddenly the rest of the platoon realizes this, and other soldiers abandon their trucks and the heavy weapons mounted atop for the safety of stagnant water.

McGinnis cuts Crump out of the wire with his

multi-tool and begins to drag him, also making for the canal, turning back a few times to wave and yell at Cassandra to follow, ordering her to, but she is too focused on firing the fifty, which she does until she runs out of ammo. She stoops inside the truck and grabs another can, heaving the steel box of rounds onto the roof. She clips the can in place and starts to feed the belt into the gun's action when more mortars come in and gouge craters in the asphalt with white-hot blasts pressing heat and pressure on her from all sides, sending sharp jags of metal whirring past her face. She quails a moment but regains her footing in the hatch and is just thinking how crazy it is that she is still alive when she sees specks of blood darkening her sleeve below the elbow, stinging, pain, and knowing it, shrapnel, it's inside me; something about this thought absolutely horrifies her and makes her want to puke, not the pain, it's not bad, still obscured by adrenaline, but the thought of her body's integrity being breached, and it has happened, and there is no taking it back.

She doesn't quit. Still fumbling to reload the new belt, she spins each way in the hatch and surveys the roundabout and gets for the first time that she is the only gunner remaining. Everyone else has broken for cover. Fifty meters away, McGinnis crouches on the canal bank, silhouetted against the black torpid water, waving her on.

The dark speckling has become a wetness, and her hand feels numb, like she has fallen asleep on her arm, dripping blood from the crook, she smears it over the belted machine gun rounds, slickening the brass casings as she struggles to seat them correctly in the extractor lever, but the fucking piece of shit won't seat right, or maybe she's what's really broken. Woozy, knowing it's now or never, she releases her hold on the fifty, the long barrel seesaws up, and she boosts herself out of the hatch and clambers down the hood, stumbling through the roundabout, through the gap in the wire, McGinnis meeting her halfway to the canal. On the banks her knees buckle and she drops. He's been supporting her and grabs the collar of her tactical vest, dragging her the rest of the way in. Her body breaks the dirty froth on the water. It feels warm against her skin, warmer than the air, reviving her some, and she's able to shrug him off and stand unsupported. She takes a step deeper into the canal, away from the bank, affording Aguirre, the medic, some room to work on Crump. Aguirre is bandaging his face with gauze, and with the blood soaking through, it looks like a botched plastic surgery.

She takes another step away, hip-deep now, boots filling with water, sinking to the ankles in the silty layer of detritus on the canal's bottom, which is steeply sloped in a V shape. The mud takes her feet until she's afraid she won't be able to free herself, that she'll be sucked in deeper and will drown with her feet stuck to the bottom like a mouse in a glue trap. With a great effort she draws her boots out and sloshes against McGinnis, where she falls again and stops resisting his attempts to render aid.

She lies against the matted cane roots growing out of the bank. She loses consciousness, seconds, minutes. When she awakes she's on her back. The clouds are moving fast as dawn nears, and they are tinged a deep slate green that reminds her of something she can't put her finger on. Something important from home had that same color, she can't think of what it is, but is lucid enough to know it doesn't matter. There are strange sounds, like popcorn in a pressure cooker, a crescendo of popping getting closer, louder, a man screams; she thinks it might be Gonzales. A rush of motion as someone else splashes clumsily out of the water, making a run for it. Popping and splashing. A firefight. Blood in the water invisible for all the black.

'Fuck this!' McGinnis shouts. 'Fuck it so fucking much!'

He's not shooting back. She realizes he's not going to. Some of the platoon are, but everyone needs to. It's hard to say exactly what is what; Aguirre and McGinnis huddle over her and block most of her view. Aguirre is cutting off her uniform sleeve with first-aid shears, telling her she's okay, to keep still, keep quiet. He is focused entirely on saving her, not on the mayhem around him, and at some level she feels grateful for that, tries to obey, to keep still, keep quiet, but her legs tense involuntarily and her boot heels gouge underwater channels. She has to fight. They all do. The medic cinches an Israeli-made battle tourniquet around her upper arm. The black nylon bites into her flesh, folding veins and arteries into themselves with a warm pain that hurts more than the shrapnel. He manages to get the tourniquet secure. Then is shot and collapses on top of her with all the ceremony of a snipped flower, warm dead weight stifling her cries.

McGinnis yanks her free from underneath and drags her into the canal, over which streams of glowing red and green tracers hurtle gracefully like a hail of burning arrows launched over the walls of a medieval fortress. She drifts away from the bank into water too deep to touch bottom and goes under, managing with one arm to unbuckle her vest that is trying to drown her, and shrugs it off, sinking deeper into the dark tangle of fluid reeking of pungent, musty life.

PART II

Every woeful story you listen to requires a
  brand-new heart.

                            — Arabic saying

2

Abu al-Hool: The Dry Time

Afghanistan: 621 days before

Jihad here is like jihad in Eritrea, Chechnya, or anywhere else. The battle is always the same: to restore peace in the war-torn, hope in the downtrodden, tenacity in the meek, and a zeal for life in the minds of those who have lost any sense of vitality. The war on the ground is — and always will be — secondary to the greater jihad, the more difficult, inner struggle.

In any honest assessment, I find I am losing. There is sadness but also a certain liberation in acknowledging this, if only to myself. Years ago, shortly before we parted last, my wife asked me when my belief began to falter, and, though I denied it ever had, the truth is, I can't remember a time when I felt otherwise. I must've been a small child in my father's house when hesitation and doubt first gouged their worrisome orbits around the same few unanswerable questions that have persisted to torment me all my life.

I should begin by admitting this. When I was much younger, at the close of every prayer, I asked for the strength to die unafraid. Now, more often, I pray to live righteously.

★ ★ ★

Summer turns to fall, and more brothers arrive in camp. They trickle in by twos and threes, eager to learn how to field-strip a Kalashnikov, how far to lead a helicopter with a rocket, to sing the *nasheeds* like true knights under the Prophet's banner, to perform ablutions when little water is available. Some have traveled from Africa, others from the Kingdom, Egypt, the Gulf states, and there is the odd European among them, these especially hopeful to become *shaheed*. Even an American from California, a place I have never been but always wanted to see, managed to bribe his way through the checkpoint at the Khyber. After a week with us, he did not find the brotherhood to his liking and moved on to train elsewhere.

Our numbers swell expectantly, though we aren't sure what to expect. Dr. Walid says it is a good problem to have, and I tend to agree. We accept each new brother with gratitude, but as time passes and the days grow cooler, the nights longer, and still they arrive in greater numbers — so much so that securing food for everyone has become difficult — I cannot help but wonder when this will end. The Afghan winter has a reputation even in the London mosques. Soon, the Khyber will close.

The other day we were slowed there by new-fallen snow as I guided a truckload of recruits across the pass. The new brothers, six in all, had been vetted in Peshawar by our man at the guesthouse, who judged them fit for training.

Among them was a beardless Yemeni, fifteen or sixteen years old. He wore a fine down coat and was also marked as a child of the rich by the haughty look on his face when he was ordered in no polite terms to ready himself for inspection.

He was pale, slight, hardly like a soldier. It is human nature to keep ourselves at a distance from most people, but every once in a while, we come across someone who passes directly from the periphery to the center, who strikes the core of us like a mallet setting a tuning fork to resonant agitation. This may or may not derive from any extraordinary qualities possessed by this person: it's an interplay of external and internal states. We must be receptive to the other to receive him.

Which is to say, I identified with the boy immediately. I must have seemed equally unlikely, traveling to the front so many years ago, a privileged brat eager to fight the Reds, an al-Azhar University dropout fresh off a backpacking tour with stops in Istanbul, Rome, Paris, Madrid, Amsterdam. Wandering stoned loops around gray spidered canals, I passed aimless hours in hostels and museums, train stations and bars and coffeehouses and brothels, those that would serve an Arab.

This shameful lark was financed with the last of Father's fortune that he saw fit to allot me for tuition and expenses before realizing I was never going to finish school, was a basket case, a bad investment, and, like the shrewd banker he was — responsibly, with regret, and once and for all — he wrote me off. That winter, as I contemplated in poverty the wreck that had become of my young life, the Soviet 40th Army rumbled across the Afghan border like a deus ex machina, lifting me up and offstage. Exit, war. People who knew me were surprised by what I did, but in a broad sense the move was in keeping with my personality. Joining the mujahideen was — at first — less a religious obligation and more like running away with the circus, only more daring, nobler, and with the added benefit of enraging Father, who believed progress came not through violent resistance but in the form of three-piece suits, Chopin études, quiet atheism, and extra-dry martinis at the cocktail hour. Father was a man bent double from the weight of his polish.

Two decades are more than enough to erase an identity, and for me they have, almost. The part of my life that the Yemeni recalled is closed off like a wing of rooms in a mansion whose upkeep has become too much for its insolvent owner. It was something in his young face that brought it back, what I was, before I was this: a kind of pomposity mingled with fear that told me he had never known hardship, not like these mountains could provide, but he wanted to know it, he had come here for that very reason, but was afraid.

I inspected his baggage, ready to find any fault, to make an example of him in front of the other new ones. He carried two leather bags as rich as his coat. I rummaged through and found nothing blameworthy with the exception of a pair of Italian sunglasses and a Swiss Army knife, both of which I confiscated.

'Your eyes will grow strong in the mountain sunlight, but not if you hide them like a woman,' I said. 'And this?' I held up the Swiss knife mischievously. 'Why in God's name would you carry a weapon with the Crusader's cross to this place? Are you a Christian or just a fool?'

The boy pointed to my rifle. 'Didn't the *kuffar* make that, too?'

Abu Annas moved as if to strike him for his insolence, but I signaled that this was not necessary.

'You've put your finger on it,' I said to the Yemeni. 'We're fighting our battles with our enemies' weapons. Maybe one day you will design us a better rifle. Until then, I'll keep this one handy. I hope that won't be a problem.'

The boy shook his head no. I noticed him continuing to admire the Kalashnikov. 'These?' I patted the stock, tracing the notches with my finger. 'Carved when I was your age.'

I raised the rifle and fired a shot in the air without warning, and the boy startled; the more seasoned brothers laughed. Their hardness pleased me, but I also felt some remorse for scaring and embarrassing the boy, an impulsive thing to do, as much to snap myself from nostalgic contemplation as to impress upon him the seriousness of what he was about to undertake.

'I no longer carve notches,' I said, once the gunshot had stopped echoing off the mountainside. 'That kind of pride is abhorrent to me now. I hope you haven't come here just to learn how to kill.'

31

'No, Emir.'

'What's your name, boy?'

'Omar ibn Saeed.'

A few brothers scoffed and remarked at his naïveté. Even his fellow recruits, encamped all of a half hour, realized his transgression. So green, I thought of him, just a child, wondering, lest I grow hard-hearted, if I should send him back over the pass, back to his mother, who, wherever she was, surely missed him.

'Little brother, that's not your real name, is it?'

The Yemeni nodded, confused.

'Don't use it anymore. When you come here you must take a new one.' I nodded at Abu Annas. 'That one there, the ugly one with the thick head? He is called the Father of Friendliness.' I turned to Abu Muqhatil. 'And this man is the Father of Fighters. I'm the Father of Dread. Do you see? When you come to us, you give up your family, your home — even your name, your birthright. Look around. This is your new family. These are your new brothers. At this moment you are like a newborn child, but soon you'll learn to walk again. We'll teach you how to dress, how to pray, how to fight, and how to die. You may question our orders, but you may not go against them. The door swings both ways. Leave if you don't like it, understood?'

He assented.

'So, what should we call you?'

With care he considered the choice of name. 'Father of Lion Cubs.'

'There it is. Everyone, welcome the Father of Lion Cubs. He has joined us today in our jihad.'

'God has willed it, God has willed it, God has willed it!' the brothers cheered the newly named Abu Hafs.

* * *

Abu Ali broke his leg early this morning on a moonlit run along the northwest ridge of Takur Gar. Hopping from boulder to boulder in the dark, he slipped and fell and after he tumbled out of view was feared dead. The brothers found him lower down the slope, splinted his leg, and carried him the five kilometers back to camp. He arrived barely conscious, looking ashen, the sharp edge of his femur protruding. When the sun rose, some of us drove him across the pass to hospital. I took the opportunity to scold Dr. Walid, whom I have placed in charge of physical training, reminding him that these night runs on the mountain are not worth the risk. He listened to my complaint but did not seem concerned. And why should he be? What is one broken bone when new bodies are always forthcoming? Today it was a father — son Uzbek pair: the father I could take or leave, but his boy, Abu Bakr, has the makings of a fine soldier. Dr. Walid and I watched from the shade of my tent as Abu Annas put them and the other recruits through their paces.

'That one's the best of the lot,' I said, indicating Abu Bakr. 'Look how he's stopped caring about what the others are doing and is concentrating only on his own form. Impressive self-possession. Ones like that always make the best leaders.'

'And fighters,' Dr. Walid added.

There were years when we would have received only a few like that in the course of a season. Now, it is regular. The influx continues to astound. The doctor and I project unity, satisfaction, confidence, but privately reveal ourselves to be just as befuddled as everyone else. There has been no new front opened in the struggle, not since Chechnya, and the second paroxysm of that terrible war is years old and more or less stalemated. Some say we have grown stronger as the Taliban has risen to prominence, but their rise and ours are merely incidental, two different flowers sharing the same soil. We are guests among the Pashtun, for whom I have much affection, but the Taliban itself I find distasteful. Its commanders exert an iron-fisted rule over the peasantry that will backfire in time. They waste their days patrolling for contraband, ribbons of confiscated audio- and videotape tied to the roll bars of their trucks, the black magnetic strands fluttering like shredded banners in the wind.

'They are innovators, not to be trusted,' Dr. Walid says, whenever the subject comes up. 'The Taliban are too strict in their application of the law.'

For him to accuse anyone of harshness is rare, and accurate in this case; we abide the Taliban, and they us, but that's the extent of it. We take no side in their war against Shah Massoud and the Northern Alliance. It's not a true jihad, despite their claims. We're in Afghanistan not to fight but to train for the struggle elsewhere. A beacon has been lit in these mountains, and mujahideen from around the world are hastening to it: in days like these a man might be forgiven for believing he lives in an auspicious moment, that he has discerned a pattern in the chaos of events, a clear signal where once was only static. If history shows us anything, it's that — for reasons obscure or obvious — movements of people combine and act as one to shape the world. I take comfort in being part of something larger than myself. It is one reason I am still here.

The mysteries of religion may confound me, but history is something I know better, a discipline in which I've rooted my command. God is an idea employed to talk about what we cannot know, but the logic of what happens on His earth throughout time can be studied and relied upon. Change is the only certainty, death the end: each generation passes away, while another, more fit for the age, is born to it. The things men build, the machines and the systems, may likewise change, but their other, more essential qualities remain immutable. The strong march against the weak. The oppressors torment the oppressed. When placed in contradiction with the truth, falsehood loses its authority.

★   ★   ★

Last night we heard the news on the BBC out of Peshawar. Manhattan lies in ruins. The Pentagon, destroyed. I find it impossible to believe. It's said that tens of thousands of *kuffar* may have perished and that the towers of the World Trade Center have fallen and burned to ash.

'Praise God for this justice,' Dr. Walid muttered, huddled near the shortwave with the rest of us, listening to the reports.

'You call this justice,' I said chidingly. 'To kill women and children.'

With the choice of target, the disregard for civilian death, there is no mistaking who has done this. I've never sworn fealty to Sheikh Osama; I met the man only once, near Tora Bora, years ago, and to my knowledge Dr. Walid never has. Nevertheless, he was as proud of the attacks as if he had planned them, pleased beyond seemliness that Afghanistan had, in one fell stroke, become the most relevant country on earth. He looked at me unnervingly, his tone riding the razor's edge between deference and condescension. 'This is the greatest victory for us since the last Soviet dog was driven across the border into Uzbekistan. Didn't the Americans bring us Hiroshima and Nagasaki? Weren't innocent women and children in those cities? Sheikh Osama is simply taking the method of fighting the West invented and visiting it back upon them.'

'You could be right' was all I said, mired again in doubt. My heart is torn. How can I lead these men if I appear weak? How can I lead those who do not share my mind? My inborn nature tends more toward the philosophical, but my duties demand a rigidity of thought that forbids too many points of departure from the crowd. God knows there have been enough of those that I've tried to keep hidden. I wonder if I am, at middle age, already a relic from a bygone era. I wonder if Sheikh Osama will be proven correct. Great men tend to inhabit the extremes of thought, and that is one reason for their greatness. I myself have managed to vacillate between extremes without inhabiting them long enough to allow anything truly impressive to coalesce.

★ ★ ★

There is no denying that Manhattan changes everything. Listening to the radio, the rough talk, Dr. Walid and the other brothers gloating, I foresee a war to dwarf even Chechnya, the worst I've ever known, where still my own Hassan rests in that ice-hard field south of Grozny. My precious boy, the only one of my sons who insisted on following me down this path. With the towers knocked over, there will be a hundred thousand more like him in a hundred thousand shallow graves. Dr. Walid seems thrilled about it. I find him increasingly revolting, yet hide my misgivings like a corrupt judge. I don't know how long I can maintain this mask. Before Manhattan, I'd been thinking of stepping aside and letting him assume the emirship. I know he's wanted it for years, and it's past time for new blood at the helm. Now, however, with the way he exults over Manhattan, his succeeding me has become much more problematic.

In the early morning after the attack, the brothers, charged with emotion, ascended the mountainside, whooping, scrambling over boulders, and in celebration emptied their rifles and launched volleys of rockets that shrieked and whistled across the valley, deafening me, recalling past battles; I worried in the chaos some careless recruit might burn another with the backwash from his rocket. The moon was large and close, our shouts and the explosions echoing from peak to peak, revealing in flashes and sound the vastness of the nightscape. The boy Abu Hafs was handed a launcher and for the first time fired a grenade that went crashing through the pines and into the river below, sending up a column of water and flame.

'Excellent shooting, cub,' Dr. Walid said. 'I've always liked the sound of an RPG.'

Our munitions spent, we returned to camp. Like a tattered stage curtain, the line of dawn descended the serrated ridges of the Hindu Kush until at last the valley floor was illuminated and night's chill forgotten. Lambs were slaughtered, and juices and sweets distributed, enough for several days, though our stores ran low. Now is the evening of the next day, and we have only begun to prepare for the counterattack. We didn't sign on for this offensive. Regardless, I suffer no illusions that our ignorance or prior restraint will mitigate what the future holds. Blood must have blood. We are Muslims training in Afghanistan, and for the Americans that will be enough. Only a fool would deny we are now enemies.

3

Cassandra: Communications Blackout

Kuwait: 36 days before

In the cool dark of the bunker they shelter uncomfortably close, waiting for the Scud drill to end and the war to start. Cassandra is the only woman among them — though, in army-speak, never a woman but a *female* — crammed alongside men and boys packed like wriggling cordwood to fill a blast shelter a meter and a half tall, three meters wide, ten long. Other, identical bunkers stretch in an ellipsis across the moonlit Kuwaiti desert.

Camp New York has been placed on communications blackout, which means the invasion will begin any day; the Scud drill, the increasingly realistic tempo of their training, are further proof. Warning sirens mounted on telephone poles ring the camp's perimeter berm and blare three short air-horn blasts, followed by a moment of silence, the pattern signifying *Gas gas gas!* and repeating itself in off-time rhythm with the empty protective mask case that jangles at her hip as she duckwalks and shimmies her way deeper into the black, narrow space. When she can go no farther, she squats back on her heels and props her rifle beside her. Men surge in behind, and suddenly there's no room to move; to get out of here, she is beholden to the people near the entrance. Bad luck to be claustrophobic right about now. These bunkers, in no way designed for comfort, were constructed by overturning preformed arches of concrete originally made for culverts. Right side up, the shape would sluice water. Upside down, they provide what defense contractors have deemed acceptable coverage from indirect blast effects and shrapnel.

An hour past sundown, the final wispy trails of lavender and blue fade from the expansive desert sky. The stars are magnificent, the Milky Way a smear of bioluminescence, but inside the bunker is only blackness, all the soldiers masked up, drawing labored breaths through biochem filters. In addition to the masks, they're also encumbered with charcoal-lined chemical suits, plastic hoods, rubber gloves, rubber overboots, forty pounds of Kevlar and ceramic-plate body armor, a combat load of smoke grenades, frag grenades, and seven M16 magazines, and some are carrying light machine guns or radios or combat lifesaver bags, but even lugging around the heaviest piece of gear is no match for the sheer stifling annoyance of the mask, which, she must admit, does possess at least one redeeming quality: sparing her from the body odor of the men nearby. No doubt many skipped showers that morning, refusing to wait in the long lines for personal-hygiene trailers.

The army camp is overcrowded, but, thanks to the ingenuity of Kellogg Brown & Root, a subsidiary of Halliburton, it's eminently expandable. Off-loaded piece by piece from ships in the

Persian Gulf, trucked through Kuwait City and into the deep desert, all of Camp New York's assemblages are modular. Steel eyelets the size of a fist, sunk into the top face of the bunker, allow it to be hoisted with a crane, loaded onto a flatbed, and hauled into all tomorrow's war zones.

Erected in a matter of weeks and in its character not unlike a boomtown, the camp houses more than five thousand American soldiers — all but a few hundred are men — impatiently living out the last days of peace in large air-conditioned tents like those where especially well-cared-for refugees might stay. Portable buildings flank the hard-pack road that spans the center of camp: double-wide trailers painted a drab eggshell white and modified to fill every organizational purpose. Trailers to sort and receive mail; trailers to treat soldiers on sick call; to house VIPs and KBR employees; a trailer stocked with a flimsy bench press, a squat rack, some dumbbells, and a treadmill so clogged with sand, the mechanism makes a sound like a coffee grinder whenever some clueless new arrival tries to jog on it. There are trailers to shower in, trailers to command troops from, refrigerator trailers to store perishables in, and the most popular on camp, a Morale, Welfare, and Recreation phone trailer (corporate sponsorship by AT&T), subdivided into fourteen obscenely well-graffitied cubicles, each with a pay phone, accepting only calling cards, no coin. For reasons of efficiency the army doesn't ship U.S. specie into theater.

Due to the communications blackout, the phone trailer has been pad-locked for nearly forty-eight hours. This is standard operating procedure for the commencement of hostilities. Turn off the phones. The brass don't want any word leaking back home about exactly when the invasion might kick off. Also off-limits is the 'Internet café,' yet another eggshell double-wide with institutional-looking desks and computers whose keyboards are yellowed from nicotine and coffee and skin oil, the keys rubbed shiny smooth and the most commonly used letters worn off. A satellite dish sits atop the Internet café. Of the uncountable transmissions sent through it, light-speed expressions of every trying shade of human emotion beamed into outer space and relayed around the world to disturb the peace at terminals back home, Cassandra has sent not one.

★　★　★

She processed into the army in Kansas City, the summer of 2001, after a daylong trip thumbing rides down state roads. Destination: Eureka Springs, Arkansas, the closest town with a bus station. She hasn't seen her grandparents' place since. Half a section of Milking Shorthorns and hog pens hedged by forested sedimentary hills on the northern fringes of the Ozarks. The land tamed only marginally over the course of five generations. The family responsible for its taming having spent itself in the effort. Nearly three hundred acres, the family's land; the family land rich, and poor in most other material.

Far as she knows, it's all still there. Prefab house. Shifty dirt road. Her Papaw and Meemaw tottering half-blind in homespun clothes like the apparitions of pioneers from an earlier century. Blankets of kudzu spreading out from the creek bed like a soft green cancer in the woods, and the nauseating smell of pig shit pressed into everything. An uncle she suspected of cooking meth as a side business, a few indolent cousins, and their broods scattered around the property in trailers and squalid bungalows pieced together with little more than salvaged materials and cunning. An occasional rifle shot cracking out over the hollows, silencing the birdsong, another deer poached; her family, she thinks unkindly: as a lot they're about as glassy-eyed and ill bred as the livestock they tend for the best legal part of their livelihood. When she was a little girl she used to tell herself she was adopted. The day after she turned eighteen, she left.

'Think of your uncle Charles,' her mom said, sitting at the kitchen table and gesturing tiredly with her cigarette at the wall, in the general direction of her brother's house. 'You know, before he joined up he used to be a football star.'

'Mom. We've haven't been at war in, what, ten years?'

'That's not the point. If there *was* a war going on, I could see how you might get a crazy idea like this. But as it is, I'm baffled. You got too much potential for this, Cass. They use you up. That's what they do. War or peace, you're just a body to them. That kind of life is gonna change you.'

Cassandra shouldered her bag and headed for the door, yet to wear her country's uniform but having already mastered one of the most critical skills of soldiering: how to say goodbye.

'I'm hoping it changes me,' she said. 'Why else you think I'm doing this?'

★   ★   ★

She'd long been accustomed to male provocations. But the sandbox, this is another level; dawn to dusk some man's gaze is always fixed on her. She's a curiosity in the ranks, a curiosity just for being a woman, forget about the rest. More than most men, she joined up strictly to escape a hard life for one she hoped would be harder. The free college money had no part in her enlisting. She wasn't interested in college and could've gotten an easier civilian job in St. Louis or KC for about the same pay. To train to fight, to kill, to prove, to defy the small domestic compassions of kith and home, was why she joined.

Some soldiers despise what they think she is and behind her back call her bitch, ball breaker, dyke. No one calls her what she really is. No one, not in a very long time, has called her Cassandra, namesake of her grandmother. In the towel-snapping locker room of the army she's become her last name, Wigheard, or, even more impersonally, her rank, Specialist.

There are the unabashed bigots and misogynists, and then there are those more common, like Sergeant McGinnis, men who feel too compelled to protect her, chivalrous to a fault.

She likes McGinnis best when he allows her to operate like just another soldier doing her job. Yet more and more, the thought of going for a twenty-year pension has begun to feel like prolonged suffocation in a cavernous, airtight room.

＊　＊　＊

As they wait for the Scud drill to end, the grunts huddled in the bunker pass the time gossiping. Or, as they might say, engaged in back-channel communications. *Gossip* being an untenably feminized word. Goddamn men. In her darkest moments she sometimes wishes she'd been born a part of their little club. Not a wish to change gender, exactly, but that she'd been given an easier birthright to power. She has to game herself to stay grounded in her own body, tensing calves, then quads, abs, lats, traps, going up and down her anatomy and activating each muscle in as much isolation as possible. Left side, followed by right. Stay asymmetrical. Stay unpredictable. Stay alert, and you might stay alive.

'Buddy of mine up at battalion, he knew about this shit,' says one of the randoms. 'He told me we'd get it tonight. Shoulda listened to his pogue ass. But no, I get two bites into my steak and then — *wanh, wanh, wanh.*' Here he does a decent impression of the hated chem-alert siren. 'So no shit, there I was, trying to pack the whole damn steak in my mouth like a crackhead swallowing the evidence.'

Their voices in the dark are disembodied and hollow; a resonator plate in the mask allows for speech but renders it metallic, thin, like talking under water, the human voice vibrating through ball bearings sandwiched between steel disks set in front of the mouth.

The conversation in the bunker livens up as it turns to one of two felonies recently committed on Camp New York. A sudden rash of criminality has accompanied the start of the communications blackout, perhaps coincidentally, or perhaps as a direct, unintended consequence.

'Heard they ganked, like, two grand worth of cigs from the PX,' one grunt says, referring to the camp store where soldiers buy tobacco, candy, magazines, CD players, disposable cameras: all the minor consumer objects authorized for sale in a war zone. 'Colonel's got our whole battalion confined to quarters until they find who did it.'

She can barely discern the glint of polycarbonate eyepieces fixed like black gleaming bug eyes in their masks. They are near the entrance, talking about the burglary of the post exchange; aside from the fact that the break-in occurred in the middle of the Kuwaiti desert in the days leading to war, it's nothing special. Typical army trash acting grimy. Seen that plenty of times. But the other felony, which is apparently unrelated, she cannot help but take personally.

Sergeant Williams, the victim, was until recently a tent-mate. And there is a fragment of a history between them, a half-remembered drunken hookup last year in her barracks room after a night out at the bars in Killeen. Just the once, then seeing each other around post from time to time, fleeting awkwardness, Don't Ask, Don't Tell, and fuck all that. But the army is worse for rumors than high school, and she's heard Williams was raped at gunpoint in a porta-potty. The location did not surprise. Few other places on camp afford even that much privacy.

It makes her sick with rage, makes her want to reach out to Williams, but the fragment of a history renders that thought too uncomfortable. When dealing with other people's tragedies, there's the risk of taking on more grief than is appropriate, of lapsing into benevolent voyeurism, of making it all about you.

Other than the rumors, she doesn't know much. She had only a brief look at Williams when, a few hours after reporting the attack, she returned to the tent they shared with sixty-two other women. At that time Cassandra knew nothing about what had happened but could see it was serious; Williams had an unfamiliar colonel chaperoning her, and a black eye and her arm in a sling. She collected her belongings from under her cot and left without talking to anyone. People said the CO had moved her out of the tent to private quarters until she could be flown home. The guy who did it was still at large. Still is.

The group of men trading gossip in the bunker don't seem to know Williams by name, swapping stories that match up pretty closely with what Cassandra has already heard. They mention the porta-potty — there are rows of

47

them on camp like those at a music festival — and they wonder out loud why she didn't use her own M16 to fight off her attacker. There's a cruel innocence in how they talk about it, reminding her of the way children sometimes torture each other.

Their hard talk, this bleak transient life in the desert, mustard gas, VX nerve agent, Scud and al-Samoud missiles, mechanized warfare, the communications blackout, it's bringing out the dog in them, she thinks: no wives, girlfriends, or mommas on hand to temper their manhood. Strip them of their satellite connection home and leave them to their own devices, and watch them go feral, the camp assuming qualities of a penal colony. Forty-eight hours is apparently about how long it takes for untended men to descend to the level of beasts.

'So. Who you think it was?' one man asks after a lull in the banter. She had just started to tune them out. Someone itched himself through his chem suit, making a swishing sound, and someone else ground his rifle butt slowly into the gravel underfoot.

'What I look like, fucking Miss Cleo or some shit?' says the one who started it.

'Shit, dude. Don't take psychic powers to figure out who it was. Not like there're that many females around.'

'Think it's that little thang from the 115th?'

'Fat ass, tiny tits? One Silver fucked in the barracks before we left?'

'Naw, bro, not her. I mean that half-black half-Asian one.'

It takes Cassandra longer than it should've to realize they're not speculating on the identity of the rapist. *Who you think it was?* Resentment, an electric charge prickling her scalp, the pressure rising behind her eyes — Ignorant fucks. Not one of them has voiced any outrage that one of their own has been attacked, that an able soldier has been taken out of commission on the eve of battle. They want to rubberneck, to pick out the victim as a kind of contest to see whether their killer instincts are honed enough to know her weakness by sight and rumor alone.

'Half black, half Asian?'

'Yeah. A cook, I think.'

Cassandra shifts against the bunker wall, flexing her rubber chemical overboots on the seam where concrete meets gravel, leaning forward until her weight rests on the balls of her feet like rounded bone fulcrums. There are two-hundred-some-odd women on camp, and one of these assholes has just guessed Williams's identity. This gets her blood up as much as anything, the fact that they are good at this game. They don't even care, she thinks. Talking about it is just something to pass the time until the Scud drill ends.

She feels her hate sink to a dangerous place and wishes McGinnis were here; he would've ended their little guessing game before it got to this point. He would've ended it by appealing to decency, and if that didn't work, the weight of his stripes. If he were here he could humiliate these guys without losing face. She could not: if she were to shame them, she would look weak

49

herself, overly sensitive. *We're just talking,* they'd say. *What's the big deal?*

Her typical response to a situation like this is silence. Prove herself through action, the army's universally accepted currency. Shame them without speaking. It's a trivial kind of revenge, she knows, taciturn, passive. Still, she'll take it. While the men around her prattle away, she endures stoically, the truest grunt of them all, disaffected and hard.

★ ★ ★

Three days later, riding shotgun down below, McGinnis reaches up and pounds on the Humvee's roof to check whether she's still alert and okay. She stands above and to his rear in the gunner's hatch, breathing in the stale desert road-wind and the exhaust fumes blown by the Abrams tank ahead of them in the convoy. She reaches forward and pounds back on the roof to let him know, yes, she's fine. She has brought her fist down harder each time they've had this exchange, hammering the truck's bouncy fiber-glass roof with increasing force in an attempt to express her growing annoyance with McGinnis for not trusting her enough to let her do her goddamn job and scan her sector for at least fifteen minutes at a stretch without his constant oversight, which borders on coddling.

The two of them have devised this crude code, the roof-pounding, out of battlefield necessity. To their front and rear, tank engines scream with a high-pitched whine like planes on the tarmac of

50

a busy airport. In reality, the tank engines *are* jet turbines that blow withering hot exhaust in addition to making it impossible for McGinnis to give voice commands to her or their driver, Crump.

Originally, Cassandra was slated to drive. To get out of the duty, she almost had to go on strike, as much as a soldier can, giving McGinnis the silent treatment, interspersed with earnest arguments about her superior gunnery scores, compared to Crump's, before McGinnis agreed to assign her to the more dangerous position manning the fifty.

The sonic roar of tanks on the ground, of jets flying sorties above, blots out all other sounds and means the war is on. In the dead of the previous night they crossed the sand berm marking the border with Iraq. As they rolled through a dozered breach in the berm, she ducked low in the hatch, half expecting enemy shells would start to fall around them at any moment. So far, none have. No sign of the Iraqi army. The sun has been up for hours, and, even though it's March, she's sweating in her chem suit, the third of four layers, counting the Kevlar.

Abrams tanks and Bradley fighting vehicles stretch one after another in a long column that disappears over the next dune on the horizon. Set beside that heavy armor, the trucks like hers look almost like toys. If the tanks can't handle whatever's coming, neither she nor any other Humvee gunner will be able to protect the convoy. Still, she's satisfied to be rolling with a cavalry brigade; combat arms, she knows, is the all-male heart of the force: tankers, scouts, artillerymen, special ops, infantry. All other soldiers merely support combat arms. She would've enlisted for one of those jobs if she could have. Now, effectively, she has.

She scans her sector, twelve o'clock to three, the tint on her scratched desert goggles making the dunes look like dirty frozen waves. She glances back down the column, catching in her hair and teeth the grit of road dust rising from whirring tank tracks. The dust settles over everything, coating the goggles' lenses, her lips, her hands and neck, with a fine white powder. It's grueling, but she feels enlivened to be in the thick of things, finally pushing into Iraq, relieved that the interminable waiting has ended. Yet something irks her, unfinished business that eats away at the Tightness of their movement. Leaving Kuwait means Williams's rape is never going to get solved. She knows this in her gut. With each passing mile, they travel farther away from the scene of the crime. It's been three days since the last Scud drill, four since the rape itself, and still no arrest. Riding somewhere in this long line of trucks, tanks, and armored personnel carriers, some asshole is putting distance between himself and what he did.

After another hour on the move, they stop for a break and to take on fuel. The platoon leaders and company commanders confer on the ground about a change in the operations order. The precise location of this place where the brass has chosen to halt their advance seems like a bit of war tourism, too. On a scalloped ridge to the

52

west they have caught the first real sight of the enemy: Republican Guard tanks line the distant high ground, a snaking mess of earthworks and T-72s annihilated by preparatory air strikes. She saw them the night before from northern Kuwait. From so far away, the bombing raids were indistinguishable from natural phenomena. They looked like the diffused white flashes of heat lightning on the horizon.

Now she takes up the binoculars hanging around her neck and focuses on the ridge. Black specks stand in contrast to the desert floor, where the only demarcation between earth and sky is a different shade of faded orange. The small black things are scattered among larger forms, the burned-out tanks, their turrets popped off like champagne corks, lying upside down or sideways, gun tubes drooping limply where their steel softened in the fires, the hulls heat-stripped of paint, now silver-gray, the color of raw ore, and after a few beats of looking, she realizes the small black things are corpses, torsos with arms charred to nubs, carcasses like the husks of beetle shells scorched into the earth. When she recognizes one, she sees them all. Bodies hang in gibbeted charcoal lumps from tank hatches. Others, unseen, did not make it that far and were trapped inside the turrets, armor becoming an oven, reducing them to ash and teeth. Those who escaped the tanks and ran for it are arrayed unnaturally, as if in the aftermath of a volcano's eruption, of a thermonuclear flashbulb. There is no flesh left on their charred bodies to turn and bloat with that sickly-sweet smell. Burned to slim carbon shadows that died low crawling and grasping at the sand in many different poses but always aligned like the spokes on a wheel, with their heads facing away from the tanks, since all they knew at that point was get away from the fire.

She sets the binos on the truck's roof and boosts herself out of the hatch. She hops to the ground and approaches McGinnis, who is poking around under the hood.

'We should go up there and do a battle damage assessment,' she says, gesturing casually to the ridgeline, the destroyed hardware, the dead. She's curious — and who can blame her for wanting to see them closer? Good soldiers are by their nature morbid. For good soldiers, death is not a taboo but a stock-in-trade.

'Naw, you don't need to be seeing that,' McGinnis says in his quiet way, not even looking at her, his attention focused entirely on the engine. He draws the dipstick through a folded rag. 'We're a quart low. Again.'

She goes to the rear of the Humvee and opens the hatchback. Unlucky enough to be issued a thirsty truck, they've got two full cases of oil stowed on top of all their other gear: five-gallon jugs of water, spare barrels for the fifty, weapons-cleaning kits, MREs, duffel bags for their uniforms and personal effects, a POW-handling kit, and ammo cans packed with linked and belted rounds.

She returns to the front of the truck carrying a quart of oil and hands it brusquely to him, not bothering to do him the favor of using her multi-tool to notch a spout.

'What's got your goat?' he says, fishing in his pockets for his own multi-tool.

'Nothing.'

'Come on, Wigheard.'

'*You don't need to be seeing that?* Like I'm some delicate flower.'

'That's it? We're not here for goddamn tourism, Wigheard. The fuck. I need you here with me, doing precombat checks in the little time we got left before we move out again. I do not need your ass off gaping at the goddamn dead.'

'Roger, Sar'nt,' she sighs, knowing he's right about not taking frivolous side trips away from the truck, but not quite believing him about why. Can't help the way he was raised, she thinks. A Southern boy, best and worst of the army, his daddy supposedly some hotshot time-share developer in Florida, and McGinnis the blue-collar-by-choice black sheep who enlisted instead of enrolling in an MBA program. At least, that was the word in the platoon. McGinnis kept pretty quiet about his own origins.

He looks at her expectantly, conveying an unspoken request for something, for the funnel she has forgotten to bring. She grimaces and goes back to the rear of the truck to get it.

'Appreciated,' he says when she returns to the sliver of shade created by the Humvee's propped-open hood. The oil glugs down the funnel, into the warm ticking engine. He looks across his shoulder and regards her in the reluctant way she has come to associate with him disembarking the laconic territory in which he's most at home. 'Whatever responsibility I have for you has got everything to do with my rank and nothing to do with the fact that I'm a man and you're a woman. You're my soldier. I'm your superior. That's the bottom line. My main job in this thing is to bring us home safe. Everything I do, every decision I make, that's it.'

'Shouldn't you worry more about winning the war than keeping us safe?' she asks sarcastically.

'No way,' he says, shaking his head steadily. 'Winning and losing is on Higher. Our game is a lot simpler.'

'Let me guess. Life or death.'

'Correct.'

'I don't know,' she says mock-chidingly. 'Sounds kind of weak to me. Maybe we should play to win. What do you think about that, Sar'nt?'

He stops fiddling around with the engine and gives her his full and undivided attention, a quizzical glare that asks why she's acting so annoyingly difficult and whether he's done anything to deserve it. He snorts and scowls and resumes his work, removing the funnel and flinging out the last drops of oil. He screws on the engine cap and tosses the empty can into the desert, where it rolls across the sand. No room in their load plan to pack trash, the whole brigade will be littering all the way to Baghdad.

He walks a careful oval around the Humvee, inspecting the tires, checking the lug nuts, assessing the cracked rubber on the hood latches, and, kneeling to lie flat, crawls beneath the truck, peers at the undercarriage, the brake lines, attuned to every key mechanical detail. He's tall and lanky, a half generation older, with fast-moving eyes.

She waits for him to offer an opinion, but he doesn't. 'You think they'll ever catch that guy, the rapist?' she finally asks.

'Maybe,' he says, judiciously wiping grease off his hands with the rag. 'They might get a hit in the all-services DNA database. Sample he gave at MEPS will be what nails him. If — and this is a big *if* — those jokers back at New York didn't fuck up handling the evidence. I've seen some ate-up police in my day, but those jokers were something else. They've been in the sandbox way too long.'

Cassandra hears him, but not really, eyes glazed over from exhaustion, locked on the faraway ridge, scorched metal and flesh; squinting, noticing something nonhuman moving around up there, some kind of animal, a wild dog, she guesses, shuddering to imagine what it's feeding on.

'It could be any of these guys . . . ' She trails off, her gaze moving closer, to the soldiers up and down the column, who are themselves busy doing the same things she and McGinnis are, pouring oil and fuel into their machines to be burned.

'It's a big army,' he says. 'Takes all comers. Some are rotten.'

One of the brigade's fuelers pulls alongside, and she gasses up the Humvee and returns the hose to the soldier manning the vehicle the size of an eighteen-wheeler, laden with thousands of sloshing gallons of diesel: it rumbles away in a cloud of greasy exhaust, one of several fuelers driving down the line, topping everyone off. They just took on twenty gallons, and that is nothing compared to the capacity of the Abrams tanks, each capable of burning through five times as much in an hour. Nearly a hundred tanks in this column alone. She does the math. Think about so much oil. Got to burn it to get it.

The radio mounted inside their truck blares with a staticky warning from the commander. 'All stations, Crusader Six. Prepare to move out in fifteen mikes.'

There is a flurry of activity up and down the line.

'Wake up Sleeping Beauty there,' McGinnis tells her, indicating Crump, in the driver's seat. 'And let's slap a fresh coat of CLP on the fifty before we get rolling, shall we?'

She climbs in the gunner's hatch and nudges Crump awake with her boot before attending to her weapon. She holds her tongue but wants to tell McGinnis that applying more lubricant to the fifty will do more harm than good at this point. The gun needs to be stripped down and detailed. Another coat of oil will do little but attract the dust that gums the action and never seems to stop falling over everything all the time.

4

Sleed: Trophies

Iraq (Highway 1; Palace Row):
32 days before

I'll never be able to forget. The desert that day was so empty of any living thing, it looked like the sandblasted side of a dead planet. We were halted on a rest-and-refuel, killing time messing around on some destroyed Iraqi armor not far from the highway. That's when it started, if you had to pick a point. Back when we thought memories would not be enough.

Galvan and Fitzpatrick, and yeah, me too, wanted souvenirs for the grandkids yet to be born. A helmet or bayonet to take home and prove we were in the shit. Trouble was, everything good on those tanks had burned or melted. Crews, too. Galvan had already gotten a few pictures with the digital camera he'd been carrying around everywhere since he'd bought it at New York, probably for this exact reason. He took some more of this one guy and went in for a close-up. The man's teeth were coal black, his hands like two claws planted into the sand that had gotten so hot in the fire, it crunched like thin ice when you walked on it. That was the first time in my life I'd ever seen anything like that, and the war felt really fucking real all of a sudden. I got this complicated feeling that has bothered me ever since. It's hard to describe, but it's like knowing every decision, even something dumb like what to eat for breakfast or what route to drive to the store, might be the thing that kills you or saves you or gets somebody else killed, and there's no way to know. Like everything matters so much, it's pointless to worry about anything.

* * *

Photographing dead troops fell under a gray area of the law of war. Whether or not it was legal depended on why you were doing it. Like, a combat correspondent would be allowed to take a picture, it would even be part of his job, but for ordinary joes, that same picture could get you busted down. You could safely kill them but not take pictures of what you'd killed. Made sense to me. Once you start in with trophies, even photographs, the nastier shit is bound to follow.

I hoped Fitzpatrick would stop Galvan with the pictures, but no. He and Galvan were thick as thieves. On their own they could have been okay, but they fed off each other, and that made for bad news. Galvan was our tank commander. Fitzpatrick, the driver, was this big arrogant bastard we called Rooster for how cocky he was. Not for no reason. Dude was smart, seemed like he basically got what the world was like, how to make his ugly piece of it better, but the truth about war is, some people are good at it, and people tend to enjoy showing off their talents.

Me, I couldn't stand the army, felt like an idiot for ever believing left-right-left would solve my problems. Grinding pills to snort in my parents' basement, working nights in a video store. I thought enlisting would give me a higher purpose, something to fight for, but as it turned out I was the same person anywhere. A watcher. Usually the wrong-place-wrong-time kind. To my credit, though, I did get tired enough of Galvan and his pictures to speak up. Said, 'You ain't worried about those Geneva Conventions or nothing, huh, Sergeant?'

Galvan just laughed.

'You heard me, though, Sarge?'

He acted like he didn't, took another picture just to rub it in, and then rose to his full height, which wasn't much. This scrawny Puerto Rican dude, but not scrawny in a weak way, he had that wiry workingman's strength. Held the camera close to his mouth and blew the dust from the lens.

'Geneva Conventions? That's good, Sleed. Real smart. Don't you know this whole fucking war is illegal?'

He shook his head like I was too much of a fool to bother with, looking at the screen on the camera, scrolling through what he'd gotten.

'Well, I just wanna go on record,' I said. 'All respect, I think this is some sick-ass bullshit.'

'Noted. Now fuck off.'

We hung around till we spotted Sergeant First Class Blornsbaum, our platoon's head honcho, making his way up the ridgeline from the road where our own tanks were parked. Seeing him put the fear back in us. Galvan stopped with the camera and slipped it in his chem-suit thigh pocket, playing it cool, but Blornsbaum had not just fallen off the turnip truck yesterday, as he always said about himself.

He was a lifer. Veteran of Gulf War I, Kosovo, and peacetime posts all over the world. Skin the color of a toad's belly that refused to tan and would only burn in the desert, so he was always slathering sunscreen on himself, real diligent about shit like that, personal hygiene. He stood there trying to look tough, but it came out painfully confused, like someone had just smacked him on the back of the head, his eyes passing over Fitzpatrick, me, Galvan, the dead bodies, the burned-out tanks, and finally back to Galvan and his pocket, where the camera was stowed. He knew we knew he knew.

'Lemme guess,' he said. 'You been playing war reporter.' He unscrewed his face and spat on the sand. Shook his head and chuckled, the one reaction I'd not expected. The sound of his growly laughter made me feel light-headed, and I could practically hear the vein in my forehead throbbing. He'd thrown me. Thought for sure he would take Galvan's camera and make him delete the pictures or even report him for violating the regs. Instead, he snapped his fingers at him.

'Hey, Ernie Pyle. Get one of me.'

He stood by the destroyed T-72 with a big shit-eating grin and flashed the peace sign. Galvan took his picture and then started a series of shots that would make a panorama if he stitched them together. He took one of our tanks in the distance, one of Fitzpatrick holding his rifle, like something out of a recruiting commercial, and finally came around to me. That lucky bastard managed to catch the exact moment I started to drop. I felt myself stumbling and swaying, my vision fading all white and hairy, and one of my knees buckled out from under me, my head so light, it was like my body was stretching into gas. It sort of felt nice. Because I thought that if a bullet did happen to hit me right then, it would pass clean on through without doing any harm. Just like I was a ghost.

★ ★ ★

I revived, laid out on the desert floor. Gritty sand pressed on my cheek and nose, and there was something wet scraping across the other side of my face, into my ear.

Blornsbaum was shouting like he was enjoying himself. 'Get that dang thing off him!'

I sat up and saw it was a dog licking me that had snapped me out of it. Spit all around my mouth, disgusting. I shoved it away. Its rusty-yellow fur felt greasy. A desert pariah dog, kind of a mongrel cur like an oversized coyote, it wasn't trying to bite, just licking crazily like it had already loved me for years.

It ran circles around us, yipping and rolling its eyes. Blornsbaum managed to snag its neck and hold it in one place between his legs so it had nowhere to go and nothing to do but whip its tail over the sand.

'What the hell?' I said.

'Dude, you just dropped like a fucking rock,' Fitzpatrick said. He handed over his canteen and I washed out my mouth, then took a swallow, the water tasting like dust and plastic. He went on, 'For a second we thought you'd been shot or something. So we're all taking cover, wondering where the fuck is the sniper, and then that dog comes trotting down the wadi.'

'Sleed, Sleed,' Blornsbaum said. 'Sleed the Gentle. Sleed the Meek. Wild animals flock to the poor son of a bitch like he's Saint Francis wrapped in Kevlar. We have absolutely got to get this fainting business checked out, Sleed.'

He let the dog loose. It rushed me again, bowing and scraping in the sand.

'You're a good boy,' I said, running my fingers like a comb through his fur to work out some of the mats. I found myself already growing fond of the damn thing. It'd been so long since I had touched any living creature in a gentle way.

Galvan took a knee and petted the dog. Even he couldn't resist some canine affection. 'Well, Frago,' he said, scratching him behind the ears and naming him at the same time, 'considering your only food source out here is these barbecued motherfuckers, you might wanna roll with us awhile. Today's your lucky day.'

'Is that cool, Sergeant?' I said to Blornsbaum. 'Can he ride in our tank?'

'Galvan wants that dirty mutt in his turret, it's his problem. Never did care for dogs myself.'

The battalion was leaving soon, and we made our way down the steep side of the high ground where the sand was loosest and deepest. We took sideways steps, and the dune gave way and rolled in little avalanches. Frago followed, zigzagging a switchback. It already felt like he belonged. Funny how in five minutes you can get so fearsomely in love with a dog. He was our first trophy, a mascot for the hard times ahead. A scavenger, a mutt, a survivor of uncertain pedigree.

Correction. He was our second trophy, counting Galvan's photos.

★ ★ ★

Couple klicks outside Baghdad, we took Palace Row without a fight. The bulk of our brigade headed on into the city, while Higher ordered our company to hold at the Row, 'to secure the area and search it for possible high-value targets,' in their words. When done with that, we were supposed to stick around and serve as a quick reaction force. QRF. Kind of like an ace in the hole, backup in case our guys in the city got overrun and needed the armored cavalry to come charging to the rescue.

On QRF we got a lot of free time, compared to before. We spent it sleeping, and when we'd had our fill of that, we poked around the Row. Place was like nothing I'd ever seen. A battalion staffer found Saddam's solid-gold toilet in our headquarters palace. The news spread, and a long line of soldiers formed up to see it. They said it weighed eight hundred pounds. Said it was worth five mil, at least. The line stretched through the palace all the way to the front gates, which looked like they were also made of gold but really were gilded brass. Outside was a checkered marble porch that looked over a man-made lake no more than a couple feet deep. A fake lake, like at a golf course. The palace with the gold toilet was just one of many near it. The most unusual one was built out over the lake on a concrete pier supported by tall pilings. We called it the water palace. Our battalion translator, whose name was Mohammed but who went by Moe, said its actual name was Victory over America Palace. It'd been built by Saddam to celebrate the end of Gulf War I and was destroyed in the first days of part two. Victory, my ass. Thing looked like a ruined temple. Cruise missiles had pounded the walls and the pier, and the section connecting it to the shore had fallen. There was no way to get inside without wading into the lake and using grappling hooks or something to climb up. Higher had absolutely forbidden us from doing that. So you know we were thinking about it.

★   ★   ★

On our second day at the Row, our battalion took a casualty. Fluke type of thing. It happened in the headquarters palace, the one with the gold toilet. A kid named Private Simmons pulled a life-sized painting of Saddam from the wall, triggering a booby-trapped grenade lodged in a carved-out hole. Whoever had chipped away the plaster and placed that grenade behind the painting had been pretty smart. He knew we would take it down first thing. The orders had come straight from Lieutenant Colonel Easton. 'Remove and consolidate for demolition all artwork bearing regime imagery.' There was a ton of the stuff. We had a pile going in the main lobby.

Upstairs, before the explosion, Galvan had found something good. A trophy room filled with mounts. Antelope, giraffe, an elephant-foot ashtray. A full-grown African lion, stuffed and posed on a boulder. I went to see it. Frago came with. The big cat startled him and he barked at the lion until I went over and knocked on its skull with the muzzle of my rifle to show him it was just old skin.

'Ho,' Galvan said. 'Jackpot.'

Against the wall was a display cabinet filled with ancient artifacts. He took out a dagger a foot long, sheathed in a brass scabbard. I could see why it'd caught his eye, the scabbard all studded with gemstones.

'Those have got to be fake,' Fitzpatrick said.

'They look real enough to me,' Galvan said.

It was like something an Arab prince might have carried tucked in his belt. Galvan unsheathed it and used the tip of the blade to pry at an emerald on the scabbard. Fitzpatrick reached into the display case and picked up a small clay statue of a woman whose breasts drooped over a pregnant-looking belly. She was headless. Her hands and feet had also broken off sometime long ago. He held up the statue and eyed it like he was some kind of art expert.

'Fertility goddess. Probably Sumerian. You want, Sleed? She do it for you?'

'Why would I want that?'

'Come on,' Galvan said. 'You know how much a thing like this is worth?'

'No, and you don't, either.'

'I know it's more than you make in a year. Like ten times as much. Damn, kid. Don't you ever go to sleep at night, like, wanting something more out of life? You ever dream about something bigger and better, or are you just too much of a pussy?'

'Yeah,' Fitzpatrick said, thrusting the idol at me.

Frago growled.

'Why do you care if I take it?' I said.

'Because. Then you've got some skin in the game. Then we're sure you're not gonna rat.'

I thought about it and decided I was not entirely against the idea. Everyone else was getting some, even the Iraqis, looting hell out of the Baath Party ministries, carting off copper piping and light fixtures and wires ripped out of the walls. Artwork, furniture, satellite dishes, spare parts for Russian-made flight simulators, law books, filing cabinets, arc welders, and second-generation fax machines that they hoisted like the greatest prizes ever won. Not to mention the other side of the coin. The U.S. contractors and mercenaries setting up shop in our AO, trucking in porta-potties and crates of frozen hamburger patties and concrete blast barriers and bottled water and ten thousand other things you need to run a comfortable modern war zone. The Row felt lucrative, like walking into a casino with a buzz on and your pocket fat. You had the feeling a man could make a fortune with a minimum amount of work, but only if he had balls.

'I'm not a rat,' I said. 'Or a puss. But that old clay shit don't do it for me.'

'Oh yeah? What you want, then?'

I told them I'd do it the smart way. Maybe snag a couple gems from the scabbard if Galvan would let me. Sew them into the lining of my uniform. Something like that, something small, easy to get home and sell. Cash would be good. 'Got to be a hoard around here somewhere.' We talked about what we would do when we were rich, messed with the dagger, and about that time, Private Simmons, working downstairs in another part of the palace, took down the painting of Saddam. The walls shook with a walloping *boom*.

* * *

I had a close call myself not too long after. I was riding with Fitzpatrick, Gal van, and Patterson when it happened. We had use of a Humvee that we took on supply runs down the highway to Camp Zopilote. Place was named after a soldier who'd rolled his Bradley into the Euphrates and drowned. It was nothing special, just an old Iraqi army base that we'd taken over, and we were headed there to pick up hot chow for the QRF. That was what we were risking our lives for. Any meal that was not an MRE was a luxury, and it made as much sense to risk your life for food as

69

for something as vague as Iraqi Freedom. Plus, it was worth the trip just to get away for a while. The Row looked impressive, but things there were starting to get weird. Two dudes from First Platoon, Crocker and Jenkins, had been prowling around, dry-humping guys while they were sleeping. It was part of a gradual slip in our standards. Everyone had stopped paying much attention to manners or decency. We wiped our snot on our sleeves or pinched our noses and blew strands of it to the ground. There weren't enough water buffaloes for us to shower or wash clothes, so the smell was like the monkey house at the zoo. Conditions at Zopilote, while not great, were a grade better, and with hot chow in the mix, I jumped at the chance to go.

IEDs were still rare at that point. No one expected to get hit, although we knew we could. I was riding in the rear passenger seat and we'd traveled about halfway to the camp when the bomb went off and all I saw was orange. I can't remember exactly what it sounded like. I guess like nothing at all, an empty space followed by ringing ears and Galvan shouting at Patterson, 'Don't fucking stop here! Just keep going, floor it, fucking go!'

Our truck emerged from the dust cloud, and everyone was fine. Second Platoon's gunner had taken a sliver of shrapnel to his right hand. Like a splinter. Hardly any blood. We continued to Zopilote and radioed in the location of the IED. Later we heard that ordnance disposal had been sent to the spot and they'd discovered the primary device still intact, undetonated. Two

70

155-millimeter Soviet artillery shells wired together, over a hundred pounds of high explosive. That would've obliterated us, for sure. The blast we had driven through was only the crude primer going off.

We sped away knowing we'd been lucky but not knowing just how big a break we'd caught. We laughed like it was the funniest thing in the world. Too hard, like crazy people laugh, the way you do when you almost died but didn't, not even a scratch. Believe me, I've tried it all, and there's not much that will get you higher.

5

Abu al-Hool: The Time When Camels Are in Calf

Pakistan; Syria; Iraq (Haditha):
103 days before

The previous winter, within a matter of days, the Taliban had fallen in a rout. Most of the old camps, including ours, were destroyed, forcing us over the border into Pakistan like mice avoiding the trap. Death came to the surface everywhere: the latest were the Uzbeks — Abu Timur and his son Abu Bakr, the boy I had once found so promising when he had joined the brotherhood in the days before Manhattan. The loss of the youngest and most vibrant among us was a hard blow to take; it happened across the Afghan border near a settlement at the head of a valley not far from our old camp. Several kilometers above the little community of shepherds, inaccessible by road, the Americans had set an outpost commanding the low ground. A group of us had traveled there to observe their position and study it for weaknesses, arriving at night disguised as merchants, rifles hidden in carts. We brought no heavy weaponry and during the day took care not to congregate in open places: each morning, I sent a three-man patrol

72

to ascend the mountain and glass the enemy outpost from below the tree line. These men were armed with only a radio and binoculars, both of which were to be used sparingly.

The first few patrols passed without incident. On the fourth day, I sent Abu Hafs the Yemeni, along with Abu Timur and Abu Bakr. A few hours after they left, those of us remaining in the village heard the shrieking of a rocket, an explosion on the mountain. We retreated inside the guesthouse and for some time heard nothing except the crackling of fire in the stone hearth. The voices of children playing outside the door. We all knew the strike had targeted our men, but there was little we could do for them, not even to recover their bodies; the Americans might be watching and would kill us if we tried.

We agreed it was best to wait out the night indoors before attempting any other action. We had lost hope of survivors, then after nightfall Abu Hafs returned to us alone, wounded with shrapnel in his legs but still able to walk. He threw open the rough-hewn door and I embraced him, kissing his cheeks.

'The Uzbeks are dead,' he said stiffly, not returning my affection.

★ ★ ★

He was treated, given refreshment, and told us how Abu Timur had insisted on approaching the Americans closer than any of the other patrols, more brazenly toward that nest of vipers, until he'd led the boys to the tree line. Abu Hafs

73

realized the danger and told Abu Timur as much, but the older man dismissed the complaint as cowardice, claiming the Americans never fired on unarmed men who weren't in uniform; he'd supposedly learned this through trial and error in Bosnia.

'Abu Bakr knew I was right, but wouldn't leave his father,' Abu Hafs said. 'God forgive me, but I was not ready to become *shaheed*. I refused to follow them into the open.'

'Peace,' I said, trying to comfort him; by now he was in tears. 'There's no shame in what you did. I would've done the same thing. We're up against men who won't show their faces to fight. You aren't the coward here.'

* * *

We crossed back over the border near Peshawar and made camp sprawled in the dusty soil under the shade of a Himalayan cedar that once again had grown tall and strong after being stricken decades ago, cleaved in two by a lightning bolt, an errant Soviet shell, or some other calamitous missile. Under that persistent tree we made the *fajr* prayer. It was Friday and Dr. Walid's turn to deliver the talk. By the way that he'd avoided me after the death of the Uzbeks, I should've seen what was coming, but my mind had grown cloudy with sorrow and fatigue after so much hard living in the field. I also found myself preoccupied with broader strategy, the Americans' good fortune. The turn in the war had left the brothers discouraged.

74

You wouldn't have known these troubles, seeing Dr. Walid that morning. He assumed a position of authority at the base of the cedar. There he sermonized, the brotherhood gathered around. Boys from a nearby farm spotted us and crossed a hay field to hang on curiously, captivated by this warrior-priest, this leader and scholar, his face lovingly formed, eyes clear and calm, beard black as the feathers of an alpine swift. I could not hold with him for sheer charisma. I was well aware of that, and of my other shortcomings, which went a long way to explaining what happened next.

'Brothers,' he said. 'I tell you that the last days of the Abbasid Caliphate were much like our own. The faithful were rare as diamonds scattered across the vastness of the Empty Quarter. Many were discouraged. They had left the cities, preferring to live instead with their wives and children in the desert. That life meant hardship, thirst, and starvation, but they preferred it to the caliphate's man-made depravities. They had turned their backs especially on the city of Baghdad, which was by then the most splendid in the world, far more sophisticated than any muddy village in Europe.

'Alas, we know the story too well,' he continued. 'Sophistication breeds vice, grandeur walks arm in arm with deceit, and triumph is always followed by a period of sloth and greed. Word of Baghdad's wealth spread north across the steppes until it reached the Mongol Khan, who demanded tribute. When he was denied, he assembled his army of horsemen and rode at its head, vowing to force the caliphate into submission or die trying.'

I saw very well what he was getting at, and it was no mere grandiloquent history lesson. For months, the symbolic importance of the fall of Baghdad in the thirteenth century of the so-called Common Era had recurred as a theme in his Friday talks. To give him his due, he had been predicting the American invasion of Iraq ever since the weeks immediately following Manhattan. It had seemed far-fetched to me at the time, and it was still hard to believe his prediction was coming correct, their forces massing steadily in Kuwait. That the Americans would be so foolish as to fulfill what I imagined were Sheikh Osama's exact wishes when he had sent those jets smashing into the towers — it seemed too easy, too simple, to trap them in this way.

Dr. Walid's historical analogy was equally unqualified, yet powerful ideas often are. My tendency to dwell in nuance was no doubt one reason I had lost the brothers' confidence. The doctor was nothing if not sure of himself. He paced in the dappled shadows and shook his fist.

'And I say to you that even as today British dogs and Saudi princes lick American boot heels, so too did the Mongols have their Tatars and mercenaries riding in their train. And, even as Bush warns and threatens the Great Syria, so too did the Mongols conquer al-Sham after riding out laden with spoils from Baghdad, the city sacked, its women raped, warriors and children put to the sword, the House of Wisdom

76

destroyed, until the Tigris ran black that day from the ink of all the books flung in the water — '

'Brother Walid,' I interrupted rudely, and more than a little unwisely. 'We all know the story. Forgive me, but I lost the connection with the theological point you were following.'

'The point is simple, Emir. The point is that the past repeats itself. I've often heard you say this. And, although things may look dark now, my brothers, you should take heart. Because, even as the fall of Baghdad will again come to pass, so too did armies from Syria and Egypt, together with Arab volunteers, join forces two years after the sack of the capital, defeating the Mongols at the Battle of Ayn Jalut. We must have faith that God in His goodness will punish the Americans as He did the khan. There's really only one question. When will the new Ayn Jalut take place?'

The brothers waited expectantly, thinking this yet another rhetorical flourish on his part. But the silence extended until it became obvious he had finished his sermon and wanted an actual answer.

Abu Hafs the Yemeni stood and spoke. 'Soon, God willing. Soon we'll make the Americans the new Mongols.'

The brothers proclaimed the *takbir*, hearts bursting with pride to think they might be the lucky ones to restore the caliphate. Dr. Walid seized upon that moment of solidarity to topple me with supple skill, the thing so smoothly done, there was no violence in it, no need even to denounce me or my legitimate faults as reasons why he should be chosen and I deposed. Over the past ten years, my command had been affirmed several times by voice vote, the last before we traveled to Chechnya. That campaign ended in tragedy; by all rights, my term should've ended then as well. I suppose I was overdue.

The doctor placed his hand over his heart and approached. 'Emir, you must know we'll have a better chance in the Iraqi cities. We're too exposed in these mountains; our power is too diffuse. In the cities — with all the other brothers who are bound to travel there — together, we can strike the enemy a real blow. How many more like Abu Bakr must give their lives before we realize this?'

'There's some truth to what you say,' I agreed, masking the anger I felt toward my former right hand, this usurping, blackguard physician. Before this day, he and I had argued long and hard, but always privately, about whether to take the brotherhood to Iraq if the Americans were to invade that country. I'd been against leaving Afghanistan, but my reluctance was largely the kind of conservatism that inevitably besets men my age, an unwillingness to change, a clinging to routine. Afghanistan had become my home. Over the years, I had grown to love the place and its people, the freest and purest in the world. How many empires had left their mark on this proud country, only to be shrugged off? Alexander the Great, the Mongols, the Arabs, the British, and now the Americans — and still there were valleys where outsiders had never been allowed to set foot, and people who had never been taxed by any government. This place was at the edge of the known world and at the same time, its obscure, violent nexus.

What Walid was proposing — taking the fight to the Americans in Iraq — was an obvious, if radical, change in our strategy. I could see merit in the plan and hope in the boldness of its ambition. Clearly, many of the men preferred it. I myself did not, but had trouble articulating why. I could have pointed out the risk of the unknown, the danger of biting off more than you can chew, but I held my tongue. Citing vague dangers seemed an unacceptable argument against taking decisive action in warfare, an enterprise in which the most perilous approach is sometimes the right one.

The brothers awaited my answer to the doctor's challenge. His eyes held mine steadily, and I confess I looked away first, afraid of him, not in the sense that I feared he would harm me, but afraid of the intentions I saw, of what he might become if his will were left unchecked. I knew that going to Iraq was not the only thing about our operations that he would change. There was something monstrous in him, an impenetrable jocularity that concealed a mass of ills, ruin, and error. When he spoke of our destiny and the struggle, he did not mean any spiritual battle. He meant taking heads. 'Jihad and the rifle alone,' this was his motto. No negotiation, no truce, no settlement. A man with this sort of monomaniacal focus could not lead us to a new golden age. His was a perversion of our traditions — I knew this in my heart — but I was only one man, and those of his mind in the brotherhood had become more numerous. My time as emir was up. A good commander knows when to quit the field; there's always another day to retake it.

'You've spoken, and we heard you,' I said. 'Now, brothers, I think we must take a vote. Despite what the *kuffar* might think, we are a democracy, after all.'

A few laughed nervously at my sarcasm, but I spoke the truth. Before embarking on any new campaign, the brothers always select who among us should be emir.

'Those who choose Dr. Walid to bear the burden, say aye.'

With their words my authority ended. I accepted defeat with as much grace as I could, having known beforehand that I would lose, and perhaps badly. But one voice, notable in that it was hardly yet a man's, rose above the rest to sting my pride more than any other, even more than the voices of those who'd been with me much longer. Abu Hafs, whom I had taken under my wing and treated as if he were my own departed son, even he voted against me.

★   ★   ★

I was terribly seasick. I had always had this problem, the few times in my life I had traveled by ship. I tried to keep to myself, grown more introverted after losing command, but the close quarters onboard made solitude impossible. We had sailed from Karachi eight days before, headed around the Arabian Peninsula, through the Suez, to the port of Tartus, where we would arrive after another week at sea. It was a roundabout way to get to Baghdad but much safer than the overland route through Afghanistan and Iran, and we had contacts in Syria who would outfit us once we arrived at port. Traveling with me in this rusted freighter were coarse men who had been warehoused in regime prisons (which regime hardly matters), charged with petty thievery or licentiousness, these boys stricken by poverty who became men stricken by sin, until one day, as the story goes, they were befriended by a brother and shown the path of submission, often while in jail. It is a vexing paradox that the coarsest and most sinful among us often become the most pious: itinerants, nomads, wanderers; young men banished from their homelands, lost to their parents; and older men like myself, strangers to our own families — we were all lost, in the world's eyes — and yet, at the same time, possessed of a deceptive resiliency, like the new spring wood best suited for fashioning arrows.

The path from poverty to war was well trodden, but not the only path, and it would have been wrongheaded to assume, as apologists among the *kuffar* had, that want of material things was what compelled us to this jihad. It was more the other way around. For every brother with a meager past, like Abu Annas, orphaned in the worst slum of Jordan, there were

81

two like Abu Mohammed the Jeddite, men from prosperous families, the sons of merchants and engineers in the Kingdom; they arrived seeking remedies for a spiritual poverty that wealth only exacerbates. Some, like Dr. Walid, were descended from families of middling means, though, it should be said, the doctor had received a rich man's education after he flawlessly recited one of Iqbal's ghazals in the presence of a regional governor who was then visiting his village. The governor, a nephew of the king, was so moved by the young Walid's recitation that he practically adopted the boy, eventually paying for his education at Baghdad University and later Oxford.

And yet, almost to a man, our fathers' fathers abided the time-honored codes, knew the Qur'an and the hadith by heart, and lived as their ancestors before them, concerned with tending their herds, with their families, the substance of their days stretching without much variation back to the time of the Prophet. Most of those old ones — and I am speaking of men who came of age just out of living memory — had never so much as seen a Westerner or an internal combustion engine. Theirs was an arduous life that purified the spirit in the way of desert people, for whom trials are ordinary and every gift precious.

Perhaps I romanticize the monotony of a bygone age. But there is no denying that in the span of twenty years, everything changed. The time-honored ways of the old ones were set aside in favor of modern conveniences. The oil companies, the giant engineering firms, the foreign mercenaries and the Western military advisers, with their liquor and paper money and promises of empire, they thrust our princes onto the world's stage to play the fools of Monte Carlo. Petrodollars were welcomed at all the casinos of Europe, but even as they took our money, the *kuffar* aristocracy looked down their noses at their churlish Arab cousins, laughingstocks who aped the latest fashions and exchanged an ocean of oil for newly minted fortunes, which they spent like it was a matter of principle.

I was once well-off — not royalty, though I would've been heir to a tidy sum — but now found myself poor as a street cleaner, sick as a poisoned dog, useless as cargo on the vessel. Lonely, angry, miserable, the seasickness arousing a petulance in me that could not be distracted. I should have, instead of distilling the past, concentrated on discerning the future, but the coming war eluded me. I had campaigned on three continents but never against the Americans. I'd seen the strange apocalyptic masterworks of Hieronymus Bosch hanging in the Prado, I'd seen a lovely girl walking barefoot along the Nile, but never the onion-domed minarets of Baghdad, its triumphal arch made of smelted Iranian rifles, its slums teeming with millions. It had been decades since I had even visited a city so large. We traveled to the unknown, and I wasn't sure exactly why I had come along for the journey. Maybe I did know but was too afraid to admit it and thus make it real. When I looked over the rail of the rolling ship, I couldn't help but think of throwing myself into the waves.

★ ★ ★

Fifteen days later we crossed the Syrian border near al-Qa'im and entered Iraq. Before nightfall we drove south to Haditha, along the Euphrates, which was like a sapphire gaping through a deep crack in the desert. After unbroken years in the stark wilderness of Afghanistan and the tribal regions, the lushness of the river valley was a sight to gladden my heart. It reminded me of boyhood in Cairo and the river that the ancients simply called River, because which else would they be referring to? The Nile had been a short walk from Father's stately villa in the Maadi District, broad avenues shaded with eucalyptus trees planted to repel mosquitoes, the district itself a fairly recent development, carved out of mango plantations on the riverbanks; the first residents were Jews and British military officers. After the occupation ended, it remained home to the city's European expats and well-to-do natives, their children mingling at the Lycée Français du Caire — with classes taught in Arabic, French, and English — and at the nearby sporting club, where I passed countless afternoons playing squash and swimming in the pool within sight of the Giza Pyramids.

The present Iraqi scenery, riverine and so reminiscent of home, lifted my spirits and appeared to be having a similar effect on Dr. Walid, who rode with me and a few others in the lead truck. More animated than usual, he from time to time wiped the dust and sweat from his face with a handkerchief as he reassured us of his many contacts and supporters here, friends he'd met while studying at Baghdad University, where he took his baccalaureate nearly thirty years ago. From our guesthouse in Aleppo, the last stop before we crossed into Iraq, he recently had been corresponding with one of these men in particular, a fellow doctor practicing in Haditha, which was why we were headed there.

We traveled several hours and arrived at the physician's estate, outside town. I found Dr. Walid's old schoolmate pleasant enough, if a little full of himself, a fault common to men of that profession. We hid our trucks under cover of his palm grove and retired to the main house, where our host fed us *masgouf*, the national dish, which was new to me. After dinner he gave us the name of a cleric in Fallujah whom we might seek out for a base of support closer to Baghdad, our ultimate goal.

Darkness fell. Some of us went to town for coffee. The streets of Haditha buzzed with anticipatory liveliness, and, surprisingly, few people appeared afraid, even though all the talk in the café was about the air war, the Americans' 'shock and awe,' which we all knew would surely commence within days, if not tonight.

Just now I've been talking with Abu Hafs, his pallet situated beside mine on the recessed roof of the doctor's home. We've heard jets flying overhead, although it's unclear whether they're American or Iraqi, and no bombs have yet fallen. The night air is cold, and I write by penlight, wool blanket hooded over me.

Over the past weeks the Yemeni and I have

repaired our friendship. He's grown comfortable around me again and has gone so far as to confide that he only voted for Dr. Walid for emir because that was what all the other brothers were doing and he was afraid to go against them. Whether or not this is true, I don't know; the boy is earnest enough in his desire to please. I willingly blind myself to his flattery. He fulfills in me something that I thought had died with my son in that forest near Grozny. He's revived my manly desire to teach. There was a time when I took great pleasure in instructing the youth, but after Chechnya I tended to distance myself from them.

Tonight, laid out in the open air under a bowl of stars, Abu Hafs asked if he might take a wife in Iraq. Throughout the evening spent in town, I'd noticed him making eyes at a certain girl outside the café; I'd thought to correct this behavior, it was asking for trouble, but his glances were sly, never rising to the level of impropriety. More than scandalized, I felt sorry for him. He's at that transitional age when the blood runs hottest, yet he finds himself least able to secure a marriageable woman, the best matches being reserved for older men with greater means.

'I've heard even the rich ones practically fall over themselves for the honor of marrying mujahideen,' he said after I'd told him that, like anyone else, he would be permitted a wife if he was lucky enough to find one. 'I've heard the normal rules don't apply. That the engagement might only last a few days. Is that true?'

'Oh?' I teased. 'Is that why you decided to

make jihad? Who would've known. All along you were angling for a wife.'

'No. But why not? This could be my last chance.'

'With luck you'll have all the time in the world. You are barely a man, my son.'

'I'm more of a man than most of these Iraqis,' he said. 'They wouldn't fight for their honor if a knife were held to their throats. They've lived under the heel of the tyrant too long. Their spirit is broken. You can see it in their faces.'

'I'm not saying you aren't brave. But how would you provide for a wife? What would happen to her if you become *shaheed?* Would you be satisfied with your widow living on charity?'

'If I'm *shaheed*, she'll praise God she once had such a husband.'

'Praises won't pay her bills.'

'Do you think so little of women, Father of Dread?' He sounded genuinely curious, not reproachful. 'Do you think that all they want is to be rich and comfortable? Don't they want the same things we do? Their hearts burning for justice?'

'No,' I said plainly. 'Their hearts aren't the same as ours at all. Marrying a mujahid is like taking a crown of roses that starts to wilt as soon as you put it on.' I gestured at the flat, broad roof where the other brothers were sleeping. 'How many of them do you think are married ?'

'I'm not sure. I know the emir has a wife back in Afghanistan.'

'He does,' I said. 'And one in Medina. And I have a wife myself, in Pakistan.'

He seemed surprised to learn this. 'You never talk about her,' he said.

'We've become estranged. For all I know, she's divorced me and remarried. I write her from time to time, but it's been years since she replied. By now it's very possible I'm actually a bachelor.'

'You don't miss her?'

'Of course I do,' I said. 'Though I miss my children more.'

'They're with her?'

'That, or grown. Or dead. My eldest was martyred in Chechnya.'

An uncomfortable silence hung between us, as if Abu Hafs was unsure whether to express sympathy or congratulations on my son's distinction.

'Think long and hard about what you really want,' I continued, now in a softer and more reflective tone. 'Do you pray for a glorious death, or is it a home, family? Comfort, safety and wealth, God's favor — it's nearly impossible to have all those things in one life. Choices must be made. No one will think any less of you if you marry and decide to leave the struggle. You made a good jihad in Afghanistan. You did your duty better than most.'

'I won't leave my brothers,' he said, not even thinking about it, possessed with all the stupid confidence of youth. I felt sure he was reliving his shame over the strike that killed Abu Bakr on the mountain. He rolled over on his pallet so as not to face me; we spoke no more. In time his breathing grew deeper, settling into the rhythms of an easy sleep. To be so young, when bodily fatigue is enough to erase one's troubles; at my age, they are, rather, compounded.

Awaiting another insomniac dawn, I realize I've been a fool to speak to him as I have. Tonight's impromptu lesson on the fickleness of women was a travesty. I have to restrain myself from waking the boy and telling him that everything I've said was a lie — prudent but wrong — and he would do well not to listen to the ramblings of one bitter with too much life. The point is not to avoid pain but to follow the right path, however painful. He should take one more wife than he thinks he can afford, father one more son than he can possibly mind, fight one more battle than he has the gall for, and then go to his grave with no regrets. How can a great man do anything less? What boy does not wish for greatness? How would we ever know our limits, if not for constantly overstepping them?

'What's gone is dead,' I tell myself, needing the reminder. I gaze on the sleeping form of Abu Hafs and ponder the mystery of the generations, how one's hour forever draws to a close. Our time is short, twenty thousand days. I think of my son who will remain forever young in death. Sometimes, I try to imagine how he would've changed and grown if he'd survived Chechnya, but it's as difficult as imagining oblivion.

But there — that's just the thing. A child is nothing if not a projection of oneself through time, a wish for immortality made flesh. I look at this proud Yemeni boy, whom I've come to adore as my own, and I see beneath the level of

89

analogy: I see myself, glimpsed through an infinitude of filters, so to speak, which is the world. Life gazing on life and wishing it could live forever.

Praise God that is impossible. Praise God for not giving us what we want. Praise God that what is gone, is dead.

6

Cassandra: Suffer the Children

Iraq (Triangletown): 1 day before

Some wiseass dubs it Triangletown, and the
name sticks. None of the GI topo maps show it
here, this gnarly growth on the side of the
highway, cinder-block compounds, mud-brick
and sheet-metal shanties, goat stables roofed in
white-painted straw, open sewers, hand-dug
wells, a communal rice paddy watered by an
irrigation canal that runs parallel to the highway,
traveled by a detachment of Cassandra's
platoon, on their way to set a roadblock west of
Palace Row. The hinterlands, cordon security.
Control the traffic into and out of Baghdad.

The villagers are warned of the platoon's
approach by their ascending dust cloud. Some of
the Iraqis drop what they're doing and kneel,
weeping, on the roadside: the emotional display
disingenuous, a stylized expression enacted for
the benefit of authority. Others keep their
distance and stare sullenly or gape-mouthed, like
what they're seeing is impossible, a ghost army
booming down the highway, the war and the
Americans finally here, Baghdad having fallen
mid-April after little more than a week of
fighting, and only three weeks after the platoon

crossed over from Kuwait with the second wave of troops to enter the country. Everyone is in the streets. Cassandra makes eye contact with an old woman who holds up a sick-looking girl, bundled in a blanket, like she wants one of the gunners to take her. The woman shouts at the convoy as it passes, growing more frantic as no one acknowledges her, ululating, now crying out to God, one of the few Arabic words Cassandra understands. After first detecting *Allah* in the greater cacophony, she hears it on everyone's tongue in tones variable and only guessed at — exclamation, plea, blessing, joke, curse; she finds it difficult to discern the prevailing mood in the crowd. Everything inside them pouring out in a rush.

For Triangletown's children, the Americans' arrival is less serious. More like a carnival train steamed into town. The kids, some shod in tire-tread sandals and some barefoot, run along the cracked asphalt, trying whatever English they've picked up.

'Hello, I love you! Mistah, I love you!'

'*Ameriki nam!*'

'No no Saddam! Saddam donkey! Yes Bush, Bush good! One water, please, mistah?'

They call her *mister*, just like the rest. From a distance, the Humvee in motion, it's a common enough mistake. Her size-medium body armor draws her breasts uncomfortably tight against her chest; the chemical suit smooths the curve of her hips to baggy uniformity. With the Kevlar helmet overlarge on her head, hair the same length as the average Iraqi man's, and desert goggles bulging like frog eyes to hide her cheekbones, she does look like a baby-faced boy suited up for high school football in pads too large for her. Which means she looks like many of the young men riding in the convoy's three other Humvees.

Her truck closely trails Lieutenant Choi's, and together with the others they crawl down the heaving street, slowing to navigate the crowd. Crump nearly runs over a toddler who darts in front of them at the last second. He curses, slams on the brakes, and thrusts his palms on the Humvee's horn, which makes a pathetic bleating sound like a Model T Ford. There are a few other near misses; the Iraqi kids press in close, their begging claustrophobic, but soon the platoon clears the throng and after that the far border of Triangletown, speeding up again on open highway beyond, big knobby tires humming over asphalt, the low roar of road wind sucking at the eaves of her helmet, morning sun just risen high enough to hit them sideways, like the light in a bad dream.

They arrive at the roundabout, splitting the highway four ways. Holding this intersection for a twenty-four-hour shift will be their small part today in securing the capital city, about a fifteen-minute drive east. Shit mission to draw, just one step up from getting stuck pulling guard with the quick reaction force back at the Row.

Crump parks their truck near the center of the circle, where stands a monumental statue of Saddam greened with copper rust. This President Hussein, unlike the one toppled and

93

televised last week, is costumed with an eye to please the local, traditionally minded population, robed as a sheikh in a long flowing dishdasha.

'Look at him in his fucking man dress,' Crump says. 'Shit's gay.'

Cassandra doesn't bother responding. With the exception of a couple of refit breaks, she's been cramped in this truck for days, pulling what could be called combat missions, sent here and there to set up snap checkpoints and roadblocks, but hasn't yet fired a shot. McGinnis has warned them repeatedly to stay vigilant. Keep up with weapons maintenance. Hydrate. Watch for blood clots forming in your legs from too much time behind the wheel. That last one seemed like an unlikely thing to worry about at first. Not anymore.

They waste no time dismounting, moving around to get the juices flowing. McGinnis fires up his camp stove, puts on water for coffee, and spreads his laminated map of their sector over the hood of the truck, where he meets with his fellow noncommissioned officers and Lieutenant Choi. They pore over the map, fretting over grid coordinates, defilades, enfilades, the emplacement of wire obstacles, and other tactical arcana.

Crump does not dismount with the rest. He conks out in the driver's seat almost immediately after ratcheting up the parking-brake handle. Cassandra is continually amazed by how he can fall asleep on cue. He's spent nearly every spare minute of the war sleeping through it. Fastest way to get to the end, she guesses. Above him in the hatch, she considers a little kick in the shoulder to startle him awake. He should be awake right now, adding oil to the truck, doing something, anything, but the malicious urge passes, and she busies herself with weapons maintenance, using a dry paintbrush to dust off the fifty.

Pulling security, she takes stock of her surroundings. A bleak landscape, not so much a desert but a poisoned wasteland that looks as drab and disordered as an abandoned construction site, it stretches flatly and with little variation into fields of brittle gray clay, the kind that would turn to gumbo mud in the rain and cling to your boots by the pound. Debris is strewn everywhere, mounds of jackhammered concrete, garbage hauled from Triangletown piled here and there and set aflame, some of it still smoldering, big black steaming mounds of trash like the devil's shit. Judging by the amount that's accumulated, this area near the round-about must've been used as a dumping site long before the war started. Rotten plastic sacks blow in the wind. A goatherd trudges through the middle distance, driving his flock from a trash mound abuzz with horseflies to a cesspool where the animals lap up verdigris sludge. She looks through the binos and sees that one of his goats has four horns, four looping horns — a genetic freak. No grass to speak of, not a green living thing in sight except for a narrow margin of canes rooted in the banks of the canal, so the goats would appear to feed primarily on garbage. She knows their meat must taste foul.

'Let's go, people,' McGinnis says, refolding his

map. 'Make it nice and obvious this thing's closed to all civilian traffic. I know our tasking here isn't the sexiest, but it's important — we can't afford any screwups.'

After delivering this tired motivational speech, he launches into constructing the roadblock, directing the work and doing more than his share; in less than an hour they transform the neglected crossroads into a makeshift citadel. He assigns one truck to each of the four spurs radiating from the center of the roundabout, with every machine gun on every truck oriented outward, and in the middle of it all, the statue of Saddam offering his unmoving blessing.

They put on leather work gloves and unlash hoops of concertina from stowage on the trucks' hatchbacks, drawing out the wire in looping barricades to close a perimeter around themselves. Fifty meters farther they pop road flares and set them in a burning red line across each spur. Those mark the point of no return. Drive your vehicle through it, and expect to be fired on.

As the work continues, the kids from Triangletown descend on them like buzzards to carrion, having followed the platoon almost a mile down the highway. Pretty soon there are dozens of them past the flares, jockeying for prime spots close to the concertina that separates them from the Americans. It isn't just curiosity that draws them; again they're begging. Feeding the local nationals has been forbidden from on high, and Cassandra can tell that McGinnis disapproves, but she and some of the other soldiers take pity — charity as relief from boredom — and tear into their less desirable MREs: bean-and-rice burrito, jambalaya, chicken à la king. They rip open the plastic pouches and toss the contents piecemeal to the kids. Within minutes an economy develops. Most valued are the miniature glass bottles of Tabasco sauce and any dessert item: minipacks of M&M's, Charms hard candies, pound cakes, and chocolate bars manufactured with a higher-than-normal melting point for high-temperature environments, desert, jungle.

The children crowd around and shout requests for MRE items like ecstatic commodity traders working a pit. A large group gathers near her truck. Even more fascinating to them than the prospect of candy is her sex. Her short blond hair matted with head grease and dust, its texture having coarsened to something like tawny fur, still manages to exert an entrancing power, especially over the little boys. They chatter and point. 'Emirah'at Ameriki' at jundi!'

A blond American woman: this is something they've only seen captured on film before today, the day the war comes to their doorstep and carries with it an American blonde — not many would call her a bombshell, but she's youthful, pretty, armed, and in uniform, all of which qualities taken together elevate her status to something grand and exotic, a reclusive celebrity, a mythological being.

'Allo, madam! I am Haider! What is your name?'

The boy is very thin, with brown eyes that at

97

first glance appear bright but are actually just fierce. He reaches across the wire, shouting at her, missing both front teeth, jabbering with mouth full of the chocolate she has just given him, the last she had. She claps empty hands together and shows her palms to him and the others.

'I'm out, guys. No more. Sorry.'

They understand much of what she says, most of all her empty hands, and everyone except the little boy, Haider, moves off to Corporal Treanor's truck, parked the next spur over. A few soldiers there are still tossing out food. But Haider stays, holding one hand forlornly over his heart.

'Madam. What is your name?'

To her mind the kid seems off. Too friendly, given the circumstances, talking to her across razor wire, and sort of robotic sounding, with little variance between the first and second time he's asked this same question.

'Specialist Wigheard,' she says.

'Special-ist,' he repeats, mulling over the name incredulously.

'My rank.' She tugs on the sharp black insignia pinned to her collar. 'Like my army name. Wigheard is my last name.' For a moment she feels more an elementary teacher, less a soldier, pointing to each letter of the name tape on her uniform, announcing in turn, 'W-I-G-H-E-A-R-D. Wigheard.'

'Yes. Army,' he says solemnly, reaching with his chocolate-smeared hand for her rifle. '*Jundi*.'

She takes a quick step back from the wire so

98

he can't touch the weapon, hefting it, readjusting its strapped weight on her neck, pinched from the constant load; she smirks at him in a kindly sort of way, not wanting to rebuff him too harshly but at the same time wary of anyone, even a child, who lacks sense enough not to grab for a soldier's gun. Maybe a cultural thing, she thinks. The Iraqi men she's met so far have been close talkers, with a different conception of personal space. And he's just a child, seven, eight. But still, should be old enough to know to keep hands to himself. If this place isn't the school of hard knocks, she doesn't know what is. Maybe it's the fact that she's a woman that makes him feel free to take dumb liberties.

'My friend, madam, I love you. Please, chocolat-tay.'

She chuckles, having been in country long enough to detect a pattern and find pleasure in its repetition: for all his simple appetites, Haider speaks in the ingratiatingly polite way of Iraqis taught with British-made textbooks, transposing Arabic conventions into the second language. Words and phrases like *madam, mister, my friend*, are not genteel placeholders but vital ways to show respect when addressing a stranger.

She's been surprised at how formal the kids sound and also by how many of them know at least some English. Haider's face beams with hope as he removes the candy wrapper from his pocket and displays it to show proof of need.

'Sorry, kid. Like I said, it's gone. Maybe there'll be some more tomorrow.'

'Tuh-maura?' he repeats, having trouble with

99

her accent. 'Ah.' He nods agreeably, getting it. 'To-morrow. *Inshallah.*'

He flings the wrapper to the wind, and it tumbles into the canal that passes through a galvanized culvert near the spur of the roundabout where their crew stands watch. Crump is awake now, perched on top of the Humvee like a lanky gargoyle, his long legs draped over the windshield, rifle resting unprofessionally across his lap. To the rear of the truck, McGinnis has lowered the tailgate to use it as a shelf for holding his canteen cup as he shaves in the reflection of a handheld signaling mirror.

'My friend, where are you from?'

'We're, uh — ' She almost says *Fort Hood.* 'Not really supposed to tell you that. But I'm originally from Missouri.'

'Where is Missouri?'

'Dead center of America. Pretty much the middle of nowhere. Kind of like this place. Dead. Not really, but not much happening, you know. So we've got that in common. No offense.'

'My friend, I love America. Soon I am going to the Missouri with you, yes?'

If you say so.

'I am eight years old.' Small for his age. He holds up his left hand and flashes five fingers, then three. For the first time Cassandra notices the defect in his other arm, which he has been holding close to his side, pressed against a careworn soccer jersey. The boy's right arm is normal except for the very end, shriveled and misshapen. Without a hand or fingers, it tapers to a diminutive paddle like a fleshy spoon. Her

100

first thought is trauma, but she doesn't see any scar tissue. She keeps her gaze moving, not wanting him to grow self-conscious, and with the pretext of stretching her lower back, which does in fact ache like crazy from the rifle and her body armor, she looks around the traffic circle at some of the other children. In that hasty survey she sees two more with obvious birth defects.

'My friend, you are Christian?'

'No,' she says flatly.

He tilts his head, regarding her with newfound suspicion. 'You are Jew?'

'No.' She decides to preempt this tired line of questioning. 'I'm not a Christian, a Jew, or a Muslim, Buddhist, or anything. I'm nothing.'

'You have no god?'

'Right. I'm not religious.'

'This is very bad,' he mutters, shaking his head and looking genuinely concerned. He shuffles his feet and glances away, like he might move on and search for another soldier to talk with, but something keeps him from leaving.

'My friend, how many sister you have?'

'None.'

'I have two. One is sick. She need hospital.'

'I'm sorry to hear that.'

'My friend, you are doctor?'

'No.'

'He is doctor?' Haider points at McGinnis, still shaving behind the Humvee.

'None of us are doctors. But that guy over there, Aguirre, is a medic.'

'Hey, don't go telling him that!' Crump chimes in from his perch on top of their truck.

'Little bastard might be a spy for al-Qaeda or some shit. Can't trust these dirt kids for nothing.'

'Seriously?' she says, voice heavy with sarcasm.

'He's right, you know,' McGinnis says, though not with any immediacy. 'Maintain op sec, Wigheard.'

Haider seems lost in their jargon but does realize his talk of a doctor has provoked some kind of kerfuffle, so he switches tack, returning once again to a less controversial topic, the previous one, their respective ages, not yet exhausted. 'I am eight years old. How old are you?'

'Nineteen. One nine.'

'Her birthday's next week,' Crump says. 'You should get her a present. Something that really says 'Iraq.' Let's see. Whatta y'all make around here other than piles of fucking garbage?'

'*Happy bird-day to you, happy bird-day to you.* Yes? This is right?'

'*You look like a monkey, and you smell like a bag of assholes,*' Crump sings back sneeringly. He pinches the bridge of his nose. 'Dang, not even kidding, son. You ever heard of a bath?'

'Like you could really smell him from up there,' Cassandra says. 'Like you smell any better.'

McGinnis peers around the back of the truck with razor pressed against cheek, shaving cream bearding his lower face. 'Knock if off, Crump.'

'Your bird-day is soon. My bird-day is soon. We are like this.' Haider crosses the fore and middle fingers of his good hand, looking pleased with his logic, apparently unbothered by Crump's teasing. A look of transgression comes over him, as if he's just thought of something wickedly clever. 'He is your husband?' He thrusts his chin toward the back of the truck, McGinnis.

'Nope. She don't have one,' Crump says, happy to make this known. He lowers his voice to a deep bass, faux pidgin English. 'She, no-man. You, yes-man. You like the cock. She, no likey. You, she, no-same-same.'

Haider scowls in confusion and anger at the gag being played on him. He turns from Crump to Cassandra, seeking guidance: she purses her lips, eyes wide, nodding, yep, no husband here, and kind of glad to blow his little mind with that. He lets out a wan huff and silently mouths words, searching for the right ones with which to inquire further, when Crump cuts him off.

'See, little G, in America the ladies got the power. We don't make them wear those black beekeeper suits and work in the fucking fields all day like fucking slaves. And they get to choose when they wanna get married. Ain't like here. Can't just trade in a few camels and cop yourself a wifey from your uncle.'

'Go fuck yourself, Crump,' she says, picking up a small stone and winging it at him, and, while missing deliberately, sending it close enough to make him duck.

Haider laughs, voice liking, taking joy in the petty violence and also in learning a new English phrase that probably means something obscene and most definitely produces a combative response.

'Oh, I'd love to,' Crump says. 'If I could get a minute's peace, I'd rub one out for you, Wigheard, no problem.' He sets the butt of his rifle in his crotch and pretends the weapon is a phallus, jerking off the barrel into the overcast sky.

'You, Ali Baba,' Haider says, wagging his finger at him. 'You, fuck yourself.'

'Wrong again, dumbass. It's 'go fuck yourself.' Little mutant fuck-tard, fucking dirt kid — you're the only Ali Baba around here.'

He springs from the roof to the hood of the truck, vaults to the ground, and feints a charge at Haider, who sees it coming in plenty of time and is already dashing away. The boy stops and turns to make sure they're watching. Then, very purposely, points his left index finger at his shriveled right hand, which he holds at his midriff. It looks like a fixed, meaningful gesture. He directs it at Saddam's statue, then at Crump.

'You, Saddam, like this!' Satisfied the message has been received, he runs off to join the other children, now mobbing Treanor and his crew for their private stash of beef jerky.

'I think that little bastard just flipped me off in Iraqi,' Crump says.

McGinnis wipes off the last of his shaving cream, not dispensed from a metal can of Gillette like most of the men have brought, but a tube of something expensive, organic, ordered off the Internet and shipped from California to Fort Hood; in addition to several common dyes and industrial fragrances, McGinnis is allergic to nearly everything. Tree nuts, gluten, shellfish, penicillin, the dander from more or less any furred mammal. The dust in Iraq has been giving him hell, and he takes an antihistamine twice a day. Symptom of growing up rich, Cassandra thinks — high strung, with HEPA filters and live-in help to scrub everything clean. Whatever the cause of the allergies, she can't remember ever meeting a poor kid who had them that bad. McGinnis's Achilles' heel. He carries an epi shot in his thigh pocket at all times and has a list of his most serious allergens, penicillin right there on top, pinned to the inside of his helmet where a medic might find it if McGinnis were too fucked up to convey the information verbally.

He tosses out the sudsy gray shaving water from his canteen cup and slams shut the tailgate, truly angry now. 'Get your ass to parade rest, Crump. Didn't I just tell you to knock it off? I catch you treating any more civilians like that, you'll be in the front-leaning rest until *I* get tired. Roger? These people's good graces are all that's standing between us and a shit storm. You show them respect. Better yet, just keep your mouth shut. We clear?'

Crump rogers him petulantly.

'Good. At ease.' McGinnis drops the sanctimonious drill sergeant routine. 'Kid didn't flick you off, though. Not exactly. When they do that, point one finger at five fingers all bunched up like that? — it means one into five. Like, your mom was such a slut, she was with five dudes in one night. Then you were born.'

'Except the way he did it with that hand was more like one into two,' Cassandra says.

105

'Yeah, I saw that.'

'What's wrong with them?' In the short time since Haider has darted away, she's spotted yet another deformed child, a girl with a stooped back who throws out one leg in an exaggerated circular motion with each step. She wonders if this could be Haider's sister, the sick one he mentioned.

'Who knows,' McGinnis says, eyeing the canal. 'Could be some toxin leaching into the water. I wouldn't even wanna guess what's buried out here. Hell, could be good old-fashioned inbreeding. Case you didn't notice, the gene pool back there in Triangletown wasn't too big.'

'Fucking hajjis are bass-ackwards,' Crump says.

They ignore him, their attention catching on Treanor's spur, where Haider and a tall kid with big ears have started to fight. The larger boy throws Haider over his hip and snakes an arm around his neck; Treanor hovers over the two like a wrestling referee, shouting pointers that are completely lost on them due to insufficient vocabulary — 'Fist in your elbow! Lock your fist in your elbow!'

Haider struggles gamely, but it's impossible for him to escape the hold with the use of only one arm. He flails the bad one blindly over his shoulder, the withered hand a blunt object useless for anything other than striking. The big-eared boy chokes him until he submits. A disputed piece of beef jerky is the prize of this fight.

'That's about enough of that,' McGinnis says.

He buttons up his uniform blouse, which he removed while shaving, grabs his helmet and weapon, and heads across the roundabout to Treanor's truck. As he approaches, he yells, '*Ishta! Ishta!*' and the mob of kids shrieks and scatters like a flock of gulls disturbed into flight. He takes careful high steps as he crosses through a hidden gap in the wire and, when on the far side, picks up the pace, driving the children down the road, in the direction of Triangletown. 'Don't come back here! It's dangerous! *Ishta, ishta!*'

The kids retreat, begrudgingly ceding ground, but some will not take him seriously until he runs down the road after them like he's on fire, holding his rifle at port arms, charging the last few holdouts. They backpedal down the highway, taunting him in Arabic. One boy throws rocks to no effect.

She's impressed by their fearlessness. She imagines what she would've done as a girl if an invading army had shown up and closed down the intersection where county road meets state road near the turnoff to her grandparents' land. What her mother and father would've done in the same situation. Probably locked the doors and drawn the shades and absolutely forbidden her from going outside. What parent in their right mind would let their kids come down here? Struggling to understand, she recalls one of the briefings they suffered through at Camp New York, 'Understanding the Arab Mind.' Typical army class, taught from PowerPoint slides, delivered by some public affairs officer flown in from Central Command to school the grunts. He lectured them on the Arab sense of fatalism, the whole martyrdom thing, how it fits into Islamic beliefs, the Five Pillars, jihad, the hajj, circling clockwise around the black cubic Kaaba, praying five times a day, abstaining from pork, graven idols, the whole bit.

She found the cultural-sensitivity training by turns maddening and intriguing: there was enough of both to make her pay attention. She remembers an Arabic word explicated by the public affairs officer; Haider just used it, *inshallah*, meaning 'God willing.' A word employed in the same way an English-speaker might say 'I hope so' or 'maybe' or 'only time will tell.'

The proof was in the language, the public affairs officer claimed; Arabs literally thought nothing was left to chance because in their minds there was no such thing, all events already divinely predetermined. This doubtful insight came as a bullet on the final PowerPoint slide, followed by 'A firm grasp on the Arab mind will be your key to winning Arab hearts.'

The sentiment sounded recycled and hokey, if vaguely plausible. Even more so when compared with the cultural analyses proffered by some of the soldiers in the audience, including the chaplain's assistant, a nebbish altar-boy type who was usually gentle but who would rant with appalling vehemence about 'ragheads,' denouncing Islam as a 'barbaric and savage religion' to anyone in the battalion who would listen.

Now, as she looks out across the parched and brittle fields and the poisoned water going stagnant in the canal, the smoldering trash pits giving off a dusty orange smoke probably laden with heavy metals, she thinks that when it came down to it, the public affairs officer understood next to nothing about this place or these people. How could he have? He himself admitted he'd never been here. He took his knowledge of Iraq from briefings and books, which weren't useless — his class did teach her plenty she wouldn't have learned otherwise — but there was nothing in what he said about the Sunni — Shia rift or the basic Islamic customs that even hinted at what it was like to live in a mud hut by the side of the highway, to give birth to stillborn monsters with twisted bones and exposed spinal cords, all the while knowing how comfortably safe the good life could be in other parts of the world where lived other, more fortunate people, because television is everywhere, even here, and you wouldn't have to watch much to realize this place you had chanced to be born into is terrible. That it exists as if a nebulous and malevolent force has been directed expressly against it. You couldn't explain that by learning the fucking Five Pillars of Islam.

She watches McGinnis return down the highway after running off the last of the kids, who are fearless, lighthearted, and not much bothered by a seemingly crazed foreign soldier screaming at them to get the hell away. What they have missed in worldliness, they make up for in courage; at ten years old they have more balls than the average American badass she's known. Crump, who aspires to badassness, called them dirt kids, and, while that name lacks any human kindness, there's something more vital in those two words than in anything the public affairs officer said during his hour-long lecture. There's nothing abstract about *dirt kids*. Which makes it a much safer idea than *the Arab mind*. More than childish insults, pleasant-sounding abstractions are the thing to get large numbers of people killed.

McGinnis arrives at the truck breathing hard, sweating. She passes him a canteen, and he takes a swallow, leans back, and pours some water over his hair, casting it off like a wet dog.

'You all right, Sarge?' Crump says. 'Never really seen you go ape like that.'

'For their own good,' McGinnis says, still panting a little. 'We're a great big target, sitting here. Waiting on whatever comes down the highway. Let's say the shit does pop off. We start taking incoming. Maybe a suicide car bomber blows through the concertina. I don't know about you. I'd rather not have a bunch of dead kids on my conscience.'

Crump says nothing but chews his lip, tilting his head thuggishly.

'They come back, you tell them to get lost. The word for that is *ishta.*'

7

Abu al-Hool: The Forbidden Time

When I was twelve, Father took the entire family to London. It was my first trip to Europe, just another business junket for Father, but on behalf of his children, he seized every opportunity to make it an education; that was the kind of man he was, never abiding a wasted minute. Unlike most of his peers, he didn't follow the cricket matches. His dinner table was no place for diversionary chatter but a venue to instruct us in political philosophy, literature, the fine arts, whatever he'd chosen as the day's subject.

In London he behaved no differently, rushing us hither and yon like some combination of dapper patriarch and mad tour guide. We saw Parliament, the British Museum, the Tower and the Crown jewels, Buckingham Palace, and many more attractions, but the one that made the most vivid impression on me was Westminster Abbey. The statuary cluttering the walls shocked my sensibilities; I'd been taught graven imagery did not belong in sanctified places. I was fascinated by the tombs of the English kings, the reliquaries that compelled me with a boy's morbidity to

111

wonder at what their regal, mummified bodies must've looked like inside those crypts after so many undisturbed centuries.

I moved through the nave and into the quire, exploring every nook of this monument that rose up toward heaven and our striving and common pain. The place awakened something in me. For the first time in my life — at least, the first that I can recollect — I had a physical sense of the divine, the feeling welling in my chest until I thought I would cry tears of joy. I climbed the flight of stairs to the Lady Chapel, where I was struck motionless by the delicate beauty of the space, the fan-vaulted roof, the stained glass, the misericords carved in oak, upon which the monks had leaned during especially long services. A placard explained that these upturned seats were normally kept out of sight and so were free to be engraved with all manner of nonreligious subjects: male and female nudes, a fox riding a goose, winged dragons, foliated corbels, mermaids, boars and squirrels, malignant-looking apes, devils, and a monster chained to a stump.

'Beautiful, aren't they?'

I turned and saw her — at first I'd not even registered that she was speaking to me — a peripheral voice, distracting from my contemplation of the carvings, a woman in late middle age wearing a docent's uniform. Helped along by my boyish imagination, I thought she looked a little like the queen: thin bony nose, brown hair tightly curled, pinned under her hat.

'Very beautiful,' I said. 'I like it here.'

'That's wonderful, darling. Why don't you run

along and find your parents now.'

'Oh. I'm sorry.'

My soaring religious feeling, my affinity for all mankind, soured into confusion and soon annoyance at being bossed around by yet another adult. It wasn't until much later that I thought there might've been something else at play in the docent's suggestion for me to find my parents. I wondered if she would've said the same thing to any other twelve-year-old boy who lingered too long in the Lady Chapel. Or if the mere sight of me, brown-skinned and unaccompanied, had offended her in a way that even she was barely conscious of. I couldn't say. I didn't have much experience with overt racism. Father had warned us about the skinheads, a new British youth cult that had sprung up, but we'd not seen one. I remember sort of wanting to, the idea of it so bizarre; the British and French expats who lived near us in Maadi were friendly with Mother and Father, even deferential to their political connections, wealth, and education. One white couple or other came over for drinks almost nightly, and their children always treated us as equals. I suppose I was young enough then to be forgiven for believing that the way people speak to you and treat you accords at all with how they think of you.

*   *   *

Today, for the first time in years, I thought of that trip to the abbey. Among other things, it made me realize just how seldom I've felt the

113

presence of God, an indecorous thing for a mujahid to admit, and not to say I'm an unbeliever.
There've been times when I've been moved to
holy ecstasy, glimpsing in my mind's eye the
knotty heart of the infinite, mystery of mysteries,
beyond what we're given to observe with these
meager organs of flesh.

Afforded little more freedom than a prisoner,
holed up a month now in this Fallujah mosque,
waiting for our new emir to decide the time is
right to begin operations in Baghdad, I have had
ample occasion to drift through the eddies of the
past. There's not much else to do: I spend most
of my day in the prayer hall. Adjoining it is a
large storage room that Dr. Walid has made his
own; before he appropriated this dim and mostly
empty space, it had been used to store firewood,
a jumble of rolled-up moldy old carpets, spare
wire, a few hand tools, and a dusty palanquin,
looking out of place amid shelves of fluorescent
light tubes and tins of scouring powder. Showing
us around after our arrival, the imam (to whom
we'd been referred by the Haditha physician)
had informed us that the palanquin — cedar,
gilded in silver arabesques — was once carried in
processions during colonial days, before its use
fell out of favor with the people, who judged it
an idolatrous pretension.

In this storehouse Dr. Walid has set up a makeshift television studio. Apparently he had designs
to do this all along. But until we arrived and he
unpacked his things, I'd had no idea he'd pur-
chased so much video equipment in Aleppo. The
crush-proof cases that I'd assumed contained

sensitive detonators or perhaps radios instead held, in black eggshell foam: a camera, a computer, a boom microphone and audio recorder, power cords, cables, battery packs, a tripod, and a 300-watt lamp with a lens like a crystal goblet, the light hot enough to make one sweat in its beam.

He's put the apparatus to much use already, enacting his latest scripts. The one he produced today was much like the others he's insisted on filming over the past weeks: on his orders, the brothers gathered in the storage room in front of a black felt backdrop, upon which was hung our black flag, black on black; and so too were the brothers dressed for battle in black and olive drab, with black and red and white keffiyehs, ammo belts draped across their chests, rifles and rocket launchers held at the ready, faces hidden; only our emir, fearless and self-admiring as ever, allowed himself to appear on camera unmasked. None but a fool would dispute that he wants fame for himself as much as our cause.

For my own part, I gently refuse to participate in any of the videos, lingering off-scene with Abu Hafs, who works the camera. With his youthfulness and fortunate upbringing, he is already very familiar with its use. This new generation can operate a computer more proficiently than a rifle, and the Yemeni is no exception, demonstrating quite the aptitude for all of Dr. Walid's new devices. To my chagrin, this duty has once again pulled the boy away from my tutelage and back under the doctor's wing; Abu Hafs and I speak seldom these days. When not filming, he's engrossed in editing and reproducing the material, and as often as he can, makes trips to the bazaar with some of the other brothers to buy blank tapes and supplies. He's not mentioned taking a wife since our conversation in Haditha, but I imagine him searching for that in the bazaar, too. Making eyes at the vendors' daughters. Casually letting on that he's a mujahid, then going on to make inquiries at another electronics stall — the foolishness of it! Talking about his quest for a satellite hookup that will allow him to send videos directly to the World Wide Web, without the need for couriers. He's already acquired a diesel generator, which even I will admit is becoming more useful with each passing day, power failures and brownouts rippling through the city with increasing frequency.

I find myself vexed by the boy and his new role as Dr. Walid's technically minded factotum. Although Abu Hafs seems to relish these duties and is obviously skilled in performing them, it's not skill alone that's won him the part as chief engineer in this peculiar cinematic process. Further isolating a potential protégé from my influence has undoubtedly factored into the doctor's decision to assign him the camera.

'How does it look, Father of Lion Cubs?'

Abu Hafs peered through the viewfinder. 'Father of Friendliness isn't quite in the frame. Everyone needs to get in tighter.'

The brothers grumbled but obeyed, shuffling closer together, cracking jokes about the smell. Here the front row knelt, there a tall and a short one switched places, the mass of men sweating under their costumes and combat loads in the heat of the film lamp, the stuffy room, a warm spring day in Iraq.

Abu Hafs made a few last adjustments. 'I think that's good,' he said, ducking from behind the camera. 'We're ready, Emir.'

'Very well,' Dr. Walid said. 'I'll begin.' He lifted the microphone to his mouth. 'In the name of God, the compassionate, the merciful, I wish to speak to the Americans. This talk of mine is for you and will concern the best way to avoid another Manhattan.'

Lounging in the palanquin like a colonial overseer from days not so long past, yawning discreetly, I took in the performance. The doctor claimed to speak directly to the Americans but of course that was a sham, nothing more than a rhetorical frame: his words not intended for the enemy but rather his supporters and those among the faithful who might heed his call to travel to Iraq. By ostensibly addressing the Americans, however, he meant to show his benevolence, that even as he fought to expel the *kuffar*, he was gracious enough to explain to them why.

I'd crossed out this particular passage from his script but was not surprised he'd added it back in. I followed along as he delivered the rest of the speech from memory; I knew it almost as well. Earlier in the day he'd asked me to proofread it.

'Do me the honor,' he'd said, venturing out from his dim dark cave of the storeroom to find me in my customary place in the mosque's prayer hall. I feigned no happiness at seeing him, knowing it could only mean some new imposition. He was too prepossessed with his work, however, to mind my surliness. He handed over the two-page document. 'After all,' he added, 'you are the poet among us.'

I grunted skeptically. 'I haven't written a verse in years.'

'Just take a look. If my phrasing is awkward, rework it. If an obvious point has escaped me, add it in. It's not like you've never done this for me before.'

'When do you need it?' I asked, making no effort to hide my exasperation.

'This afternoon. I'd like it if you'd appear on the tape — '

'I'm afraid you'll want younger brothers to stand to your left and right. You and I aren't nearly as fearsome as we once were. There's too much food here to eat. Too few mountains to climb. I have to say, this is the most luxurious jihad I've ever fought in.'

'You've done nothing lately but mope around and scribble in that book of yours. Maybe I should take more of an interest in it,' he said, eyes on my journal. 'I might find something there to explain how you've come by this sulky, womanish mood.'

I spoke in a strident whisper, growing heated myself but not wanting to disturb the peace in the hypostyle hall, where the high domed ceiling amplified every sound and the imam was always on the prowl, looking for infractions.

'You haven't heard any of the brothers

complaining behind your back? No? Well, you should pay closer attention. They came here to make jihad, but they're making videotapes — *videotapes*. They're amateurish drivel. We are fighters, Walid, not propagandists.'

I was exaggerating to make a point; though the doctor had still not found a suitable opportunity for us to join the war, of course we were doing more than filming videos. He had sent out daily recon patrols, groups of two traveling the highway unarmed, studying convoy routes, troop numbers, tactics at the checkpoints. This kind of meticulous groundwork is necessary, but it's hard to convince the average soldier that a month of it is time well spent. The fruits of Dr. Walid's propagandistic efforts were even more meager: hc'd sent copies of his work to every major news outlet operating in the Gulf and some beyond, but to my knowledge not a single frame of a single tape has aired thus far, nor has a single drop of ink been spilled by any journalist writing about us.

'You may be right, Father of Dread,' he admitted, ego clearly wounded, a glint of anger in his voice. 'The tapes may be no good. But we must crawl before we can walk. The world has changed since we started on this path. You're shortsighted not to see it.'

★ ★ ★

Yesterday was a brief but heavy downpour, the kind of rain in which the last drops, fat and smelling of ozone, fall from a clear blue sky.

119

Afterward the sun baked the earth, and the rising moisture steamed the air, complicating our restlessness. The brothers caviled at Dr. Walid's orders to clean weapons after the rain, and it didn't take any special clairvoyance to realize things would be coming to a head soon. What I'd told him was true: the brothers have tired of inaction. They hadn't come all the way to Iraq to wait out the war in a mosque.

Before evening prayers, the imam caught Abu Annas smoking outside the ablution room. A stupid infraction, trifling but at the same time egregious; the diminutive old cleric hectored Abu into the courtyard, forcing the larger man to retreat before his fury.

'You dog!' he cried. 'You dirty lout!'

None of us should be smoking. It would be improper for a man to enter this place reeking of spicy food, let alone tobacco, but some of the brothers, in our present period of lassitude, have fallen back on old habits. Discipline has lapsed; the cigarette-smoking is only the most blatant and easily detectable manifestation. I have no doubt some of the men are engaged in all manner of other vices. Just the other day I overhead two discussing rumors of a brothel in the city.

'I made you my guests,' the imam said. 'And you repay me this way. Unbelievable. You, who call yourself mujahideen. Smoking in the mosque.'

'I didn't do it indoors — ' Abu Annas started dumbly.

'Speak another word and I'll have you in bastinado,' Dr. Walid said. He'd heard the commotion and come out from the storeroom with a look that could have killed a cat. 'I assure you, *sayyidi*,' he said to the imam, 'no man of mine will disrespect this place again upon pain of flogging, so long as I'm in command.'

The imam seemed a little pacified by this ultimatum but made clear that another transgression would force him to reconsider our arrangement. Once more, Walid promised a reformation. He upbraided Abu Annas in front of the brotherhood and ordered us, in an act of mass contrition, to scrub the mosque top to bottom; with buckets of soapy water, rags, and bristle brushes, we scoured the mihrab, the minbar, the minaret stairs, the fountain (after first draining it), the columns in the prayer hall, and the tile floors. The imam took a quiet but apparent pleasure in our ordeal, pointing out spots we'd missed, going around from man to man and ladling water into our mouths so that we might work longer without breaking for refreshment. Our penance lasted into the night, and even as a new day has dawned, and the smoking incident has resolved itself, with everyone exhibiting a renewed abstinence from tobacco, I believe yesterday's events have caused Dr. Walid to reexamine our state of affairs. He must know now that I wasn't sulking or spinning lies when I informed him of the brothers' dissatisfaction, his authority threatened by any number of unforeseeable, seemingly inconsequential turns. These men came here to fight. One way or another, we will.

* * *

Several days later, we left the mosque around noon, taking little-used roads south and east of Fallujah, making our way toward Baghdad. The brothers who had been scouting knew of a supply route relied upon by the Americans, and several ideal places to set an ambush along it. Dr. Walid had selected one of these, an isolated area about an hour's ride south, and we headed there. I was in the lead truck with him, Abu Annas, and two other brothers.

'The shamal,' the doctor remarked pedantically, 'is a study in the patient accumulation of force. As long as the wind shall hold, two will become four, four will become eight, and in time, eight grains of sand will grow heavy enough to hobble a giant.'

'God is greater,' I muttered. The storm he was referring to was forecast to hit overnight; nature had finally given us our chance. But something always goes wrong. Twenty kilometers into the trip, about halfway to our destination, one of our Toyotas — the trucks had been a gift from a Syrian intelligence officer — began to overheat, billowing steam from its engine compartment. We pulled to the side of the highway and discovered the radiator hose split lengthwise in a way that made patching it difficult.

'A thousand cocks in this damn machine! If we miss our chance because of this piece of shit . . . damn it!' Dr. Walid ranted, the obscenities coming hard and fast as he kicked a dent in the truck's quarter panel. Back in Aleppo I'd argued we shouldn't accept the Hiluxs. Every Salafi who left Syria for the jihad in Iraq was one less that Bashar al-Assad would have to contend with when his own time came to face justice. It was to Assad's benefit to bleed both the Americans and us at the same time, hence the gift of the Hiluxs from his agent; the trucks were so many Trojan horses.

The doctor managed to contain himself and stopped abusing the quarter panel. While we were delayed, the storm drew closer, diffusing the sun until it was indistinguishable from red-and-gray sky. Finally the radiator cooled enough to be uncapped, and Abu al-Deehar, who had served as a ship's mechanic before joining us, wrapped the split hose with most of a roll of electrical tape, topping off the reservoir.

'It'll hold for now,' he said, finishing the repair. 'But it's going to leak. We'll have to stop every so often to add fluid.'

Dr. Walid ordered everyone to be on the lookout for any Toyota that might provide a suitable replacement hose. We remounted the trucks and set off down the highway another ten kilometers before entering a village too insignificant to merit a garrison of American troops but which did appear to contain an assortment of well-used automobiles. Our prospects of finding another hose seemed fair.

We drove the narrow streets, taking stock of the place, laid out in a rough triangle. A gang of children, some grotesquely deformed, trailed behind, shouting and begging. We took a turn and slowed to a crawl in a constricted alleyway.

The doctor lowered his window and waved one of the boys over.

'You, child! I'll make it worth your time if you tell me where I can find a man who owns a truck like these.'

His arm dangling out the window, he slapped the door. The boy looked at him boldly in his face; one day, these Iraqi street children will make the best sort of mujahideen.

'Sheikh Hamad has one, sir. Come on.'

The boy ran ahead of our truck, taking us deeper into the village. A short drive later we stopped by a rusty sheet-metal gate set in two-meter-high walls surrounding one of the larger compounds in the area: a sprawling, gauche construction, like someone had tried to build himself a mansion out of hand-fired brick.

We found the gate shut tight. The doctor knocked until a judas on the gate was slid open by another boy, who looked nearly like the one who'd brought us here. No doubt the resemblance was familial, the two brothers or cousins.

'What do you want?' this second boy said.

Dr. Walid rebuked him wryly. 'This is how you talk to your elders?'

'It's how I talk to strangers who come pounding on the gate and frighten my mother.'

'Why should a visitor frighten anyone?'

'Don't you know the Americans have come through here?'

'Have they,' the doctor said, intrigued by this news but not very surprised, as we were near the highway they had been using as a supply route. 'Are they gone already? Where are they

124

now, do you know?'

The child didn't answer, disappearing from the judas. A moment later an old man took his place. 'Peace be with you. Forgive my grandson; he has lived only in evil times.'

'And unto you peace,' the doctor said. 'God willing, the times won't remain evil for long. I assume you're Sheikh Hamad?'

'I am. And I hope you'll also forgive me for not extending the typical courtesies. My granddaughter isn't well. What's your business here?'

Dr. Walid's eyes brightened at the mention of an illness in the household: clearly, we needed an inroad with this old man, who had already shown he would not be intimidated easily.

'God is merciful, my sheikh. I'm a physician.'

'What?'

As proof, Walid called for his medical bag to be brought from the truck, and he opened it and held it to the judas.

'God brought you!' the sheikh exclaimed, admitting us into his home. For the first time, we got a good look at him, stooped and frail, and we could see by the disarray in his courtyard that the family as a whole had also fallen on hard times: there were brightly dyed dresses hung out to dry, but they were dusty, as if the wash had been neglected for days. A few potted palms drooped along the walls, and there was a fig tree with fruit rotting underneath, and in the air, the stink of clogged sewage pipes. We were pleased, however, to see that our boy informant had led us to the right place. Parked under an awning was a Toyota truck only a few years older than ours. Dr. Walid noticed it, a covetous gleam in his eyes, but tactfully made no mention of the truck, the true purpose of our visit. He asked the sheikh to show us his ailing grandchild, and away we went into the house. The old man must've been overcome with grief, as he did not ask why we'd come or how we'd known who he was. It was good if he took it on faith that God brought him a doctor in his time of need. That's one truth of what happened, however poorly the business ended.

He led us to an upper floor of his crumbling manse and from there to the sickroom where lay a girl no more than five years old. She was being attended to by her mother and grandmother.

'This little bird has never been very strong,' the sheikh said. 'But the last few days it's gotten bad. She can't take any food. What comes up, doctor, is like coffee grounds.'

'What's her name?' Walid asked, kneeling beside her, opening his bag.

'Fatima.'

'A good name, sweet one. It'll give you strength.'

He took her vitals, glancing at his wristwatch, two fingers pressed on her neck, her skin beading sweat over a grayish pallor marred by bruises and spots like dark-red pinpricks. Dr. Walid felt the nodes in her stomach and underarms and helped her to open her mouth so he could take her temperature.

'Thirty-nine,' he said disapprovingly, returning the thermometer to its case. 'Does she complain of pain in her joints?'

'Constantly.'

'And these bruises . . . '

'Just from touching her. We had to move her today. My wife — well, it doesn't really matter why she moved her. But a woman's touch is enough to cause them.' With some difficulty the sheikh bent down and stroked his granddaughter so tenderly, it was as if his fingertips brushed no more than the downy hairs on her forearm. 'Do you know what it is?'

'I couldn't be sure without the proper tests,' Dr. Walid said, now engaged in auscultation to discern the murmurings of her heart and lungs, moving the stethoscope's chest piece from place to place. 'But I can tell you this. It's serious. She must be taken to hospital immediately.'

The sheikh's wife and daughter, mother and grandmother to the girl, exchanged a distressed and knowing look, as if the doctor had touched on an already sore point. At the mention of a hospital the sheikh also grew agitated and moved away from the sickbed. He thumbed through his prayer beads, pacing the one window in the room, peering out over his decrepit courtyard and our trucks, parked in the alley near the gate, studying them like he had noticed for the first time the mortar tube strapped in the bed of the rearmost Hilux, the black flags, the Kalashnikovs carried by the brothers who milled about on the street, teasing the children.

He turned to the sickbed in anger. 'You'd have me drive her into Baghdad with what's happening there? The hospitals filled with the maimed and dead and dying? Anyway, it's impossible. The Americans have closed the road.'

'Where?' the doctor asked, doing his best with the succinct question to maintain a magisterial, barely interested tone. I was probably the only one in the room who realized how the sheikh's answer might shape our immediate future.

'A few kilometers east of here at a traffic circle.'

'How many are there?' Now Walid could barely mask his excitement. The prey was close; he had feared our opportunity had slipped away, but luck had found us again.

'Fifteen, twenty. They had four trucks. My grandson told me one of them was a woman, carrying a rifle just like the other *kuffar*. A woman, can you imagine? Anyway, that's all I know. But, doctor, *you* know what's wrong with Fatima. I can see it in your face. Speak, I beg you.'

Dr. Walid sighed and looked at the girl; he seemed truly sad to be the bearer of bad news, but there was more to it: surely he had hoped for something easily treatable, a quick fix that would earn the sheikh's gratitude. It wasn't to be.

'Possibly rheumatic fever. But, more likely, cancer of the bone. There's no way to be sure without more tests.'

I could tell he was hedging; he was quite sure it was cancer, and that meant I was sure of it, too. His leadership qualities may have been doubtable, but his prognostic capabilities were not. During the jihad against the Soviets, he had gained a reputation among the Arab Brigade for medical genius. His professional skill, in fact, had occasioned our first meeting. For some years of my youth, I suffered mysteriously from low blood pressure and required daily glucose injections to keep up my strength. After our field medic was martyred by a Russian tank, Dr. Walid personally took it upon himself to make the perilous drive over the Khyber, traveling to the front lines from his clinic in Peshawar several times a month. This was before he fully dedicated himself to the armed portion of our struggle, still harboring idealistic ambitions to uphold his oath to do no harm. But he could help in other ways, and did. He treated the wounded brothers, ferried new arrivals, and delivered shipments of painkillers, bandages, IV bags, and other medicaments, including my glucose. It was often in short supply, and so it was not uncommon for him to arrive in camp and find me lying on the floor of the cave in painful delirium. While he administered the treatment and restored me, I would regale him with tales of the latest miracles witnessed at the front. It's difficult to remain dignified while being treated by a physician, and so, in the airy darkness of the cave, its entrance sealed by a boulder that we moved in and out of place with a bulldozer, I turned the doctor's attention from my failing body to those of incorruptible martyrs uncovered in their graves, men whose flesh would not putrefy in death but would, even weeks later, still smell sweetly of musk. I told of brothers who returned from ambushes only to find bullet holes in their waistcoats but no commensurate wounds on their bodies. I relayed the well-known account of a wounded mujahid whose dying groans were drowned out by the humming of an angry swarm of bees, millions of them, though none could be seen anywhere. I spoke of a patrol pursued and overtaken by Soviet jets, the brothers cornered in a steep-walled valley, but when all seemed hopeless, they were spared at the last minute by a flock of birds that took wing and formed a dense canopy overhead, a shield of beating feathers that forced the *kuffar* pilots to avert their attack. To these and other reports of preternatural events, Dr. Walid listened by my side, enthralled. The following spring he forsook his medical oath and took up the rifle.

Seldom had I seen such a willing disciple. One might suppose, given his Western training and scientific cast of mind, that he would be skeptical of miraculous tales, but this was not the case. The doctor was the proverbial study in contradictions. On the one hand, he refused to drink ice water, complaining it was a European luxury with the tendency to weaken a man's vigor. Yet before selling all his possessions and traveling to Peshawar to establish his clinic, he'd been a foremost expert, at least in the Arab world, on the subject of using immunosuppressants to increase the odds of success after an organ transplant.

If he had determined the sheikh's granddaughter was suffering from cancer of the bone, I didn't question his judgment, not in the slightest. The girl lived, but I thought of her as dead already, my mind moving to other problems: the radiator hose, the coming storm, the enemy on the road a few kilometers east. I wrote her off. A harsh thing, but so is war.

The bleak diagnosis had the opposite effect on Fatima's mother, who clung all the tighter to her daughter and prayed; the grandmother wailed and tore at her own breast and hair, cursing the earth, blaspheming God for the children He had taken from her in the past and now this one, their poor little bird, who would die before she'd even lived, who would starve to death while the cancer feasted on her bones.

'You and your cautiousness,' she said to her husband the sheikh. 'You who were too afraid even to speak with the Americans. We might still go to them — '

'Silence, woman!' the sheikh roared, with more potency than he had theretofore displayed. His wife demurred straightaway and assumed a more compliant attitude. One got the feeling, watching them, that they had gone through this argument many times before and that it had, through sufficient rehearsal, become something of a pantomime, albeit one fraught with dangerously real consequence.

'How long does she have?' Fatima's mother asked.

The doctor had finished packing away his kit and pulled himself wearily to his feet. 'Weeks. Days. Only God knows.'

'Can't you do anything?'

'I could leave morphine for her comfort. But with her being so weak, even a small dose would probably kill her.'

'Would that be the worst thing?' I asked, shocking the sickroom into silence. There was only the wheezing of a small, dying child. Probably the others had forgotten I was there; I hadn't spoken once since entering, and with my black fatigues and stillness of body, it was as if I'd blended into the darkness of the corner in which I stood.

'My brother,' Dr. Walid said, shifting his attention from the girl to me, his eyes belying the politeness of his tone, 'what you're talking about is unlawful. Illness is sanctification, a blessing in disguise. 'Have no fear, the ailment will prove purifying from sin if God wills it so.''

'There's no need to lecture me on the Sunna,' I said. 'I know it well.'

'Then you'll agree it absolutely forbids what you are talking about.'

'Who are we to make their decision for them?'

'The sheikh is a good Muslim. Plainly, he agrees with me.'

'So he does,' I said, looking the man over, already regretting that my discomposure had afforded Dr. Walid such a chance to rebuke me. 'You're right, he does. Forgive me. I'm not myself today. How can one look at such suffering and not despair?'

★ ★ ★

In light of these grave developments, bringing up the subject of the radiator hose was a delicate matter indeed. We'd left the cloistered sickroom for the open air of the courtyard; the sheikh had chairs and a table brought out, and we were there being served chai by his grandson, the same one who first appeared at the door, and who seemed less than ideally suited to wait on us, due to an unusual deformity of one of his hands.

'Thank you for the hospitality in this difficult time,' Dr. Walid said. 'We only wish we could do something more for your family. Maybe we could. Here's a thought: Maybe we could drive ahead. Test the American blockade. If it's possible to reach a hospital in Baghdad, we could send word. You could follow with the child.'

'How would you send word?' the sheikh asked. 'All the telephone lines are scrambled.'

'Abu Hafs, bring me one of the satellite phones.'

'Is there no end to your generosity?' the sheikh said, but with some reservation.

'It's nothing.' The doctor flicked his wrist dismissively. 'But we're afraid we do need some help, if we're going to make the journey.'

The sheikh indicated with a nod that he was listening.

'Your truck. The radiator hose. One of ours has broken down.'

'I see now,' the sheikh said, narrowing his cloudy eyes. 'I see you would barter with my granddaughter's life.'

'I'm only seeking a solution that benefits everyone,' replied Walid smoothly. 'Let's call the one-eyed man one-eyed. I need that hose, and you need the road to Baghdad. Do me this favor, and I'll pay it back in gold. You have my word.'

'I'm sorry, but I can't. My family needs that

133

truck. I have a duty to them.' The sheikh sipped his tea and placed the cup carefully on its saucer, which he rotated a quarter turn. He rose from the chair and smoothed his dishdasha where it had bunched around his waist. I could tell he was the kind of man who moves and speaks slowly, who does not mind if others mistake this slowness for insipidity, and who may even accentuate certain deliberate aspects of his personality, inviting this mis-judgment, realizing its advantages. He motioned for his crippled grandson to collect everyone's cups. 'That's all I can say on it. Thank you for looking at Fatima, but the time has come for you to go.'

For the second time that day, I spoke out of turn. 'You talk about duty. Do you think I wanted to give my own boy to this struggle, to have the flesh of my flesh shrouded in a funeral robe? And yet he was, and I went so far as to celebrate his martyrdom, because that was my duty as a Muslim, which is greater than anything I owe to family. So what are you doing? Why aren't you fighting the Americans, who even now are plundering your country? Or, if you are too old and weak for that, why aren't your landsmen under arms? You know, it would be lawful for us simply to take that truck of yours. We'll take what God demands and no more. And if you stand in the way, I'll have your head for a traitor's.'

Dr. Walid looked at me crossly but not without some pride at being able to lay claim to a subordinate with such a brutally stern streak, one that had lain dormant a long time. 'You see what my men think,' he said to the sheikh. 'But we won't let Abu have your soul. Despite your weak faith, you are no traitor. It would be a sin to take your head, but my brother might be right: it is lawful for us to take your truck. With due compensation, of course. Abu al-Deehar, give it a look over. If it runs all right, we'll trade it for ours. Surely you'll be able to find a radiator hose among your neighbors soon enough.'

'Now there's — '

'No, no, sit back down. We'll just be another minute.'

Walid had drawn a pistol from beneath his shalwar and pointed it lackadaisically at the sheikh's gut.

So it was we solved the problem of our transportation. We left the village in search of our first engagement with the *kuffar* — the roundabout, not our intended target, but one of opportunity. I was purified with water and blade, having shorn every hair on my body the previous morning. We moved to seek the enemy: at our backs was a ruddy sun that cleaved the gulf of earth and sky, illuminating bilious red clouds like wet clay smudged over the horizon. A wall of dust and sand crawled behind and carried with it uncountable specks of grit swept up by the wind to roil a while before falling and dislodging more of the earth with the force of their saltating impact. The atmosphere was electric, a combination of the weather and the battle to come. I was out of my body. I was willpower hurtling through space. The past receded to mean nothing; the future was all. There was the sense of the existing order overturned, a feeling of wild possibility.

8

Sleed: Victory over America

Iraq (Palace Row; Triangletown):
day of

Jonesing in the dead of night I flicked my Zippo
and lit a Miami, this off-brand cigarette made in
China. Galvan had bought a couple cartons from
a local national after our supply of Marlboros
had run out. I dangled my legs off the back deck
of the tank. We'd run the engine earlier to do
some maintenance and underneath me it still
gave off heat like the coals of a buried campfire.
Crickets chattered in the palm groves, the sound
throbbing like the slow scattered heartbeat of
one big creature. I smoked and petted my dog in
the light of the moon that'd risen high over the
lake at the Row and put a glazed look on the
water. Victory over America Palace was a black
shape out there not too far.

I'd woken up craving a smoke and found I was
alone on the tank. It was Galvan's turn to pull
duty as sergeant of the guard, we had posts set
up on the roof of headquarters and in five
sandbagged hooches on the perimeter, but that
didn't explain why Fitzpatrick was missing, too.
If I hadn't known better I might've thought
something bad had happened. Instead, my mind

136

went straight to them foraging. That's what Fitzpatrick called it. Some nights he and Galvan liked to go out and explore the palaces and sometimes I went along to see what they might find. Once it was a suit of chain-mail armor, another time, a brand-new big-screen plasma TV that we lugged over to headquarters and presented to the sergeant major, who was happy as a pig in shit to get it.

I wondered what it'd be tonight. Nothing to do but find out. I grabbed my weapon and battle rattle and a pair of night-vision goggles that I hung around my neck on some parachute cord. Frago tagged along as I hopped off the tank and we walked the lakeshore to Bunker Six on the perimeter of the secure area. I ducked under a sagging plywood roof covered with sandbags. The bunker was empty, a couple cigarette butts floating in some stagnant ooze that'd filled the grenade sump. Frago hopped on the firing platform by the machine gun and raised his hackles, growling softly. He stared into the night and kept up that throaty purring. I shushed him and strained to hear what was out there in the dark. The wind gusted like a storm was on the way and made it hard to pick out any sound. I stood listening for a minute like an idiot before remembering the NVGs. Powering up, they made a faint electronic whine, then I saw a cluster of bushes along the water. Next to them, two dudes about the right shape to be Fitzpatrick and Galvan, heads on a slow swivel.

What happened next was strange. They sat on the shore and took off their boots and pants. I didn't know what to think about that. I thought maybe I'd seriously mistaken the nature of their friendship.

They got up and stood half naked. Each one tied his bootlaces together and slung his boots along with trousers over his neck, and Galvan also carried something that looked like a long walking staff that he held for balance as he waded through the muck. Fitzpatrick went behind him and I watched as they slunk into the water. The way they did it made me think of Vietnam, at least what I'd seen in movies, rice paddies and muddy GIs with peace signs and kill counts painted on their helmets. Some things change. Most don't. I tracked them through the goggles as they kept moving offshore to Victory over America Palace.

★ ★ ★

Frago hated getting wet and had sense enough not to go venturing into a strange body of water at night. I could just barely hear him worrying about me as I sloshed around the palace's pilings, no clue how Fitzpatrick and Galvan had climbed up and gotten in. I'd seen them do it from a distance through the blurry NVGs. Stumbling through the water I banged my kneecap on a concrete block hidden below the surface. Pain shot through my leg, I bit my lip, and craned my neck. Then I saw it. On the underside of the pier beneath the palace, a maintenance porthole was busted out. Next to it was a piling with a service ladder attached.

I waded over to the ladder and climbed the narrow rungs, sharp on my bare feet. I had slung my boots around my neck like I'd seen them do. At the top of the ladder I dragged myself over the lip of the porthole, into a dark room like some sort of pump house, pipes and metal tanks stained with rust trails.

'Sergeant Galvan. Rooster. Y'all in here?'

My voice sounded too deep in the hollow concrete room, like talking at the bottom of a well. No one answered. As I put on my boots I decided it'd be dumb to panic them with whispers in the dark, take a bullet in my lungs for the trouble. I clicked off the goggles and lowered them to my chest. I had a red-light headlamp on my helmet and used that instead.

Footprints in dust led away from the porthole. I tracked them through the pump room and a T-shaped hallway to an industrial-sized kitchen with stainless steel countertops and pots and pans hanging in racks from the ceiling. Everything coated with plaster dust and grime. Big cracks had opened in the floor and I made out a rat skittering through one, catching its red eyes in my light. The air was stagnant, humid, with the whiff of spoiled meat, and I hoped the smell was coming from a refrigerator somewhere and not bodies.

The kitchen was next to the palace dining hall. The footprints disappeared on the moldy carpet there but I headed for the only other way out, a set of double doors blown off their hinges that opened to a domed lobby with a black-marble goldfish pond, the stone shattered, water leaked out, and fish rotted on the bottom. A cruise missile had crashed through the ceiling, left a gash in the dome, brought down half of it, and the falling ceiling had sheared off the bottom of a staircase on the other side of the lobby. The upper stairs were still attached to the next-higher floor. Broken glass and tile crunched underfoot as I headed that way, adjusting the beam on my lamp to focus on the staircase where there were more marks disturbing the dust.

I slung my weapon and went for it, jumped up and grabbed one of the wrought-iron spindles, hung there in midair rocking side to side enough to throw a leg on the bottommost step. I got a knee up, an arm, and the rest of me. At the head of the stairs was a long hall. Falling sheets of wallpaper drooped down and made it look like a path cut through jungle.

'Hey, fucknuts. You guys up here?'

Nothing. I started checking rooms. I hadn't gotten far when a clanging came from the other end of the hall, a steady muffled clanging like someone was trapped in the walls, banging on pipes. I followed the sound till I found the door where it was coming from and pounded on it with my fist.

The clanging stopped.

'Sergeant Galvan! Rooster!'

Footsteps, and Galvan spoke from inside. 'What the hell. Sleed? You scared the piss out of us.'

'I wouldn't have had to if you'd told me you were going out tonight.'

'I can't have a snitch,' Galvan said.

'I keep saying, I'm not gonna snitch. Just let

me in. I'm not chicken-shit like you think. You scored something good, I want in.'

He opened the door a little and showed his narrow face, looked at me and thought about it.

'Fine. You want in, you're in. About fucking time.'

He opened the door, and I saw a desk and a dresser with drawers and cabinets dumped out, but I zeroed in on the king-sized four-poster bed. With my red headlamp the gold rifle lying there looked the same color as a sunset.

'Pretty badass, right?' Galvan said.

It was an AK-47. I picked it up and pulled back the charging handle, turning the weapon in my hands and admiring it.

'This thing legit?'

'Gold plate,' Galvan said, like it was no big thing. 'Check this, though.'

He pointed me to a walk-in closet. No clothes inside, like no one had ever really lived in the room, just another empty one in a big-ass palace. Propped in the corner was a tanker's bar, an oversized crowbar four feet long. It was the thing I'd seen Galvan carrying like a staff, and now I could tell why he'd brought it. The closet had three safes in it. The smallest one was a fireproof model with a carrying handle and its lock mangled, the lid jimmied open, the inside empty. The other two were identical floor safes with thick steel doors and combination locks. They were shut tight.

'I busted this one earlier,' Galvan said, and toed the fireproof safe. 'You won't believe this shit.'

He grabbed a stack of papers from a dusty bare shelf in the closet and handed them to me. I scanned the first page and looked at him. The writing was in Arabic. None of us spoke a lick, let alone could read it.

'Keep going.'

I flipped through. Most of the paperwork was in Arabic but I found some in English, account statements and real estate deeds, the kind of stuff people usually keep in fireproof safes. What blew me away was the name printed on them. *Uday Saddam Hussein al-Tikriti.*

'How'd you find this?' I said.

'Same way we found everything else. Climbed up in here and started messing around. I went back and got the tanker bar and Rooster tonight, to get at them safes.'

'Damn.'

'Yeah. Crazy, right?'

'Seriously,' I said, excited but also beginning to experience major doubts. 'Maybe we should forget about this and head back to the tank line.'

'Damn, Sleed. Cold feet already? Thought you were in, tough guy. Do what you want, but I'm not going anywhere till I crack these.'

'He could be right,' Fitzpatrick said. 'Let's call it quits for now and come back tomorrow night with an acetylene torch.'

'Who says we'll even be here tomorrow?' Galvan said. 'We might get orders to roll anytime. This QRF gravy train's not gonna last forever. We'll be back in the shit before long. We gotta seize the moment here.'

He took the tanker's bar and jammed the

chisel end between the safe door and the frame and threw all his weight behind it like he was hitting the tackling dummies at football practice. It barely budged.

'You two gonna help or just stand there and jaw jack?'

★ ★ ★

Cash, jewels, guns, drugs, Uday's collection of self-produced snuff films, or maybe empty space, nothing at all, we couldn't say. We beat on the safes and jimmied the doors and dragged one down the hall and heaved it off the balcony, and it crashed into the empty marble goldfish pond, but nothing worked.

'We'd better leave soon,' Fitzpatrick said, checking his watch. 'We're officially on QRF as of twenty minutes ago.'

'Chill,' Galvan said. 'When's the last time they activated QRF? Let's just try one more thing.'

He ripped open a Velcro pouch on his tactical vest, took out a grenade, and grinned.

'You've lost your damn mind,' I said.

That was when Blornsbaum ruined the party, barking our crew's call sign over the walkabout radio clipped to Galvan's belt.

'Two, this is Four. Where you at, Two?'

I could tell by the background noise on Blornsbaum's end that he was in his tank with the engine fired up, which could only mean one thing. QRF was rolling out. Soldiers outside the wire were in trouble and needed our help, but the three of us, messing around in the palace,

143

had missed the call. Missing your unit's movement was no joke. You could get court-martialed for this shit.

'Fuck. What're we gonna do?'

'Don't answer him yet,' Galvan said. 'We need to get back to the tank.'

We hauled ass out the palace, down the ladder, into the lake, and splashed back as fast as we could toward shore. As we hurried back, Blornsbaum tried to raise us on the handheld every thirty seconds or so, getting more and more pissed. Finally, he said the platoon was pulling out without us.

★   ★   ★

We were screwed. Knew the situation was real bad when we saw a snaking black curl of smoke, the heat signature from the checkpoint at the traffic circle ten klicks west of the Row. It was impossible to miss, bigger and brighter in infrared as we pushed the tank to its limit, hitting sixty miles an hour before the governor on the transmission kicked in. We weren't supposed to leave the Row with any less than a two-vehicle convoy but there was no choice. It should've taken us only a few minutes to make the traffic circle once we got the call. It took almost twenty, and fifteen of those were us getting back to the tank from the palace.

We got on scene and dismounted. Two Humvees were burning, the smoke smelling toxic, making my eyes water. Soldiers from the MP platoon, guys whose names I didn't know

144

but whose faces I recognized, just stood around in shock, watching everything burn. One kid missing his helmet looked like he'd just crawled out of the shit canal and I saw a couple bodies down that way. They were so still. Like mannequins.

'What happened?' Galvan said.

'What's it look like?' Blornsbaum said. 'The MPs got hit hard, mortars and small arms. One truck and six joes are still unaccounted for. Now that you all finally decided to show up, we can go look for them. Where in Christ were you anyway? Why're you all wet?'

'Long story,' Galvan said.

'Save it, then. I don't even want to hear it right now. You even know what could happen if Higher finds out about this? You're lucky I told them we were having engine trouble.'

To be sure, it wasn't like he'd covered for us out of the kindness of his heart. He'd lied to Higher to cover his own ass, too. A leader who couldn't account for his soldiers was in almost as deep as the soldiers themselves.

* * *

Two of our four tanks stayed at the circle to treat the wounded and secure the area while more platoons at the Row were spinning up to come help. The other two tanks, including ours, went to look for the MIA. We followed Blornsbaum as he tore down the road. Before long it dumped us in a little village of mud-daubed huts that everyone called Triangletown. The streets were narrow, unpaved, empty, and it wasn't long before we found the missing truck. We spotted a heat signature and deep tire tracks in the mud by the side of the road. The Humvee had crashed through a low brick wall and rolled in a ditch, engine still running, bullet holes all through the cab. We looked around and called out for survivors, but there were none. Three killed, two in the cab, and this dude I knew named Worthy. I'd been in a long-running spades game with him and some other guys.

Worthy had made it out of the truck. We moved him to check for a pulse but didn't bother anymore when we turned him over enough to see his face. Splintered teeth and pieces of skull scattered in the mud like tiny broken pieces of a smashed plate. There was no fear or pain or emotion of any kind that you could read into that face. Hard to believe it was the man I knew. A deep pain beat at the center of me, and I thought I was going to faint again, but all I did was retch up water.

Blornsbaum called in a status report. 'Three more KIA, grid to follow. I say again, three more KIA. Three still unaccounted for.'

We moved the tanks to defend the position from any attackers who might still be out there. When help arrived, some of us dismounted to consolidate the bodies. After that was done, Blornsbaum went to the lowest point in the ditch and squatted down to clean his hands in the tacky mud. He coated his palms with the stuff and rubbed them together until the friction dried the mud and rolled it off his skin, blood with it.

We followed his example and cleaned our hands. Rubbing them with the mud brought out the smell of iron and salt even worse. I felt myself getting light-headed again. Couple seconds later, I was out.

PART III

Money is ammunition.

— United States counterinsurgency doctrine

9

Cassandra: The Prisoner's Dilemma

```
Iraq (Fallujah): 1 day after
```

She comes to at the worst possible time, in the middle of the procedure. It's thirst that does it, thirst that drags her out of anesthetized black, somewhere past sleep but not far enough. Her tongue is practically glued to the roof of her mouth, a sweet chemical taste as she pulls it away, rolls it around, a dried-out worm roasting on pavement.

That she's alive at all surprises her. That she's been rescued and evac'ed to a field hospital is her first wrong assumption. Her vision skews like she's looking through a lens smeared with petroleum jelly, eyes focusing at cross-purposes but she can see enough to perceive a bright white light and masculine, vaguely military silhouettes working together toward some purpose in a procedure that centers on her. Everything feels ambiguous and faraway, disassociated monstrously like a bad trip on cough syrup. She strains to raise her head but the force on her shoulders, slim bony fingers, thwarts her too easily. Is that all the fight she can summon? Must be in real bad shape.

The last thing she remembers is the canal, the way the clouds looked like green slate, and sinking into the mud of the bank, Aguirre dead on top of her. She tries to speak McGinnis's name, to ask him for water, she's so parched, but renders nothing intelligible, just a little bubble of spit to wet her lips, a draft of cool air passing over her legs. They're bare. Her feet are as well. Toes work. Good, not paralyzed. Again she makes a go at sitting up.

You don't quit until you're dead, Wigheard. You don't lose until you're dead, so don't quit.

'Relax. You'll only make it worse.' It's a man's voice, rich and almost sultry, pitched in a British accent, which is absurd. She must be hallucinating, because whoever he is, he can't be a Brit. They're all the way down south near Basra. No way she would've been transported to one of their field hospitals.

'*Nahnuf e-haj jahwore hydurt upthere adhokethen.*'

Now the voice, by its timbre and direction of origin the same man's, gibbers not in the queen's English but a nonsense language that feels immensely more comforting to hear, the one incongruity confirming the unreal totality of these other sensations: She's out of her mind on drugs. Painkillers. That's it. A red blinking dot like the LED on a video camera, tracers of light circling, bobbing, pupil dilated to the edge of the iris, something cold and wet pressing against her arm, the smell of rubbing alcohol, a needle prick going almost unnoticed in the bright cacophony of pain. The cords of her neck slacken, eyes rolling back; the drug does its work, burying her once more beneath cave-dark silence, blackness light as air.

152

Next time Cassandra awakes the room is still and quiet. Into her forearm an IV bag drips a solution of saline and whatever substance is capable of obscuring agony. The line runs down her forearm into the crook of her elbow, the catheter sunk like a clear plastic vein extruded from her body. That is what she fixates on, the line, the catheter, the coolness of the drip into her arm marking time. She manages to tilt her head enough to look down her torso and what she sees there startles her, though even incipient terror is substantially dulled by opiates.

She's not laid out in a hospital gurney. Not even a proper bed. No longer wearing her uniform but some kind of plain long dress like a nightgown, lying on wool blankets arranged into a pallet on a dingy tile floor. A thickness of gauze is wrapped around her right biceps and the blood spotting through the bandage looks black in the low cold light. The wound. She was shot. No, it was the mortars that did it: but she may have been shot, too. She passed out. There's time unaccounted for.

Somewhere nearby a muezzin sings the call to prayer through a loudspeaker. It's so close it could be coming from another part of this building, the walls of cinder block transmitting sound well. In time, dawn diffuses through the one visible window, barred but not paned, enough light for her to distinguish the different-colored threads in the dress she's wearing. First she can tell blue from white, then blue from green, the colors forming a childish pattern, triangles stitched down the front. The dress perplexes her. She has to muster an immense concentration to focus on it or anything else but does manage to conclude that it's an entirely inappropriate garment for someone in her situation to be wearing. The next inference does not follow, one logical extrapolation too far for this amount of morphine. Nor do words like *captured* or *prisoner* yet enter her mind. And dozing off again she never does spot the quiet boy in the shadowed corner sitting guard in the room, a vigilance over her.

★ ★ ★

Whatever this is comes in waves. She allows one to take her under, to roll and drub her on the bottom like a surfer bashed in slow motion over a reef. Fantastic pixelations form and shift behind her eyes, rods and cones uninhibited in the darkness and by the drug and so free to resolve themselves into whatever the brain chooses, patterns plucked from white noise, a biochemical Rorschach test. Black smoke, or is it clouds? or is it the night-black water of the canal? and McGinnis like an anchor pulling her in deeper. Crump's wounded eye like a misshapen pearl, the reflection of fire on broken glass, the mucky feel of the water, the smell of shit, fear, what is beneath fear, disease, infection, and water snakes and snapping turtles — wait, that's it. The weird-looking slate-green clouds — she's hit on the association: they were the precise color and texture of the mat of algae grown onto the shell of an alligator snapper her cousin once hooked accidentally while fishing in the marshy end of the stock tank on her grandparents' land. Her cousin using chicken necks for bait. Beaching the strange saurian creature and pestering it with a tree branch until it extended its neck with alarming rapidity and cleaved the offending object in two.

From somewhere far away she feels pressure on her arms, legs; they're bound together, slung, her body being moved. She strains to open her eyes but there's trouble there, a tight blindfold. Men speak. Talking among themselves and taunting her, she supposes, by the venom in their laughter. She'd know what they were up to even in this inscrutable language, the way soldiers mock the vanquished.

It's Arabic, not gibberish. A point of rare clarity for her at this moment of embarkation. She's alive, not dead. Alive and entombed, alive and buried alive and drugged and shut inside a dark airless prism rushing through space, diesel exhaust and burning-trash smells, honking car horns like random shouting in a crowd, shitty Arabic pop music broadcast from radios overheard from the next lane over of gridlocked traffic. Mutedly, through insulation. The rattling idle of a truck engine; soon they're moving again. Whatever she's trapped in feels like slick plastic on the bottommost corner where her palms are bound behind her, slowly suffocating, drugs wearing off as the journey drags on, her wound throbbing aguishly with each returning beat of her heart.

The fever breaks on the evening of the third day, although she might've guessed a week or only hours. Given the other menacing unknowns she's facing, Cassandra finds it surprisingly concerning, her complete inability to reckon the passage of time. If she's going to maintain her wits, she'll have to devise some way to divide the day from the night. The call to prayer would be the perfect thing but she hasn't heard it in how long? — which points to one of several possibilities. Could be they're holding her somewhere in the countryside far from any mosque, or else this place is deep enough underground, she wouldn't hear it. Or both scenarios could be true. There are no windows, it's pitch-black, and her limbs are free now, unbound. Condensation wets the concrete walls dank as a cave's but warmer. Definitely feels subterranean. Her cell, as she first thinks of it. The red fog of infection having cleared enough for her to realize very well that she's a prisoner and in serious trouble.

* * *

Every time the door opens, she's jolted with fear. The obvious, that they will rape or kill her, rape and kill her. This is something that she thought about plenty before the invasion: what might happen if she were captured. Arabs do have their reputation. This time it's the man with the British accent, the one from her fever dreams, who enters her cell. He has a workmanlike manner and carries a satchel in one hand and a kerosene lantern in the other. He sets the lantern on the floor, the tubular cotton wick burning a lively orange. Even that much light is painfully, blindingly bright as her eyes acclimate. Behind him is another, taller Arab who leans against the door and never speaks. He carries a rifle slung on his shoulder and sniffles from time to time as if he has a cold. He looks at her with aristocratic curiosity, the hint of disdain.

'Feeling better?' the British one asks.

She nods, grunts, and it's the truth.

'I can see. Excellent.' He kneels beside her and searches through his satchel, producing a small glass bottle and a syringe. 'Penicillin. You got quite a nasty infection, I assume from that filth you and your comrades were cowering in.' He inserts the needle into the membranous lid of the bottle and pulls back the plunger to draw liquid into the syringe. Taps it. Gestures at her arm, the bandage soppy, smelling like ripe cheese. 'Will you permit me?'

She could refuse to cooperate, resist every little encroachment, but to do that right now would be in total contradiction to her will to live, which is as stark and unvarying and immense as a prairie. And she believes him. Doesn't feel like a dirty trick. Probably is penicillin in there. Whoever this man is, whatever he has in that syringe, under his care her fever has broken.

'It's perfectly safe. I know what you must think, but be careful not to confuse what you see for what is.'

157

That's indisputable. She allows him to give her the shot with only a passing worry about the cleanliness of the needle.

He tends to her wound, swabbing her arm with alcohol, replacing the dressing with a fresh roll of gauze. No fumbling with anything, assured, like he's done this many times; he examines her pupils with a penlight and seems satisfied by what he's seen, packing his instruments back into the bag. He's close, squatting on the concrete floor. He wears a pair of sturdy brown shoes, slacks, a collared shirt, his beard a bit scraggly but not too long, a face that could pass for Spanish. She can smell all three of their bodies. She's never been more aware of a man's in relation to hers, never more completely beholden. He snaps his satchel closed and, taking up the lantern, rises, his tall and silent, sniffling companion holding open the door to a glimpse of a bare passage beyond.

Before they leave she manages to croak out a few words, her first coherent statement since the traffic circle.

'Please. Can I have a light? It's so dark.'

'We'll see. Anything else?'

'Who are you?'

There are fifty other questions she's burning to ask, and Cassandra doesn't really expect he'll answer her at all, but then he does, pausing in the doorway like a harried mogul who's stopped for a moment to deal with a minor problem before moving on to more pressing business elsewhere.

'I'm Doctor Walid.'

Crump is screaming through the floor. Crazy, but that's how it sounds, like his angry, stupid, irreverent voice is rising from the floor somewhere toward the back corner of her cell, projected there as if through a tin-can radio.

'Hey, you fuck! You stay away from me with that thing! Fuck! Fuck! Motherfucker, I'll fucking stomp your hajji ass! Ah, man. Fuck. Ahhhh . . . '

Amazed to learn he survived his injuries and is here, at the same time she's terror-stricken by his cries, by whatever awful torment has befallen him. She calls his name instinctively and drags herself to the corner of the cell from which his voice came, feeling her way in the dark, leaning on her left side to keep the pressure off her wounded arm.

Her fingers find the seam of the wall and, searching farther, a small circular grate sunk into the floor in the corner. The grate must be covering a drain, Crump's voice literally piped into her cell. She can no longer hear him, even when pressing her ear to the grate, only the steady roar of resonant hollow places, the sound of the ocean in a seashell. She thinks of cupping her mouth and speaking into the grate but is afraid of who might overhear. She listens with her ear to the floor an indeterminate time, until her throbbing arm forces her to shift position, to sit with her back against the wall. Whatever just happened to him is over and might happen to her next. She isn't sure whether to explore the possibilities there or to have no thoughts at all, no guesses about the immediate future, to keep her mind empty, at least that way to gain some kind of Zen mastery over helplessness. She finds it impossible. Can't stop ranging from one scenario to the next. Eventually she gets around to a thought that all prisoners, sooner or later, trouble themselves with.

How on earth did I get here?

★ ★ ★

It was a mercy killing, although she didn't know at the time those exact words for what she did. In the black, she abandons the unknowable future for the past, one of her strongest early memories, a story there in the past to be followed, her mind trying to discern what her unconscious is telling her in moral, symbolic terms with this memory bubbling up.

How old was she that day — seven? Her cousin Jessie about four years older. The day of the alligator snapping turtle. After catching it and tormenting it with a variety of sticks, he went and got his Christmas present that he'd set nearby, a .22 rifle, which he'd used to entice her out into the fields to play. He was odd and lacked for friends, and even back then, as a small girl, she was fascinated by the gun, by its precision, the weight of it, the cold mechanical potential, the adultness. Jessie had promised to let her shoot but had reneged and gone fishing instead.

That day by the stock pond she told him to leave the turtle alone. It stood its ground dumbly. Long tail like a rat's, hooked beak gaping, a defensive posture that might've succeeded over an evolutionary time-scale but did nothing to deter the assault of a creature such as her cousin. 'What'd that thing ever do to you, Jessie Statler?' she said. Using his full name, aping the way adults, her father, scolded her. Growing up with hogs and cattle she was no stranger to slaughter and the kinder way to do it. Quickness was paramount; minimize the struggle. Misdirect the animal's attention. The unexpected blow of the sledge. Stealthy slip of the knife across the carotid.

Her cousin's underpowered rifle was anything but kind, the pop of it no louder than a firecracker. It made clean holes the size of pencil erasers in the ridged leather of the turtle's carapace, with clawed feet swiping methodically to escape the torment, its defensive posture abandoned but the hook and line preventing it from reaching water.

She let him shoot it maybe five times before stomping off to a rock wall around the nearest pasture and fetching a big enough one to bash its head in. The first creature besides bugs she can recall killing. And not for food or to defend herself or for any other halfway decent reason, but for mercy.

'Hey, no fair,' Jessie said. 'That was my turtle.'

'I told you not to.'

'I don't have to listen to no girl.'

'I'll tell Daddy,' she said, but they both knew the threat was empty. Jessie dragged the carcass into the woods and covered it with a mound of rotting leaves in the gaps between the washed-out roots of a maple where the bones may remain to this day. This is the end of her memory. A forgotten burial site.

⋆ ⋆ ⋆

The door opens, startling her out of sleep. She shrinks against the wall, tangled in her blankets, rubbing eyes in the lantern light.

'You want sandwich?'

It's a boy this time, can't be more than a teenager. Not even the hint of a beard on his face, which is handsome, as far as boys' go — a few more years before he's fully a man, his good looks and youth especially alarming her; young men are the worst. But there's meekness, too. He seems almost embarrassed to be in the cell with her.

'Yes. Please,' she says, famished in the way of those emerging on the far shore of a serious illness. Her stomach, in knots, has been growling so loudly she heard it earlier like a stranger grumbling in the cell.

'You want tea?'

'Yes.'

'Okay. I bring.'

When he returns there's a man with him. Older and heavyset with coarse skin, he has none of the Kid's shyness, looking her right in the face, appraising her body like a pickup artist at a bar. He murmurs something in Arabic to the Kid, and given that voice and his face, she silently names him with an epithet, Pig. You can't always judge someone by looks and mannerisms, but sometimes you fairly can. Later, she'll know this man as Annas.

The Kid sets a plastic sack on the floor. 'Bread. Cheese. Olive.' He takes an old metal thermos and displays it generously. 'Tea.'

'Thank you,' she says, not quite obsequious but making an effort to show rational deference. By her formality she also hopes they may know she has some strength and dignity left in her, even in this position.

'Also this,' the Kid says, removing a penlight from his shirt pocket and setting it on the floor. It looks like the same instrument Walid used to examine her eyes. 'Emir says is a gift to you.'

★ ★ ★

They've come and gone again, taking back the thermos after she drank the last of the tea, leaving behind a tin pail, delivered without comment, although she knows very well what it's for without having to be told. No toilet paper. A pitcher of water they tell her is for drinking (*Good, good, iodine*) and one for cleaning her hands (*This wash only, no drink*) after they've departed and she's finished squatting over the pail.

Later she lies in the corner on her wool blankets, the penlight clutched in her fist like a sword hilt. She's already used it to inspect her cell, finding nothing much. The grated drain. A nonfunctioning fluorescent ballast on the ceiling. She checked it out. Standing on her tiptoes, touching the penlight to an exposed jag of wire protruding from the ballast, weighing the possibility of a shock and deciding it worth the

163

risk of discovering a hot wire, which she could fashion somehow into a weapon or a fire starter, something to change the status quo. But the wire is cold.

Now, without any good reason to use the penlight, Cassandra has to work hard to suppress the urge to switch it on. She knows she should conserve the battery for essential tasks, but after a while the darkness gets the better of her. It cannot even be called darkness anymore, since she's begun to see bluish filaments of light coiling and uncoiling like glowing threads in the space above her. Trick of the brain. Early sign of madness, maybe. When she can no longer resist — it's either turn on the light or continue to pinch her face to remind herself she has form and heft and isn't merely a pair of eyes connected to a brain in shapeless dark — the penlight throws a ghostly penumbral beam on the far wall, temporarily banishing these thoughts.

Seconds pass. She clicks it off, feeling guilty and weak as an addict. She forces herself to concentrate on something else, whatever is happening aboveground. By now the army must know they've been captured and aren't simply lost, didn't flee the ambush and take a wrong turn in some no-name village. The army will move heaven and earth to recover them. This assurance gives her small consolation. Mind boggled at the unluckiness of being the one for whom heaven and earth must be moved.

★ ★ ★

Enough time passes for her to work up the courage to try the pipe. Enough time that she can't say for sure whether Crump's screams were something that happened today or yesterday. Enough, she begins to doubt she ever heard them.

★　★　★

She's in the corner with the drain and the penlight, using the light's aluminum body to tap on the grate. She hopes the metallic clicking will be transmitted well enough through the pipe to wherever the drain leads, somewhere near Crump. Three quick taps, then three spaced further. *Dit dit dit, dah, dah, dah, dit dit dit.* She sounds the SOS exactly fourteen times.

'Crump?' McGinnis's tentative, hushed voice comes up through the drain, sounding very near, like he could be in the next room.

'No, me,' she whispers, cupping her mouth to the grate and speaking into the musty-smelling pipe. When she's done talking, she turns, ear down, to listen.

'Wigheard? I thought you were dead.'

'Me too. You heard Crump? Wasn't sure if I was going crazy there.'

'No, I heard.'

'What happened?'

He's silent a moment before answering, and she takes that for shame at letting himself and his two soldiers be taken. She assumes by his surrendering. They would surely be dead back in that canal if he'd put up an organized resistance.

165

Maybe he made the right call not to. Or maybe dead would be better.

'I think Treanor, the LT, and some of their guys got away.'

'What about the others?'

'I don't know. Jesus, we're in bad here,' comes the huskily whispered answer through the pipe. Curt, almost prideful, the kind of pride that comes from resigning yourself to out-and-out bleakness.

'Who are these guys?'

She's already spent some time on this question and wants his take. One piece of evidence is the Kid, whose name she'll soon learn is Hafs. He was wearing a fatigue-style shirt but it looked tatty to her, like surplus from two wars ago, no name tape, rank, insignia. And other than those fatigues, neither Pig nor the tall sniffling Arab nor Walid wore anything like a uniform. Fedayeen Saddam, a paramilitary force, famously disguise themselves in civilian clothes, and she assumes there are secret police and spies and other remnants of the regime still operating in pockets of resistance throughout the country. But her guess is, these men aren't Iraqi. She thinks they're the foreign fighters, the mujahideen Haider warned them about.

'Doubt they're regulars,' McGinnis says. 'One is maybe a doctor — '

'Walid.'

'How do you know his name?'

'I asked.'

He chuckles, the laughter sounding eerie and more than a little spectral coming through the pipe. She isn't sure what he finds funny but, even so, can't help but join in. It's a strange thing. In a tight spot, with everything riding on the line, laughter is more irresistible than despair. No small number have gone to the gallows sniggering.

★ ★ ★

She and McGinnis work out a code to talk. Safer than using voices. She has the penlight and he a piece of loose tile pried from his cell, instruments with which to tap messages to each other through the cast-iron pipe running under the floor. The code is simple: one tap for the letter *A*, two taps for *B*, and so on, with a brief silence to indicate a new letter, and a longer silence for a new word. As with any language, idioms and other shortcuts arise organically to solve flaws inherent in the code. By the end of the first day they've devised a grid-based tapping system: two rows and thirteen columns of letters, with one or two taps indicating the row, and the second series, the column. That speeds things up some, but tediousness remains a problem. The length of time it takes to relay a message means that many of them don't need to be wholly articulated for the listener to infer their meaning. So, they come up with a signal to let the other know when this happens. If, for example, McGinnis guesses the word before Cassandra finishes tapping it out, he interrupts, tapping rapidly on his end to signify a movement toward the letter Y, an affirmation, as in, 'Yes, got it.'

Hearing this, she then skips ahead to the next word unless the entire intended message has become obvious.

He has light in his cell, not from a penlight but a window. This fact comes out early on. They talk about it for a long time in the context of escape. He tells her his window is small, barred, and at the top corner of his cell, which has a high ceiling. He thinks it's ten or twelve feet. It feels as though the part of his wall — concrete under tile — that he can reach while standing is, like hers, buried underground. Feels solid when you knock on it. Thick, a weight of earth behind.

He describes several rows of shelf mounts without shelves attached, the mounts like runners bolted onto the entire length of his back wall. He believes it might be possible to climb them and reach the window. But the window bars look made of iron or steel, something that rusts, and set close together — no way to squeeze through.

He balks at her suggestion to climb the wall immediately and further assess the bars. The bolts affixing the shelf mounts look sketchy and might shear off under his weight. Not much purchase. Fingertip's worth.

The tile in his room is blue. The room itself like it could've been some kind of washroom or small kitchen. Grimy shadows on the walls where fixtures were once mounted but no longer are, wires and pipes and hoses cut, all appliances and cabinets stripped out, hauled off. A tall empty room with a window.

He's sorry she has no sunlight. She tells him what it's like without it. *Light is life*, she says.

Crawling out of her skin, waking up and not knowing if someone or something has snuck in the cell with her, the contradictory sense that the cell is both smaller and larger than it actually is, she tries to explain it, but there's really no way he can know, not unless they lock him in phantasmagoric dark for days. He says he thinks it's been five since the traffic circle.

S-E-E-M-S — L-O-N-G-E-R, she says, then badgers him about the window until finally he promises to attempt a climb up to it when he thinks the time is right.

O-K — S-O-O-N — P-A-T-I-E-N —

She cuts him off, racing to Y.

★   ★   ★

Then there's Crump. Much of their talk in the days to come centers on him, sharing their concern and speculating over his condition. He has so far refused all communication, verbal or code. McGinnis thinks he's being held next door, maybe two doors down. But neither he nor Cassandra can say whether Crump's refusal to communicate stems from an inability to hear, maybe some side effect of his head wound, or, more disturbingly, whether he's well aware but chooses not to respond. Would he somehow save himself by sacrificing them? Is this why he won't answer? Or is there something he knows and they don't, which makes any interchange too dangerous or pointless to attempt?

In any case, the problem is not that he's silent. His latest outburst was the worst so far.

Cassandra woke to him screaming and throwing himself against what sounded like his cell door, making enough of a racket that she could hear him plainly through her own door, the echo rising through the drain a redundancy.

'Come on and do it!' he shrieked, the kind of unmodulated shrillness that can only come from a human being pushed to a place where the lines between fight and flight approach a vanishing point. 'Just get it the fuck over with! Do it, you pussies! Do it! I know you're gonna do it so just fucking do it!'

The guards wouldn't oblige him. Neither would he let up, and she thought he must've been hurting himself with the way he was going at the door, the crashing bangs sounding intermittently; must've been running at it, putting his shoulder into it like a battering ram. For his own good she hoped he would knock himself out. No such luck. The guards were in the hall, chattering unintelligibly among themselves and also yelling at him through the door, hollering at him to shut up, which only inspired a greater apex of fury.

There was the unmistakable *clacking* sound of an automatic rifle being cocked. Spring-loaded, slick, a slim-tolerance sound. Done in the hallway, and louder than it had to be, more dramatic, as if the person cocking the rifle thought the sound itself would serve as sufficient intimidation to silence him, which it wasn't. He kept on. And even though Cassandra was pretty sure he was about to die, she felt little pity for him in that moment. Anger, mostly. Anger at him and fear for herself, because of how his actions would implicate her, because the guards would kill him first and then move on to her and McGinnis. Not necessarily because they wanted to, but because they would have no choice, these Americans turning out to be more trouble than they were worth. Once you murder one prisoner of war, you'd better dispose of the others.

She braced herself for the rifle shot foretelling her doom. But as inexplicably as he'd started, Crump stopped. He went at the door to the point of muscle failure. Or maybe he did knock himself out. The guards talked for a while longer in the hallway and then went silent, too.

Afterward she and McGinnis spent hours going back and forth on the pipe about it. McGinnis had been afraid of the same thing she had, certain that if the guards had shot Crump, they would be next. They still couldn't say for sure whether the periodic yelling from his cell indicated torture or madness or both, whether they were being held hostage for ransom, a prisoner exchange, the extraction of intel, propaganda value, or something else. But, setting aside their captors' motivations, they agreed that Crump could get them killed if he couldn't be reasoned with. The only way to mitigate this risk was to make contact, talk him down, at which task they continued to fail, tapping out SOS signals until their wrists throbbed with repetition, and sometimes, in desperation, risking verbal appeals through the pipe, calling his name softly, asking how he was holding up, but he never responded.

It was mystifying in the first days, but now she has an inkling of the reason Crump won't speak except to demand his own death, assuming that's what he means by *Just fucking do it already*. It's still crazy, she thinks, it'd never be something she'd ask for, but maybe her instincts are wrong here and Crump's figured it out: Talking to each other isn't going to end this. Won't solve the essential problem and may only compound it by making them more dependent on one another, therefore more vulnerable to threats and torture. Already, she and McGinnis are running out of things to talk about, their conversation grown stale. It's what McGinnis seems not to understand, the law of diminishing returns; they talk constantly and yet it gives them no power, no control. They talk about Crump. About home, rescue, escape, what the army may be doing to locate them, and the more they talk, the more McGinnis needs to, and the more she doesn't, because she can get no more information from him. It's hollow comfort, like spending money. Frustrated, she lapses into terseness, periods of enforced silence, while McGinnis is starting to show signs of a dangerously needy desperation.

Like now. Like right now with his tile shard working rapidly, recklessly loud, insistent, demanding her attention. She decides to ignore him for enough time to make it obvious. She would like to ignore this entreaty entirely, claim later that she was asleep and didn't hear it. But that won't pass. They've just been fed and watered, the boyish guard Hafs entering her cell to change out her waste pail, and she knows the same has been done for McGinnis, which means he knows she's awake. Other than transparently shunning him, there's no choice but to tap back on the grate. Listening, ready to receive. He proceeds with the message.

I-F — I — D-O-N-T — M-A-K-E — I-T . . .

She can already tell where this is headed. They've been over this ground several times and she doesn't know if she can bear to reassure him again that if she manages to live, and he doesn't, she will definitely, without fail, tell his wife that he loved her to the bitter end and that his last thoughts were of her and their son, whose name, she's relearned, is Matthew. She curses him, the father, silently. Need to teach him a lesson. These things don't need to be said. They're mawkish promises to make. Foregrounding what is already huge and painful, talk like this can only lead to defeatism, paralysis, despair. Of course she'd do all that for him. Go to see his people, if she had to. Course she would. Stop worrying about them and worry about us. Like they need any more melodrama, the stakes to be higher. Maybe disgust is too absolute a sentiment for what she feels for him, but she finds him repellently pitiful; what he's doing makes her want to keep her distance from him, as Crump may've decided to. Being chained together is almost as bad as being alone.

Her anger gets the best of her. She interrupts him and taps rapidly on the drain and doesn't stop for a solid minute, which action in their code is roughly translatable to her bellowing,

Yes, I get it, I fucking get it, so shut up about it already!

He goes silent. She immediately regrets what she's done and taps out an apology, repeating it over and over because he doesn't respond.

S-O-R-R-Y — S-R-R-Y — S-R-Y . . .

I give up, she thinks. An hour passes. Or two, or four; she's lost her clock, McGinnis and his window and the sun. However long it's been, silence. Sulking. She thinks it's just like a man to rub it in like that. To pull back when things are at their most intense. To avoid. To punish by withholding.

★　★　★

Sex is always on their minds. From what she can tell, they're even more fixated on it than the average adult male of fighting age, a class of person she's known very well over the past few years. So, for her to believe the guards are oversexed is really saying something.

She knows they're thinking about it by their eyes and their horny awkwardness with her and because from time to time she overhears them, those who speak a little English, with McGinnis in his cell.

You have wife? What car you have? Why in America are the men always fucking other men? How many times you can do it in one night? How many TVs for your house? Where you live? What you think of Iraq? You fuck many women or just wife? What you think about this Wigheard? You fuck her?

174

* * *

She figured it would come to this. But there's no good way to steel yourself to accept victimhood. To try is only to codify the souring relationship between yourself and the world, to cement future agony like reliving a trauma that hasn't even happened yet.

It's Annas, the ugly piggish one. She knows his name by now. She's made an effort to learn all their names and has succeeded so far with three: Walid, Hafs, and Annas. Her thinking is that by using their names as often as possible, she might, by proxy, humanize herself.

This strategy is fundamentally sound and will work well with some, less well with others, and not at all with a man like Annas. Might even have backfired, in his case. To remind someone like that of his humanity is to remind him of what he hates most. Thus rage. Thus this present moment, a while in coming.

He slips into her dark cell with eyes wild and rifle held by the pistol grip, the weapon pointed carelessly toward her while he sets the lantern on the floor and with his foot eases the door shut behind him.

'What's wrong?' she says. She sits up on her pallet, blankets folded on top of flattened-out cardboard boxes, these new, a gift from Hafs. Until this present intrusion she'd been sleeping intermittently, stuck in a series of not-quite-nightmares in which she failed at one crucial responsibility after another. Snapped from that into this, the mind demands a moment to realize

175

how afraid she should be.

'*You* are wrong,' Annas says, venom material-
izing out of nowhere. 'You are very bad woman.'
He comes closer, hovering over her. 'Move. The
other way.'

He's directing her to lie facedown on the
pallet. Before she buries her eyes in the scratchy
wool she catches a glimpse of his sandaled foot
in the lantern light, curly black toe hairs
gleaming, and the rifle barrel, her senses so
attuned she can pick out the dust and
carbonization on the flash suppressor dangling
there beside his knuckled toes, inches from her
head. He's breathing hard and fast like he's just
run a sprint. Her palms are drawn instinctively
to the back of her neck, her face pressed in the
wool, eyes closed, better not to know, see,
expect. Of these, expectation is the worst. She's
reduced to paralysis, not a weakling or a coward
but a soldier, she who's persisted where others
have folded insensate. And yet the gun barrel
forces itself between two of her clinched fingers
and she allows this to happen; it digs into the
hollow directly above her spinal cord. What
jujitsu could she use to wrest it from him and
blow him away? — but that's Hollywood bullshit
talking. He'd kill her, or someone else soon
would. For the time, fighting is not what affords
her the best chance.

'You are bad,' he says again, and begins to
grope her. A callused hand slides beneath her
dress, squeezing and rooting in her flesh,
between her legs. He removes the gun from the
back of her neck to get a better purchase. She

can smell the tartness of his breath, his unwashed body, her every muscle gone rigid with revulsion and alarm. Feels like she's being robbed. The maddening unfairness of that. Never in her life has she allowed a man to do this. She's sobbing, choking hiccupping sobs.

'Please, don't. Please. You don't have to. This is wrong. You shouldn't do this. A good Muslim wouldn't do this.'

The words escape her like a stumbled-upon incantation. The way a smart person can figure the exact right move to get her way with a stranger. To wheedle, to praise, to hurt. To provoke a swift, different, and violent response.

He jerks his hand from between her legs and strikes the back of her head with the heel of his palm. She smells blood iron and sees silver. He's straddling her and cursing. 'Shut fuck up!' His tone is outraged, indignant, like she's committed some contemptible transgression against him and not the other way around. 'I do not need you. I am looking for weapon. This is it.'

It's an absurd excuse for what he's done.

'I don't have anything, okay?'

He takes his rifle and again uses the barrel to pin her head to the floor, this time with enough force she fears her skull might crack, impaled on a steel spike like rotted fruit. It was a desperate gambit, and she's said the wrong thing. Challenged his religion, his manhood. Now he'll kill her for it. Ready as she can be. Eyes scrunched, face buried, sobbing, reduced completely. But the pressure lets up. He doesn't pull the trigger. He must know he couldn't get away

177

with that much. She has value, maybe more than he does himself. He shoves her head against the floor one last time and spits on her back and leaves.

⋆   ⋆   ⋆

Cassandra walks four paces and reaches out with her wounded arm to touch the wall with splayed fingertips, then does a right-face and this time walks five paces before touching the wall again in precisely the same way. She's just traveled half the perimeter of her cell. Without pause she does the other half and adds the lap to her mental tally of how many she's completed so far this session — the number is thirty, representing 1,620 feet — having earlier measured the cell's perimeter with her hands, which she estimated to be six inches from base of wrist to tip of middle finger.

She's forgotten the exact number of feet in a mile. Sharp with numbers but never had a memory for that kind of thing, which is why she assumes the military, unlike the rest of America, is on the metric system. Not remembering the exact length of a mile, she's substituted 5,400 feet as a reasonably convenient approximation. Convenient, because it's the distance traveled in one hundred laps of her cell. Close enough for her purpose which, simply put, is distraction. She walks and lifts her arm to strengthen it and indulges in hate fantasies of what she'd like to do to Annas, the whole time keeping up with the math in her head. Her arm has healed enough for it to have stopped throbbing but the scabby shrapnel wound still itches like it's mosquito-bit. That curative sort of itch, the body making shiny new red skin. There doesn't seem to be any permanent damage to her tendons or elbow; the worst of it was to the meat of her biceps, with a few splotchy scars there, and pinprick scabs on her hip where entered flecks of steel no bigger than sand. The real damage comes later and is intangible. Goddamn men. Nature, with its two-bodied disregard for fairness. For the first time in a while she thinks about the unsolved rape at Camp New York, which she knows was just a thing that happened, and not even to her, a thing in the past that's unconnected causally in space and time from what's happening now, and a forewarning of it only in the sense that war is hell and men are men everywhere.

She walks and keeps the tally and envisions how Annas's face will look after she puts a bullet through it. Complete darkness. Trusting the sameness of her stride and the touch of the walls to guide her. It gets to where she doesn't need to use her hands and can feel a wall coming in the dark with a phantom sense like a bat's sonar. Not just her imagination, either, but something about how the timbre of sound changes as she circles the empty room. Probably the best thing she could be doing right now, distraction is good, and also there's the sheer practicality of exercise, the best way to prepare for the unknown, her intelligence consumed by the physical activity, hateful fantasy, spatial mindfulness required to navigate without sight, the tallying of distance, the illusions of forward progress, revenge, survival: together, enough to totally occupy her mind.

Five paces, right-face, four paces, right-face, now exploring a new and very twisted way to kill him: fake-seduce him and take him in her mouth and bite off his rigid cock, bleed him to death from his bitten-off cock stump; Jesus, girl; fifty more laps, and having slain him fifty more ways, she reverses direction, right-faces become left-faces, going counter-clockwise to build muscle evenly. She's amped, ready. Yesterday she did four miles before she couldn't go any farther, her wounded arm tiring before her legs. Today her goal is to beat what she did yesterday. She'll walk for seven, eight hours. Until she can't anymore.

She completes a mile and takes a break, moving to the center of the cell where she's dragged her pallet and set the plastic pitchers of water and her waste pail so as not to stumble and spill anything. She has to ration the water, especially with working out like this, but allows herself the luxury of a long satisfying drink, forgetting for a moment its questionable provenance, the taste metallic, over-iodinated. At least someone has tried to purify it. At least there's that.

She sets the pitcher down and guesses by the difference in weight that it's a quarter gone. Clicks on the penlight to check. Pretty close. Just then she's startled by McGinnis crying out in his cell, a yelp of pain and surprise. In a moment she's in the corner with her ear to the drain, listening. She can't remember hearing his door open. Whether a guard is in there. Sounds like he's muttering to himself now. She taps to get his attention.

O-K — O-K — O —

He taps rapidly to Y, as in *Yes, I'm OK*.

She taps, *W-H-A* —

He interrupts and races to *Y* again; taps, *F-E-L-L*.

How

Tried climbing cut arm on bolt falling

Cut bad

Not too, he says.

Window solid

Never reached

Sorry you hurt

OK

Sorry about before too

OK I sorry too, he says.

Why

Heard what he did to you

She takes a while to respond.

Nothing happened

★ ★ ★

There's a guard outside her cell messing around with the lock. She stops her pacing and goes to the far corner and drags the pallet atop the grated drain to muffle the sound so that McGinnis won't have to listen this time to whatever's coming. The door creaks slowly open. She sits on top of the pallet directly over the drain and wraps her abaya over her face, as they've instructed her to do whenever they enter. *No look. Cover eyes.*

'Hello. It's okay to take off.'

She lowers the fabric, recognizing the voice as Hafs's. Of all the guards she's had dealings with — besides Walid, whom she encountered more often when she was delirious with fever — Hafs is the best English-speaker. Perhaps because of this, he's also the one who's shown her the most kindness. He enters the cell and leaves his rifle propped near the door, setting it there out of reach and taking care, during their meeting, not to let her come between it and himself.

'I bring food.'

'Thanks.'

'Eat, eat.' He gestures magnanimously at the plastic sack he's placed beside her. He retreats to the door and leans against the jamb uneasily, a posture of forced coolness, watching her while she takes a bite of flat-bread. Eating in front of him feels wrong. Too intimate, like using the toilet in front of someone you've just met, but she forces herself to do it because he seems to want that, and she thinks obliging his desires could do her some actual good, that his desires are neither as cruel nor as dangerous as Annas's and might even be to help her. She does her best to savor the bread politely, and the greasy olives wrapped in the bottom of the sack, but still finishes the meal too quickly. She's ravenous, has lost a lot of weight already, ten pounds or more.

As a surprise he produces from his pocket a Jaffa orange, tossing it underhanded across the cell. She flinches at the quick movement and fumbles the catch. The orange rolls between her pallet and the wall. She reaches for it, her first fresh fruit in well over a month, since Camp New York. Rotating the orange in her hands, marveling at its salamander sheen in the lantern light: it's the most vibrantly alive thing she's seen in a long time.

Hafs has also brought one for himself. He stands in the doorway, peeling it.

'You are Christian?' he asks casually, swallowing a bite. The question immediately recalls her first conversation with Haider at the traffic circle. This time she isn't going to answer, at least not truthfully, any questions about her faith or lack thereof.

'Yes,' she says, trying to sound genuine. 'But I have a lot of respect for Islam. The little I know about it. I'd like to learn more, though.'

She makes this statement knowing that Muslims tend to regard Christians in a better light than they do atheists. Christians and Jews are the People of the Book. More factoids culled from the cultural-sensitivity brief, which may prove to be the best piece of army training she ever got.

Hafs appears immensely pleased. He's just about beaming, giving her a goofy teenage grin like she, the most popular girl in school, has just bestowed special attention on him. 'Good, good,' he says. 'You are already one-half Muslim. You know, if you say the Shahada, you go to paradise.'

He smiles again. She forces herself to smile back. His guilelessness amazes her, but then again, he's devout, even for this bunch, and devotion is the enemy of guile. Through the cell door she's heard him praying, salaaming and chanting out there in the hallway during his guard shifts; once, she listened as he prayed so hard and fervently, he worked himself into a crying jag through nothing but the power of his own overwhelming spirituality. She wonders how it's possible for him to be touched so deeply by a thing he can't even see, and yet, at the same time participate in caging a fellow human being in these conditions.

'If you want,' he says, 'I bring you Qur'an.'

'That would be good. Yes, definitely.' There's no need for her to fake enthusiasm at the prospect of having access to reading materials. Anything would be welcome, even holy scripture, a type of literature she's never been much interested in. At this point, however, she'd gladly read the phone book. 'But, Hafs,' she adds, 'I could never read in here. It's way too dark whenever you're gone.'

His smile melts into a frown and a studied look at the lantern. In his zeal he's forgotten this overriding limitation of her existence.

'Is no problem,' he says. 'Soon, I look in bazaar. I bring better light. I bring English Qur'an. Arabic is best, but I can teach. You can help my English.'

'Good,' she says. 'It's a deal.' He takes a smiling bite of his orange, the juice dribbling over his chin. She eats hers more carefully, not wanting to waste it, and thinks over what might happen if she were to tell him about Annas. That

184

one of his fellow guards has mistreated her. The calculus is whether suffering the inevitable reprisal by Annas will be worth whatever punishment he himself might receive at the hands of his superiors. Whether they'd care at all. She weighs the choice and decides it isn't worth it, not yet. Better to keep her mouth shut for the time being. What she needs now is not to set a grand plan into motion but to think smaller. What she needs is more information.

'Hafs, can I ask something? Are you Iraqi?'

He appears to find it amusing, the suggestion he might be from this place. 'No, no. I am soldier in the Islamic army. Since two years, jihad.'

'What're you going to do to me? Do you all want money? What's going to happen?'

You shouldn't have just come out and asked that, she thinks; the fear in her throat is like an invisible hand playing at strangulation. She watches him considering how to respond, probably gauging how much he should divulge, whether he is betraying his cause and comrades by telling her anything at all. The boy looks sympathetic but with a prickly sort of impatience, like she should've known better.

'There is no problem, sister. *Inshallah.*'

*　*　*

They're brought from their cells to be interrogated on video. They're brought one by one, and she's last to arrive. When the blindfold comes off she sees McGinnis and Crump kneeling to her left and right. She's also been made to kneel, swivels her head to check what's behind her — the first thought, It'll come from behind — but there's nothing there, just a bare wall with some kind of black Islamic flag hung on it. The room is lit by sunlight through a slatted window, long thin slats, the window reachable from the ground; this is some other room than McGinnis's cell. She hasn't seen the sun in two weeks, and it hurts her eyes like standing too close to a hot fire.

She recognizes a few of the guards. Hafs, Annas, an older man named Mohammed, and the tall aristocratic one who had a cold when she first saw him; there are also several others she doesn't know by name. All are armed, kitted up like they're about to go into battle. It's not hot but she's sweating through her abaya. She doesn't look closely at them or make eye contact, holding her gaze mostly at the floor, stealing sidelong glances at her friends. McGinnis and Crump are looking haggard, grubby sallow skin and neck beards, Crump especially grizzled, wearing an eye patch, face all bruised up. Each man has lost twenty pounds, easy. Makes her wonder what she looks like. Not out of vanity but it's disconcerting not to know.

There's a broad bandage around McGinnis's right arm. The cut from when he fell trying to climb his wall. The gauze is stained puss yellow in places, and the skin on his exposed arm looks sunburned, taut. She thinks of his allergies and whether Walid has something other than penicillin in that aid bag. Her eyes meet McGinnis's and then she wishes they hadn't.

The contagion, fear. She looks away, at Crump, who refuses to engage with her or anyone, staring fixedly at the slatted window with one eye bleary and angry; unlike her or McGinnis, he's had his hands bound in front of him with a plastic zip cuff. A number of things can be inferred from this. Crump is pissed. Crump is unruly. Crump has been driven berserk by the dark solitary cell.

The door opens, and the guards make way for Walid, who isn't armed. He carries a clipboard and is dressed all in black except for a white rounded skullcap. The outfit makes him look like a severe cleric. He moves confidently through the room and approaches the prisoners, punctiliously handing each one a sheet of paper as if he's an instructor distributing teaching materials.

'We're going to make a video,' he says in his British-inflected accent. 'Look at these words and put them into your heart. You must say them like they're your own. You'll have twenty minutes, then we'll rehearse and film it.'

She looks down at her paper, the print in neat block letters like those an engineer might make.

My name is Cassandra Wigheard. I am an American soldier. I have been tried and found guilty of supporting the United States' invasion of Muslim lands. My life is in danger. Please help me. This is not a plea to President Bush, because his lack of concern for those sent to this hellhole is well known. This is a plea to the people of America. I am asking for the release from captivity of all Iraqis. I am asking you to petition the government to end this war. Please, do what you can to save my life.

She looks up. The Kid, Hafs, AK-47 in hand, has wandered across the room and sidles up next to her. While Walid is occupied with staging, directing his men as they rig a tripod supporting a photographic light, Hafs smiles and leans in and pulls back the charging handle of his rifle. There's a banana clip in it, but when he operates the charging handle, the bolt slides back a couple inches to reveal an empty chamber, both the rifle and the magazine unloaded.

'See?' he whispers. 'Is okay. Is just for video. Like I say to you, no problem.'

10

Sleed: Collateral

`Iraq (Triangletown): 1 day after`

The shamal hit. Those bastards were smart to time their attack right before it did. We kept on going through the dust and sand blowing around, but it made the search almost impossible. There were a couple crucial hours we couldn't get birds in the air to spot for us, and when the weather did clear, we still hadn't found the three MIA. They weren't sheltering in the palm grove near Triangletown like we'd hoped, weren't lying facedown like Worthy in a ditch, or inside any of the ramshackle houses and outbuildings we raided. By that time, most of the brigade had been called out to help. Navy divers were on the way to dredge the canals. Psy-ops teams drove trucks rigged with loudspeakers that broadcast warnings in Arabic and messages of support in English. Colonel Easton was on scene, supervising the whole shit show.

Easton was convinced the locals knew more than they were telling about who'd taken his three soldiers. They were still officially listed as missing, not POWs, but it wasn't looking good. On his orders we went street to street, knocked on doors and kicked them down if they weren't opened fast enough to suit us. We tore through their shitty little houses, tossing closets, wardrobes, stepping over screaming babies, dumping stacks of blankets onto the floor. It seemed like each Iraqi family owned a ridiculous number of blankets, way more than you'd ever need. I still can't figure why they had so many and it's not important at all but the detail sticks in my head, searching through stacks of them so big, you could definitely hide a body in there. McGinnis, Crump, and Wigheard. By then, we knew all about them. We'd memorized their names to call for them on the streets.

★ ★ ★

Next afternoon we were still on the hunt. Our platoon had moved out from Triangletown to a spot on the highway where we set up a traffic-control point, looking for late-model Toyota trucks. The soldiers who'd survived the traffic circle reported that was what the guys who'd attacked were driving. Higher told us to keep an eye out for Toyotas but to search every car that passed. Sometime late on the first day we stopped a gold-colored Mercedes E-Class with two occupants. The driver looked nervous, too smiley. He wore a red-and-white head scarf.

'Red is the Palestinian color,' Fitzpatrick said. 'It's what the fighters like. Most Iraqis wear black.'

'That right?' Blornsbaum said.

'Haven't you noticed?'

'I ain't been paying that close attention to their headgear.'

'Car looks fancy enough to be from outta town, though,' Galvan said. 'These hajjis around here would just as soon be rocking a donkey cart.'

'True.'

Blornsbaum pounded on the trunk and motioned for the driver to open it. The driver clapped his hands together like he was dusting them off.

'Meestuh, is nothing. Meestuh, is dee-nuh.'

'Freaking open it,' Blornsbaum said. 'Now.' He pointed his rifle at the driver and tapped the muzzle on the trunk, chipping the paint. The driver winced but quickly smiled again, no problem, and turned his key in the lock and opened the trunk like he was expecting something or someone to jump out. When I saw how he did that, the hairs on my forearms stood on end and I raised my rifle, finger crooked on the trigger. The trunk swung all the way open and I leaned back, expecting to see wires and propane tanks and plastic explosives, or the bodies of three U.S. soldiers, bound and gagged, but it was nothing like that. The driver had taken care with the trunk because, while there was a creature tied up in there, it wasn't a person but a sheep, legs hobbled. It saw daylight and raised its head, bleating pathetically. The driver punched it in the neck and it groaned and lay back down on the spare tire.

'Dee-nuh,' he said, patting his belly.

★　★　★

Shit continued to get weird. That afternoon there was an unexpected visitor at the traffic-control point. Frago came ambling down the road. He'd tracked us more than five klicks from the Row. Blew my mind. You hear stories of dogs following their masters across crazy distances but I'd always thought those stories were hype.

'You ever know a dog that loyal ?' I knelt to scratch him behind the ears.

'He's just looking for a free lunch,' Fitzpatrick said. 'Besides, I'm not even sure it's the same dog. Most of them around here look like that.'

'It's him,' I said. 'Hundred percent.'

He gulped down the bean-and-rice burrito I tossed into the shade of our turret, where he spent the rest of the afternoon lying around, watching without much interest as we stopped dozens of cars and searched each one, finding nothing as interesting as the sheep. There was more drama around dark when a Volkswagen painted orange and white, the Iraqi markings for a taxi, approached our checkpoint without slowing down, so Galvan fired a shot into the front tire. The bullet ricocheted off the wheel into the passenger compartment, hitting the driver in the foot, severing his middle toe. Medic Marko cursed Galvan as he treated the wounded Iraqi, who reeked of whiskey and sobbed like a crazy person. Frago went over and sniffed at him, and the drunk toeless cabbie wailed even louder.

'Stop being such a baby,' Blornsbaum said. 'He ain't a biter.'

'It's a cultural thing, Sergeant,' Fitzpatrick

said. 'I heard the CIA uses dogs at Gitmo for interrogations and shit. Arabs are scared to death of them.'

'Really. Dumb mutt might be useful after all.'

Marko stopped the bleeding with QuikClot, bandaged the foot, and handed the man the dime-sized piece of his toe wrapped in gauze, sealed inside a plastic bag. We'd found the toe on the floorboard. We sent him on his way with a warning to get off the road as soon as possible. He was so drunk, he could barely stand.

★ ★ ★

That night we were ordered to collapse our roadblock and set an observation post on a stretch of dirt road that ran along a canal north of the village. The road wasn't used much, and we took turns sleeping and pulling watch in the tank. With the engine running, the inside of the turret was too loud for us to talk without using noise-canceling headphones wired into our helmets. We had an MP3 player jury-rigged into the commo system so we could listen to music, each other, and the military radios all at the same time. Galvan liked gangsta rap and was blasting Eminem. Not my first choice, but he was the tank commander.

I slouched in the gunner station watching the road through the thermals. Sipping on coffee to stay awake, I felt so tired from the adrenaline dump and no real sleep in almost forty-eight hours, I got annoyed, starting to forget we'd caused this whole mess. If we'd been at camp, like we were supposed to be, instead of trying to crack those safes, we wouldn't have held up our platoon when the QRF call went out. Our tanks would've gotten to the traffic circle a good ten minutes earlier, and what happened there might've ended differently. It was hard to say for sure, but we might've been the one thing that tipped the scales. The thought would pop into my head from time to time but I couldn't make it stick. Zoned out, listening to the angry music, I was nodding off when Galvan said, 'You see that?'

'No. What?'

'There.' He hit a button on his joystick and the hydraulics in the turret whirred as the gun snapped to the point he'd been looking at through the thermals.

'You think that could be a Toyota?'

'I dunno. Maybe, yeah.'

The truck was in a field about a klick away, off-roading slowly in the general direction of the canal.

'Looks like they're creepin',' Galvan said. 'Get ready.'

He called in a report and then told Fitzpatrick, down in the driver's hull, to fire up the engine. The turbine kicked on. The radio beeped.

'Blue Two, this is Crusader Six. I copy your traffic about the possible Toyota. Detain and search that vie. Over.'

'Shit,' Galvan said to himself. 'Roger that, sir,' he said to Colonel Easton.

The truck had almost reached the canal. It

turned onto the road, heading slowly for us, driving with no lights, and that was a huge red flag. We were also blacked out, not moving, and they were far enough away, there was no chance they could see us yet unless they had night vision, too.

'What's the distance?' Galvan said.

I hit a button and painted the truck with a laser. 'Five hundred fifty meters,' I said.

'Wait till they're at one fifty and then turn on the white lights.'

'Roger.'

'Now?'

'Two hundred.'

'Okay. Tell him when.'

'Rooster, hit it.'

Fitzpatrick threw the switch for the brights, and seeing our tank suddenly lit up on the road ahead, the truck stopped. Just sat there for a second like the driver wasn't sure what to do next, before the front end dipped as he threw it in reverse, backed up in a hurry and did a three-point turn, taking off.

'Get that motherfucker,' Galvan said, and Fitzpatrick dropped the transmission into drive, opening the throttle. The sound of the tank speeding up was like a fistful of pennies dumped in a blender.

'Crusader Six, this is Blue Two. Vic is refusing to stop. In pursuit, time now.'

'Two, do not let that goddamn truck get away from you.'

'Roger, sir.'

Some people might think it'd be easy to chase

down a truck with a tank, but it's not. An Ml Abrams drives like an old Cadillac, one of those big boats from the seventies. Smooth-handling and fast on the open highway, but not a lot of get-up-and-go, and there're some things it just can't do, like crossing the wrong kind of ditch. The tank is so long, it'll pitch down the slope if the sides are steep enough and get stuck in the bottom like a lawn dart.

The canal road was a long bumpy straight-away, and the driver of the truck must've seen us gaining and gotten desperate. He hit the brakes and tried the one thing that could've saved him. Headed across the canal. The water wasn't so high there and he slid down the bank and gunned it through. At first it looked like he might get swept away, but his wheels caught and he made it up the other side.

'Want me to try it?' Fitzpatrick said.

'Negative,' Galvan said. 'We'll never make that.' He keyed the net: 'Crusader Six, Blue Two. Vic crossed the canal, vicinity Checkpoint Three One. I'm stuck on the far side. Request guidance. Over.'

'Two, Six. Is it definitely matching the BOLO?'

'Affirmative.'

'Can you shoot to disable? Over.'

'Negative, sir. It's too far away and still rolling.'

There was radio silence while the colonel thought about it. A second or two to decide life or death. That's all you ever get, if that.

'Two, Six. Engage, over.'

'Roger, engaging time now. Gunner, coax, truck!'

I flicked off the safety but didn't fire. Something in me already knew what we'd find later.

'Sergeant, they haven't really done anything. And what if the POWs are in there? We sure about this?'

'Fuck, Sleed. You heard what the colonel said.'

'I know but — '

'Fire!'

I'd never physically hurt anyone in my life except for a fight in school when I was in the eighth grade and bloodied the nose of this bully who'd been picking on me because of my acne. Still, I was supposed to be a stone-cold killer, had trained for this moment for years, but when it came down to it, it was hard to pull the trigger, especially when no one was shooting at us. I just couldn't. Galvan had to. The truck was getting away, six hundred meters now. He took over the gunnery controls from his station. The coax bucked in the mount, the smell of cordite filled the turret, and I watched in my sights as the tracers sailed through the air and landed all around the Toyota, shredding it like a beer can blasted with a shotgun, the tires bursting, truck bouncing across the field before it rolled on its rims to a stop.

Galvan ceased fire. The rear passenger door opened and stuck halfway like the hinges were damaged and someone inside had to kick it free. Galvan was about to shoot another burst but when the door opened the rest of the way, it was

197

a woman who stumbled out. She moved like a puppet whose strings were being cut. Wobbled away from the truck, back toward it, and leaned into the backseat. Dragged something out. Even from that far off, but with the sights set on max power, I could tell right away we'd screwed up big.

'Oh my god,' I said. 'It's a kid.'

★　★　★

We drove farther up the road to where there was a bridge over the canal. We crossed to the other side and circled back around to the truck smoking in the field. By then everyone in it was dead. The woman we'd seen. The little girl she'd been carrying, who looked too skinny, like she'd been about to die of starvation before we killed her. The man driving, still buckled into the front seat. A boy in the back. Something was wrong with one of his arms. Like it'd been whittled down to a nub in place of a hand.

'This is so bad,' Galvan said.

I was starting to get light-headed, but this time I refused to let myself faint. Instead I walked up to Galvan and hit him as hard as I could. Sucker-punched my tank commander. Laid him out and got on top and started to choke him. We fought, going hard, basically trying to kill each other — why not add one more fucking corpse to the mix? — and even Fitzpatrick, big as he was, couldn't separate us. It wasn't until Blornsbaum drove up in his tank and dismounted and got involved that they broke up the fight.

They dragged me off to one side. Galvan the other. I sat with my head in my hands, nose snotty and bloody, and all that mixing with the tears.

'I can't believe this!' I shouted. 'We shouldn't even be here.'

'Tell me about it,' Blornsbaum said.

'Those people are wasted because we're looking for the MIA, and the only reason we're doing that is we didn't get to them fast enough.'

'Yeah. You're gonna have to live with that.'

'You wanna know why we missed the QRF call, Sergeant?'

'Shut the fuck up, Sleed,' Galvan yelled from across the way.

'I don't know if I do,' Blornsbaum said carefully.

'Well, I'm telling, regardless. We missed it because we were too busy trying to bust into some safes in the water palace. I can't fucking take this anymore.'

Blornsbaum stared at me like he wanted to wring my neck, and he spat on the ground and wiped his mouth on his sleeve. 'You kids,' he said. 'Man, you kids.' He didn't sound mad or even disappointed. Just real tired. 'Sleed,' he said, 'I want you to listen close. Never say what you just said to me, ever again, to nobody. You put that mess in a box. Lock it, bury it deep, and throw away the key. Word of this gets out, and some people, including you, are going to jail. Not for just a minute, either. I'm talking about your life is over. And the people who are lucky enough not to go to jail, their careers will be over. You three are a disgrace. I hope you get yours, but you better believe I'm not letting you take me down with you. What's done is done. The only thing left now is to stop the bleeding.'

*　*　*

The day after the shooting, Triangletown was in an uproar. Dozens of Iraqis moved on our company's makeshift outpost, spools of razor wire strung around tanks and APCs circled defensively like a wagon train in a western. The Iraqis were chanting something that could've been *Death to America*, we didn't know. They were led by this old sheikh, who, unlike everyone else, acted calm, hands clasped behind his back like a professor, skin the color of a walnut, and just as creased.

We were quickly becoming surrounded. The crowd surged forward, pushed from the rear by newcomers. Frago ran back and forth along the wire, barking at the Iraqis. Someone in the crowd threw a stone at him and missed. Somebody else threw another one that hit him in the haunches and made him yelp, tuck his tail over his balls, and scurry under our tank to hide.

I yelled, brandished my rifle and stepped to the crowd. The night before, I'd been destroyed by regret, but now it turned inside out, to anger, like when you do something wrong and get called on it.

'You shit birds wanna throw rocks? Throw one at me, and let's see what happens.'

Just then I jumped in my boots at the sound of

a command. 'At ease that goddamn noise, troop!' It was Colonel Easton, small man with a big voice. He was bandy-legged, built like a jockey but a few inches taller, and always acting unnaturally crass, probably thinking that the way he cursed all the time made it easier for us common folk to relate. Like a lot of officers who'd drunk the Kool-Aid and slogged away long enough to gain command of a battalion, he was a weird mix of motivational speaker and prison warden.

'What's the fucking big idea here?' he said, looking right at me.

'They were throwing rocks, sir.'

'Who'd they throw rocks at?'

'My dog, sir.'

'Your fucking dog?' He scrunched his face like he'd just bit into something nasty. 'You know we've got three MIA out there right now, don't you? Not to mention this mob scene on our hands. And you mean to tell me you're busting balls over a dog? You aren't even authorized to keep a dog, Specialist ... Sleed,' he said, squinting to read my name tape. 'We tracking?'

'Sorry, sir. I shouldn't've pointed my gun at them.'

'A rifle is a weapon. The only guns in the army are the big guns. You make my head hurt, Sleed. What platoon you in?'

'Third, sir.'

'Oh. You're the assholes. What've you got to say for yourself?'

I could feel Blornsbaum staring a hole through me.

'We, uh, we tried, sir.'

'You tried. Look what that gets you. Goddammit, Sleed. I'm going to personally do violence upon you if you don't get out of my sight in the next three seconds.'

'Yes, sir.'

I moved off, and he turned to Moe, his interpreter. 'Which one is he?' the colonel said, scanning the crowd. 'Yeah? Ask him what he wants.'

Moe was on loan from the State Department, an Iraqi American by way of Detroit. Rumor was, his dad had run afoul of Saddam's secret police during the war with Iran, and as a little kid, Moe had fled with the rest of his family to America. He was wearing desert camo, same as everyone, but had on metallic-colored sneakers in place of combat boots, and a pair of sunglasses with wide frames that none of us regular soldiers could've gotten away with.

He went up to the razor wire and talked with the sheikh in Arabic. The crowd quieted, listening in.

'So?' Easton said at a break in the conversation.

'He's come for the bodies of his family,' Moe said. 'His daughter, granddaughter, grandson, son-in-law. He claims your men shot them last night.'

Easton sighed. 'Okay. I was expecting this, but hell. First, make sure you let him know that I'm the one who gave the order to fire. My men were just doing their job. Second, pass on my deepest regrets over his loss. There's nothing I can do to make this right, I know that. It'll be a burden on me for as long as I live, and obviously it's much worse for him. I'm not sure what happened last night, but we're looking into it. His people were driving a vehicle that matched the exact description of one that ambushed my men. They were driving off road, no lights, evading a search. That's why I made the call. It was a terrible mistake.'

Moe relayed the colonel's message, and for the first time the sheikh brought his hands from behind his back. One was wrapped with a strand of prayer beads like a rosary, except a knotted green cloth hung in place of a crucifix. He concentrated on his hands, fingering the beads as he spoke, and Moe translated.

'He says they were driving the girl to a hospital. She was sick and got much worse during the night. Since your men have blocked all the roads, they were going a back way. He says he understands that this was not done on purpose and begs you again for their bodies.'

'Tell him I'm sorry, but I can't get them,' the colonel said more bluntly. 'They were taken to our hospital across the river. He'll have to go there to claim them. I can give him my personal sat-phone number and a letter of passage to show Third Corps.'

After Moe translated, the corners of the sheikh's mouth tightened like he'd been insulted.

'He says he'd prefer you claim the bodies yourself. He wants you to bring them here for his people to receive. They're gathered and ready to perform the burial. This must be done by

203

nightfall to keep with Islam, as you're probably aware. He says you owe him at least that much. He also hinted at *diyya*, an Arabic custom. The payment of blood money in cases like this.'

'Cases like what?' Easton said.

'Wrongful death, usually. *Diyya* is a way to make things right with the family without resorting to, well, more forceful forms of justice. But he only mentioned that in passing. He's much too correct, you might say, to get into money right now. Mostly he talked about what has to be done with the bodies to satisfy his — '

'Like I said. Tell this distinguished gentleman I'll be glad to give him all the credentials he needs to claim them, but he has to do it. They've been signed over to Thirds Corps, Division Mortuary Services, and that's where they'll stay until they're claimed by next of kin. Just tell him I don't like it, my hands are tied, but it's protocol. And we can definitely talk more about that *diyya*. I think we can get at least five thousand per casualty from Brigade for a war damage reparation payment. That's twenty thousand dollars. Tell him.'

11

Abu al-Hool: The Empty Time

```
Iraq (water treatment plant):
7 days after
```

Continuing a spate of uncanny good fortune, Dr. Walid has found a water treatment plant ideal for his current purposes. The facility, long disused, has space enough to hold the prisoners and also to quarter the brothers while still affording us a certain inconspicuous privacy. Roughly a dozen kilometers northwest of Fallujah, it's built on rotten ground near the edge of a marshy, derelict network of canals that feeds off the Euphrates like a metastasized tumor; this patch of blocky concrete over-grown with elephant grass and cypress would appear from the air as only another moldering infrastructural ruin, vestige of the sixties, a substantially more prosperous and optimistic time for this country.

The Americans keep up the search for their own. I find it remarkable, their dogged determination to repatriate three measly soldiers, their willingness to devote tens of thousands of man-hours and untold millions of dollars and materiel to the cause: they barge into homes, stores, and mosques, harassing travelers on the roads, disrupting traffic into kilometers of angry gridlock. One unintended effect of this operation has been to prove what we've argued all along — their shambolic rhetoric of liberation aside: they hold their own lives dear and an Arab's cheap.

I am, however, far from exilient: so much good fortune makes me skittish. The noise from any overflight, even an oblique one, is enough to send me to ground. Though the countryside has its benefits, in the end it's almost always safer for the guerilla to operate where the crowded hubbub of urban life offers a better guarantee of anonymity. We find ourselves in a predicament. Returning to the mosque where we'd been holed up in Fallujah is out of the question, the roads too well watched for us to risk moving our prisoners again. Nor can we sneak into Baghdad and join the fight there. If we had planned on taking captives, we might have been able to arrange a better stash house beforehand. As it is, in a real sense, they are the ones who have shackled us.

* * *

Yesterday Dr. Walid and I took one of the Hiluxes and drove into the marsh, scouting out a place that we might use to cache our explosives, the mortars and a small case of plastique, so as not to be sleeping right next to them. The excursion, I found, had an ulterior purpose as well: when the doctor had me alone, he laid out his plan for the Americans.

'I need you with me on this,' he said after I'd

expressed uneasiness with what he had in mind. 'A thing like this could divide the brotherhood. You're one-half of their heart, you know. I'm the other. They can't see us at odds.'

'It'd be one thing if they had any valuable information to give. But they don't. They're just peons. What you're talking about is a perversion of jihad.'

'Do you understand what we've got on our hands here?' he said. 'Do you realize what Zarqawi would do if he learned we had them?'

'I agree. They're a huge liability. They should've been executed immediately on the battlefield, in the lawful way. But, since they weren't, we need to arrange a trial, contact a few of the emirs we trust, and then — '

He beat his hands on the steering wheel. 'No. No, no, no. What you see as a liability is actually a blessing. This is our moment, brother. It's what we've been working for all these years. We *must* do this.'

'It would be false. A victory, maybe, but empty. You can't start rewriting the rules, Walid. It undercuts everything we stand for.'

'In your opinion. I could offer counter-examples from the Sunna. At the Battle of Uhud, who served the Messenger of God as a living shield to catch the arrows of the *kuffar*? It wasn't a man but Nusaybah, Mother of Ammara, who won that glory. But you know this. And also that in some ways this isn't about religion — we must speak to God but also into the megaphone. Argue all you want. You can't deny how powerful it would be.'

An exhausting night, troubled by dreams of the dead. I was back in Chechnya, in the field where they laid my son to rest. Except in the dream, I was the gravedigger, and it wasn't Hassan but a small boy that I was to bury. I worked quickly and without breaks, slamming my pickax into the hard frozen ground, gripped with a criminal's sense of panic; the more I thought about what I was doing, the faster I swung the ax, yanking out clods of dirt, worrying someone would pass in the forest and find me with the boy's corpse: I had no good explanation for it, no memory of what'd happened. My rifle was with me, but his body showed no sign of violence, his face familiar — but I couldn't place it — serene.

As happens in dreams, my fear realized itself at the worst possible moment. A Chechen woman appeared across the meadow just when I'd finished excavating the plot. She was dressed in an old coat and a loosely woven shawl, moving toward me with a hobbling but purposeful gait, calling, 'You! What is it you have there, what wickedness are you about?'

'Don't come any closer,' I said, not wanting to do it; but, according to the logic of the dream, allowing her to see the dead boy would be a kind of death for me as well. It was the thing I was most afraid of. I simply could not let it happen. When she refused to heed my warning, I picked up my rifle and fired a single shot.

Now I had two graves to dig.

In the interrogation room the doctor plays angel to my devil tonight. Abu Annas lurks in the background, flexing his thick forearms, a menacing addition to the *mise en scène*. The focal point of our efforts is the American prisoner Michael Crump, a boy not much older than Abu Hafs, who is operating the camera.

Shielding the prisoner's orbital socket, livid with bruising from the surgery, is a crude patch fashioned out of tape and rigid plastic; Dr. Walid did his best to save the eye but, after putting the boy under ether, determined it was irretrievably lost, then scooped out what remained, cauterizing the optic nerve, I must say ingeniously, with gunpowder. Despite the memory of this wound, the fallibility of his flesh, the prisoner has proven himself intractable, the least pliable of the three. We've succeeded in coaxing the girl to make statements against her government, and just last night their sergeant went even further and professed the Shahada on record. With these words he became a believer, supposedly — though the forced nature of this conversion invalidates it. There can be no compulsion in religion, but Dr. Walid has little time for such scruples. For him, last night's session with Zachary McGinnis was nothing less than a triumph; our emir's fight is not for souls but for footage he can accumulate, arrange, and later release to embarrass the enemy and embolden our allies.

This is a message to the people of Iraq. I know

my country has caused you great suffering. I know we have profited from your suffering. I am a simple soldier. I have found nothing good here. I am sorry for what I have done.

But tonight's prisoner refuses to speak these words, printed on a piece of card stock. Dazzled in the bright light of the Fresnel lamp, he resembles a confused, dyspeptic Cyclops. We pick him out of the chair, his hands and feet already bound, and place him in bastinado. Abu Annas sits on his legs while Abu Muqhatil uses a length of steel cable wrapped in rubber on the soles of his bare feet.

They take turns with the cable, but the doctor does not participate in the beating. He's cast himself as the boy's savior: the 'good cop' (as the Americans would say) in this farce we are playing. We hold ourselves out to be their moral betters, but what we're doing here leaves the same taste in my mouth as the atrocious reports from Guantánamo. Tit for tat, a childish and impure way of making war; with each lash they dole out, I gain further resolve to do what I should've done months ago. My time in this brotherhood, I am increasingly sure, is drawing to an end.

The boy's body shivers with pain, his feet seared by the cable. He cannot help but cry out. He's strong, but no one is strong enough to resist this. His shalwar is damp with sweat; dirty tears run down his face, poor boy; he shouldn't have come here. I run a finger along the edge of his foot to check if there is feeling. When he no longer cringes, I nod at Dr. Walid.

210

'That's enough,' he says in English. 'I want this to be easier for you. I could stop it if you helped us. But you're like an unruly child' — here he glances knowingly at me, speaking more lies. '*He* wants to bring a car battery and a capacitor for you. I tell him no, not yet. But maybe he's right. This is nothing compared with electricity.'

'Fuck pain,' the boy growls, his first words of the interrogation. 'I'm not afraid of pain.'

Anything other than his silence is an incremental victory for the doctor, who latches on to the antagonistic angle, provoking him again. 'You know that's not true. Everyone fears pain. But in a way, you're right. There are worse things.'

'You'll kill me anyway. You just want me on tape, saying that bullshit. The minute I do, it's over.'

'No. False.'

'What? You're going to let me go?' The boy's contempt is palpable, grainy and black as bile. What glowering defiance he shows, for someone who's just taken a beating like that. I admire him for it. I admire the one we have tortured.

'No, we're not letting you free.' Dr. Walid smiles wanly, hinting at the secret he's been building up to. 'Though you might live. Save yourself. Your sergeant, he's found this way.' He snaps his fingers at Abu Hafs, demanding the camera be brought forward. 'Show him, Cub. Show him how alone he is in this.'

★ ★ ★

211

Abu Hafs flips the camera display shut after the tape ends in a blue screen.

'You're lying,' Michael Crump says. 'It's just trick photography or some shit.'

The doctor allows the bald absurdity of that accusation to go unanswered. As if we had the resources for cinematic special effects; it's all we can do to keep the generator gassed up and running long enough to charge the radio batteries.

'Even if it's real, he would've never said that if you hadn't made him. I ain't no Muslim and neither is Sergeant Mac. You'll never make me say I am. You all can go to hell. Get it over with.'

'No. Not today. If and when that time comes, we'll not be the ones to take your head. Your 'Sergeant Mac' will have that honor. Then you'll know, once and for all, that we've told you only the truth.'

* * *

Terrorism is a word that's hard to define and one that's also always used contemptuously. These qualities, taken together, make it a powerful rallying cry but completely useless in describing real events with any degree of precision. During the Afghan jihad, their President Reagan called us 'freedom fighters,' and as far as I'm concerned, the only thing that has changed between then and now is which ponderous empire has begged a reminder of its founding revolutionary principles. Yesterday's freedom fighter is today's Islamofascist; the

212

Americans approved enough of killing Communists to let our techniques in doing so pass without criticism. At the Second Battle of Zhawar we harvested scores of Soviet heads. The Recitation is quite clear that this is an appropriate means of striking fear into the heart of the enemy. Nor is it unique to us; beheading appeals to the most primal fears and frailties, is the purest iteration of *I am right and you are wrong*, applied over the ages as an empire killer and as a tool for empires to use to stoke among the polis a hatred of the savage: from the Romans, horrified by the Celts, those dirty, long-haired tribesmen who were said not to fear death and who routinely beheaded their captives; to the French revolutionaries and a commoner's handkerchief dipped in king's blood; to the U.S. Marine Corps. I remember reading somewhere that 60 percent of Japanese skeletons recovered in the South Pacific were found missing their heads, with most thought to have been taken as trophies.

Be all that as it may, I've never enjoyed executions. There aren't many people who truly exult in that kind of work. Even the most ruthless man likes to think he kills only as a last resort; I am only of middling ruthlessness, and after my first trip to Afghanistan, it took no more than two and a half years for me to have had enough.

Shortly after I returned to Egypt, my mother — never one to mince words — told me that I had the look in my eyes of a wild animal. It was a dark time for me, darker in some ways than the war had been. I had no patience, no money, and was forced by circumstances to live with my parents, which I hated, taking a job as a taxi driver, which I hated even more. I believed the work beneath me; there's no creature more abhorrent than an underachieving rich boy. Looking back, however, I was well suited to the job. Driving other people around the city was one of the few things I could do all day without being overcome by a dangerous feeling of restlessness, which was alleviated temporarily by hurrying nonstop from one place to the next.

I was twenty-three and felt like eighty, my soul seized like a set of rusty gears under enormous torque, stuck between worlds; as often happens, it was a woman who tipped the balance and set me in motion again. One afternoon, driving my cab, I picked up a second-year university student on her way home from a rally in support of Palestine. She gave me the address where I should drop her. I was interested to discover that, like mine, her family lived in Maadi. She had intense brown eyes flecked with gold and wore a modest abaya at a time when doing so had become a kind of political statement among the upper classes. Sadat had been assassinated by the brothers the previous October, with his lapdog, Mubarak, assuming the presidency. Mubarak had made good on his promise to crack down on fundamentalists and leftist agitators, so naturally it was all the more fashionable to be one.

Her name was Mariam. We struck up a conversation, starting with idle patter about our neighborhood: we'd attended different schools growing up, but, as it turned out, we'd both taken classes from the same swimming instructor at the sporting club.

'How funny,' she said, recalling how all the children made light of the way this man slurped pool water from his bushy mustache when he thought no one was looking. 'I can't believe you remember that. It just goes to show how worthless it is to judge someone by his looks.'

'What do you mean?'

'Don't take this the wrong way, but when I first got in your cab, I was sure you were a refugee.'

Even after returning home, I'd continued to wear the *pakol*, a rounded wool hat common in Afghanistan but not at all in Egypt. The affected manner of my dress distanced me from my countrymen, signaling I was either a foreigner or a veteran of the jihad. It was reckless of me to wear it, given the current political climate, but the garment was a totem, a fetish, an invitation to sympathy or hate. I wasn't sure myself which I wanted.

'A refugee isn't far from the truth,' I said, and went on to tell her how I'd left university to join the mujahideen. She was enthralled, confiding in me a short while later that she was a member of the Muslim Sisterhood, opponent of the regime, supporter of our cause. I was afraid to tell her that I'd stopped caring much about our causes. I had gone to war as a desperate adventurer, not for a coherent set of beliefs. Which fact I kept to myself. It would be some years before Mariam came to discern just how troubled I was by doubt. In the meantime, I found a renewed purpose with her, the way it can be in young love, our desire fierce, bright, all-consuming as a collapsing star; each giving the other more than we were capable of, we eloped after knowing each other only the winter. My parents approved of the match — they were glad to see me take an interest in anything besides myself — but her family didn't share their enthusiasm.

She gave birth to Hassan in 1983, in Islamabad, where she lived while I fought the Soviets across the border. It'd been her idea to return to the jihad. Egypt had been no place for us; in Afghanistan I was a hero, while in my homeland, little more than a fugitive. With the telltale stamps of a mujahid on my passport, I'd had a difficult time even reentering the country. I was briefly detained. Father had had to vouch for me, to bribe officials, and after my return, the State Security Service had dropped by the house several times unannounced, a little preventative harassment, nothing too serious, but enough to ensure I lived in fear of being rounded up and imprisoned during one of Mubarak's periodic purges. Then again, there was more than stateless anxiety motivating our flight. Mariam hadn't fallen in love with a taxi driver. She thought of me as a warrior, a fighter; she wouldn't come right out and say it, but that's what she expected me to be. And that's what I became again, for a time, for her.

★ ★ ★

216

We've just gotten word over the radio that Dr. Walid's first video has aired. The sergeant and the girl, embarrassing their country with testimony against its warmongering; Michael Crump, bruised and battered, glowering silently at the camera; the doctor making vague threats. I can no longer take the men's gloating, so I wander off, eventually downstairs, where the only light is warm and orange, a kerosene lantern burning dirtily in the hallway. It reeks of fuel, and I worry about the air becoming poisoned. My shadow skulks over the wall as I join Abu Hafs in front of the girl's cell.

'How far do you think she's gone today?' I ask.

'God only knows, *sayyidi*,' the Yemeni says. 'Every time I've checked, she's been walking.'

It's common for prisoners to pace in agitation, but the girl's exercise is clearly more than idle restlessness. Some days she must walk fifteen or twenty kilometers.

'Is she still taking meals?'

'Yes, *sayyidi*.'

'Stop calling me that. Please.'

He's taken to using the honorific in addressing me. I haven't yet discerned what he means by this, but it makes me uncomfortable, separating us too much; it's like he's afraid of me. Perhaps he has reason to feel this way.

I struggle to come up with something to talk about, something small and human — it's never been my strong suit. To break the silence, to busy myself, I ask him to unlock her cell. The lantern light dimly issuing through the cracked door must appear to her deprived eyes like a fiery

217

beacon. I think of calling to her and telling her not to be afraid, but that's a foolish thought, and I don't act on it.

I peer in, wanting a glimpse. Each morning after prayers, the men argue and cast lots over who'll be the one to deliver her food that day, their desire barely masked, a paradoxical mixture of revulsion and flirtation: the condition of any woman is a strange one, at the same time venerated and reviled, powerless and all-powerful, and this is no ordinary woman. The brotherhood fairly pulses with masculine interest. They want her to teach them English. They call her a whore behind her back.

Abu Hafs is clearly drawn to her and can often be found near her cell. I'm sure that with his youth and inexperience he's even now plagued by unclean thoughts, and yes, I will admit to the same. I've stirred for her more than once; though, even while in delicto, was disappointed in myself, numbed by unsavory detachment from my body's wants. I've lusted in my heart ever since I became capable of experiencing lust — who hasn't? It's better to admit this than to hold the schizophrenic and peculiarly Christian belief that one's thoughts carry the same weight as actions. They don't, and I am not guilty, nor ever will be, of laying a finger on her.

I'll grant that thoughts do sometimes lead to actions. I have confidence in my ability to control myself, but it's only a matter of time before one of the others decides to take her, if it isn't already happening without my knowledge. I don't want that, yet here I am in the doorway to

218

her cell, curious, watching. She's lying in the corner, resting, or pretending to, her abaya drawn up around her face. To view her is anticlimactic. She's the most valuable spoil we've ever taken, she's elevated our brotherhood from unknowns to the talk of the world, but to see her, she could be any girl.

I expect she must feel equally anonymous, even if she has grasped the magnitude of what her captivity must mean to her countrymen. I myself have spent no more than a few days behind bars, detained when I reentered Egypt after my first trip to Afghanistan, but that taste was enough. It took only hours for me to begin to feel abandoned by everyone outside the prison walls, which is the curse of all prisoners, even the most celebrated. Rulers, killers, revolutionaries; iron bars and dungeons have a sly way of effacing the distinguished, belittling the accomplished, stripping the entitled, enforcing anonymity across the board. The oubliette is so named for good reason and represents one of the prime truths of confinement. Forgetting. When on the free side of the cell, the jailer turns the key; on the far side, the famous, infamous, and ordinary alike all despair of being remembered.

I watch her a moment longer before locking the door and taking a spot beside Abu Hafs in the hallway. He and I are alone.

'Do you talk to her much?' I ask.

'We aren't supposed to,' he says quietly.

'Right. But everyone does. I heard you were teaching her Arabic.' He hesitates.

'I wouldn't be angry if you were,' I venture.

219

The boy looks down at his feet, the rust-stained wall, anywhere but my face. Yes, the cub has grown fond of her, perhaps a little smitten. What is the inverse of Stockholm syndrome? — is there even a term for that?

Squatting on the floor, balancing my wrists on my knees, I tap a fingernail against the buttstock of his rifle, a familiar, conspiratorial gesture.

'Some time ago you spoke to me of marriage. Do you have your eye on any girls in the bazaar?'

'Not really,' he says, his manner precluding further discussion of the topic.

'What's on your mind, then?' I've noticed the distance in his eyes, the way they remain on the latch as if it holds a transformational power.

'Can I tell you something, just between us?'

'Of course,' I say, pleased he has come back around to confiding in me.

'It's about them. Her and the other prisoners. Sometimes I wonder if what we're doing is right.'

'Yes. I see. Well, it's good to think this way, to examine one's self. But remember, whatever the nuances of *our* situation, *they* are completely in the wrong. They chose to come here. They brought this on themselves.'

He nods thoughtfully at what I've said, but the rest of his body betrays his disagreement with it, his mouth contorted, shoulders hunched; biting his bottom lip, he grasps for a way to express what he's feeling and finds himself at a loss, reduced to uttering childlike truths. 'I always had an idea of what the Americans would be like. But they are different than I thought. They're just people.'

I have to stop myself laughing, not wanting to insult him in his moment of vulnerability but struck again by just how unworldly he is. 'Who did you suppose we were fighting? It is always 'just people.'

'When I was your age,' I continue more kindly, 'there was a Russian soldier we came upon after a firefight. He had been badly wounded. I tended to him as he died, even though our emir at the time, a man named Jawad, scolded me for it. He wanted me to put the Russian out of his misery. That might have been the best thing. It's what I would probably do now, anyway. But back then, I could see that the Russian was very afraid to die. The way he concealed his fear touched something in me, and it seemed like he appreciated what little I could do for him. A sip of water. A sympathetic face to look on as his life slipped away. It is inevitable, what you are feeling. There comes a time for each of us when we realize the truth about the enemy. Which is that he is not an idea, or some faceless demon. He is a man. And every man is much like ourselves.'

There is quiet in the hall, the distant sound of the brothers upstairs celebrating the video's release, as Hafs digests what I've told him.

'She is not a man,' he says after a while.

'She was doing a man's work.'

'So she deserves to die because of it?'

'That's not for me to say.'

'But if it were?' he asks earnestly. 'If you were emir again, what would you do?'

'I'm not sure,' I say, and this is the truth.

'Do you think Dr. Walid will have them all killed?'

'If he gets his way, yes.'

My admission seems to disturb him even more than I thought it would. His brow quickens. He cannot meet my gaze, staring instead at her cell door. 'The other day she asked me to get a Qur'an for her. Do you think if she professed belief, the emir would spare her?'

'How am I supposed to know?' I say, frustrated with his adolescent fixation on the girl. 'Walid is a madman. There's no telling what he's capable of.'

My treasonous words hang unanswered in the still, underground air.

'You hate him,' the boy finally whispers, eyes wide, but nodding as if realizing he'd known this for some time.

'You are no fool,' I say, leaning in closer, lowering my voice even more. 'And now it's my turn to seek your confidence. I'm trusting you with my life. And I feel compelled to warn you, because I've come to see you as a son.'

Here I pause on the precipice, knowing full well that what I've just said is no exaggeration; if I have misjudged the boy's loyalty, I will be endangering everything to continue.

'What?' he asks, a soothing urgency in his voice, as if he is trying just a little too hard to reassure me that it's safe to tell him.

'I've been thinking of leaving the brotherhood for some time. I've got a bad feeling about the way this is going.'

'Will the emir just let you leave?'

'No, I don't expect so. He would take it much too personally.'

'So what, you'll run away?'

'Is that the kind of man you think I am? Someone who steals away from his obligations like a coward in the night? No, Walid may not let me go freely, but that doesn't mean I won't go. There are ways of persuading him to it. Cub, look at me. It's not an easy choice for me to make. I've given my life to this. I would rather change the brotherhood from within than — well — but if I do leave, you should consider coming with me. You should strongly consider it. This may be the last chance you get.'

The boy looks surprised, deeply unsettled, even a little sick. He must feel a host of clashing impulses: honor at the trust I have placed in him, uncertainty over having to choose between two feuding mentors, and above all, the fear, written all over his face, of how their conflict will play out.

'I'm not sure I could,' he says.

'Why not? What, because of her?'

He doesn't answer, but I can tell I'm right.

'You're young,' I say. 'You have a strong sense of justice, and that's admirable. But she isn't your problem. If things turn out like I think they might, you will be throwing your life away along with hers.'

12

Cassandra: Antibody

```
Iraq (water treatment plant):
17 days after
```

Crump's screaming again and there is the furious whir of an electric drill being operated somewhere down the hall. These twinned sounds evoke horror-movie sequences of mutilation, gore splatter, panic: she was waiting for something like this to happen. Walid threatened to punish them if they disobeyed his instructions, and since Crump, even with a pistol to his head, refused to read his statement or to engage with the camera in any way other than stating his name, rank, and service number, this must be his punishment. A motherfucking drill.

Cassandra rises from her pallet and begins to pace, circling her cell a few times before her guts turn to water and she squats over the pail and moves her bowels, her body unburdening itself gracelessly before its own turn comes. She doesn't bother washing up with the pitcher of water, an unusual lapse in hygiene, and goes immediately back to pacing. The drill and Crump scream in angry antagonized bursts. The sounds give her wild visuals, blue and green fractals sparking in the darkness as she

224

completes ten, fifteen laps. At which point Crump falls silent. The drill also stops and then begins again. Closer now. Twenty, forty laps, and the drill is repositioned a second time, just outside her cell. It's biting into the wall outside her cell. It's coming through the wall. There's a beam of light as the bit emerges near the door, gouging an inch-wide hole. The bit is removed, spinning. The door opens. Hafs enters, proudly displaying the drill in one hand and a porcelain light socket in the other.

'See?' he says. 'I promise you. Now is no problem for the Qur'an.'

★ ★ ★

Got light, she taps.
　How, McGinnis replies.
　Hafs wired bulb
　Good sign
　Maybe
　No it good
　OK how your arm
　Same

She knows he tends to downplay; *same* means *worse*, the cut still infected. On top of everything else that might kill him, it's his penicillin allergy that constitutes the most pressing threat, his body primed to self-destruct. Penicillin is all Walid's got. According to McGinnis, Walid is supposedly sending men on regular trips to the bazaar, searching for an acceptable drug, but two wars and a decade of sanctions have made short supply of exotic antibiotics.

225

Find any yet, she asks.
No
F that sorry
There's a long pause.
He say maybe have to amputate

★   ★   ★

The incandescent bulb mounted on her wall burns for the several hours the guards run their generator each day. When it's dark in the cell she sleeps or paces or communicates with McGinnis. When she has light, however — and it's possible she's never been more grateful for anything — she devours the Qur'an that Hafs has given her.

The volume is a well-worn paperback with a maroon cover and the title embossed in gold: *Interpretation of the Meanings of the Noble Qur'an in the English Language*. It's no idle way to pass the time: reading takes her mind off the future better than anything else.

Even so, she finds it difficult. Compared to what she remembers of the Bible, the Qur'an has nowhere near as many discrete stories with beginning, middle, end, its message revealed not so much in parable as direct pronouncement. Giving her the book, Hafs explained that Arabs consider it the most beautiful feat of prose writing accomplished in their language, but if that were true, something must've been lost in this translation.

The majority of the verses lay out rules, warnings, and proscriptions. The first few *surahs* read to her like a long rant about how the unbelievers are going to hell. It surprises her, how harsh is the condemnation. She remembers the way prominent Muslims came forward after 9/11 to denounce the attacks and to defend Islam as the religion of peace — she remembers some called it that, *the religion*, not *a religion*. At the time she had no real opinion on the truthfulness of that claim, but the Qur'an seems far from peaceful. The battlefield is a continuing theme, and a significant number of passages set out rules for combat. Rivalry, feuding, and conflict make appearances in nearly every *surah*. If this is the religion of peace, she thinks, I'd hate to see a religion of war. Not that the Old Testament isn't chock-full of blood and guts and God's holy wrath. There's a famous psalm that ends with the image of babies' heads being bashed in, and this is supposed to be a good thing. Monotheism is funny for its sheer wrathfulness. Once you corner the market on the divine, it becomes yet another thing to fight over.

* * *

Be careful, McGinnis taps.
  About what
  Heard you two talking
  So
  Dangerous
  What
  Religion
  Lying on her side in the cell, ear to the drain, she laughs out loud, an exasperated laugh at his

227

expense, at his absurd risk aversion: right on the line between overcareful and craven. Here they are, held captive by men threatening daily to kill them in the name of God, and yet he feels the need to warn her that religion is a possible flash point in their relations. Like she hasn't already thought through the possibilities and decided to take the risk anyway, to leverage the crux of the matter — conviction — to her advantage.

Maybe they treat us better if we convert, she tells him.

If caught faking they kill for sure

Don't get caught, she taps, then immediately changes the subject:

Arm OK

Skin cracks when I touch

Sorry

Is OK but afraid

Of losing it

Yes and

Let him amputate

Not yet am waiting while longer so they find meds

They will, she assures him, but isn't so certain, though she can hardly blame him for wanting to put off the decision about the arm until the last possible moment. She'd be equally reluctant to subject herself to major surgery undertaken in primitive conditions without proper sanitation or anesthesia. Even if there is a medical doctor, or someone claiming to be one, to wield the scalpel.

★   ★   ★

Not wanting a thing never stops it from happening. She'll learn the details later, but for now all she knows about McGinnis's fate is what she overhears through the pipe. The sound of his door repeatedly opening and closing, a steady stream of traffic into his cell, the points of her hips growing sore from lying against the concrete, eavesdropping. Him talking with the guards. Although she catches only the odd phrase, the gist is they've devised a treatment and must remove him from his cell to administer it. She hears 'medicine' from both him and the guards. Why they would have to remove him from his cell to dose him, Cassandra doesn't understand. This question also bothers McGinnis, who asks more than once where he's going.

'We have better place for you.'

'It's okay here. Why don't you bring it here?'

'No, no good here. Much better with us.'

They're vague, evasive, but in the end he seems to go with them voluntarily — no sound of a struggle. It's quiet an hour or two and she's about to nod off when his door opens again. She presses her ear against the grate, hoping he'll make contact, tell her he's okay, but it's only two of the guards who've returned to his cell, speaking Arabic. She wonders what they're doing in there without him. Snooping around, probably. Whatever it is, they stay only a short time.

Moments after they leave, the light in her cell goes dark. They've switched off the generator. She has a feeling something bad has happened. If they lured him out of his cell with promises of

229

medicine, only to operate on his arm, they would have had the generator running throughout the course of the procedure; point of fact, the light was on for an unusually long time. Hard to know if it's a best or worse case. A feeling he's somewhere nearby, recovering from an amputation he didn't expect.

Hold on, she tells him silently. *Hold on*.

★   ★   ★

She feels herself getting turned around again; mealtimes and the generator cycling on and off aren't reliable timekeepers, and she no longer has McGinnis with his window to consult. She can't check with him, tap out a quick *T-I* on the grate, which two letters were all he ever needed to know what she was asking. He always answered, too, giving her his best guess. Some people would've gotten annoyed with the constant requests. She probably would've herself. Pestering him with a time check at least once every couple hours.

She misses him badly, her grief strong, and sometimes in the darkness it pulls at her like too much sedative, making the world spin, her body too heavy. Numb, aggrieved, missing her crew whom she loved and hated like family, and also home, her real family. Having as few obligations that way as possible, maintaining a certain untethered distance to home and the people there, was a deliberate choice on her part. She figured it would make the separation less painful not to have one foot on each continent. This was why she never wrote anyone while in Kuwait, not her parents, not her old friends from high school, not even the woman who'd made her promise to write: Liz, the one she'd slept with a few times in the months before deployment.

She misses them all. Even Crump — whatever he is now, it's not his old self. Missing fucking Crump — the thought of it's enough to elicit a morbid chuckle. Never would've expected to get nostalgic over that fool. One incident in particular stands out for sheer boneheadedness. The party Corporal Treanor threw at his house in Copperas Cove before they left for Kuwait. One last rager. About a third of their company was in attendance, forty soldiers, even a couple lieutenants and senior noncoms put in appearances, and everyone's spouse or date, if they had them. Two kegs of Belgian, barbecue, Doritos in plastic bowls, a bookshelf stereo bumping a mix of rap and country music in the spotless echoic garage, darts and a pool table for entertainment, the party spilling over into the front yard and back.

She'd brought 'my friend Liz' as her date. Because, fuck it. What was the army going to do, not send her to Iraq? Her inner circle in the company already knew or suspected; wasn't exactly a tough secret to crack. They were either fine with it or, like McGinnis, believed it was none of their business.

'Don't Ask, Don't Tell is their policy, and that's gotta be mine, too. Less I know, the better, for both our sakes,' he'd said once, when in a moment of weakness she'd more or less confided in him.

231

Everyone who mattered probably already knew who Liz was. Besides, the two of them weren't flaunting the rules. They didn't make out at the party or otherwise engage in any displays of affection, public or otherwise, not so much as holding hands, which wasn't really their style as a couple anyway. No one in the company who was savvy enough to guess the truth about them would give a hoot that someone he'd already pegged for gay, was. The army's actively dangerous homophobia was mostly confined to intramasculine relations. Lesbians were another breed, a tolerated curiosity more than an object of hate and fear. Cassandra had once tried to estimate what percentage of female soldiers were gay and had arrived at one in four. This, compared with the rate among male soldiers, which probably hewed more closely to the population as a whole: one in ten, one in fifteen. The difference was a matter of what type of person was typically attracted to the idea of the military: she thought the army had more than its share for the same reason that professional women's basketball did. It takes a certain kind, is all.

Crump, as part of her truck crew and therefore a de facto intimate, knew she was gay. At least she thought he had. He got shit-faced at Treanor's, staggering monkey drunk, badgering people to hoist him for keg stands, downing back-to-back shots of tequila, and those just the ones she personally witnessed.

'Well, shit,' he said, cozying up to Liz after being introduced. 'Any friend of Wigheard's is a friend of mine. Don't get mad, hon, for me asking, but hey, you got a man or what?'

It was early in the evening but he'd already benumbed himself past any minimal amount of suaveness he might have hitherto possessed. Past that — and decency — and into earnest, generally well-meaning jackassery and not giving a fuck.

Liz was easygoing, though. That was what Cassandra liked most about her. The stress-free unflappability. She laughed it off, said, 'I'm married. Sorry.'

'Shit,' Crump said, belatedly looking at her hand and finding a ring. 'My bad.'

She'd thought he knew. Was just too drunk to put two and two together. Or maybe she'd granted him powers of perception that never existed. It wasn't like he wasn't thinking about sex; he hit on pretty much every available woman there, and some who weren't. By no means alone in his horniness. The collective libido that night spiking off the charts, even for an army party. If he and the rest of them were going to be that amped up during the deployment, man oh man, it would be a long year.

Later in the night, things got absurd when he wandered up to the conversational circle that she, Liz, McGinnis, McGinnis's wife, and several other soldiers and wives had formed in the backyard near the barbecue. What a bonehead. Hitting on Liz again.

'So. You're married. Hey, tha's cool. You know I can keep it on the DL. Ask Wigheard. She knows I won't say nothing.'

Cassandra had to pull him away from the

group and spell it out in private.

'You realize I'm gay, right?'

'So?' he said.

Unbelievable. He still didn't get it.

'Look,' she said. 'Yeah, you're tanked and an idiot and everything, but you're being really fucking disrespectful right now.' She made an open face, like, *Hello, are you kidding me?* and looked at Liz, across the yard, and Liz smiled at her, and then Crump got it. Finally it clicked. He laughed and clapped her on the back like one of the guys. He hugged her and he was so drunk, his skin didn't even smell like booze anymore but like the stuff booze breaks down into, liver by-products, toxic metabolites, embalming fluid.

'Fuck me,' he laughed. 'Fucking my bad. Shit. Huh. Hey,' he said, having a thought. 'Y'all wanna come with to the Bunny Club? Some of us are about to bounce that way.'

'I think we'll pass.'

'Okay, whatever. Don't act like you're too good for it.'

'*You* don't get your dumb ass arrested,' she said sternly, starting back toward Liz and the others.

'Hey, Wigheard!' he called, loud enough to gain the attention of the entire backyard, slurring out his exit. 'Can you fucking believe it? We're going to fucking Iraq!'

⋆ ⋆ ⋆

She's exercising in her cell when she feels the familiar dull ache in her back. Getting her period here and now surprises her as much as it did the first time, when she was twelve. Going to the bathroom and seeing she was bleeding and calling out to her mother, 'I got my period!' and her mother calling back, 'You know what to do, right?'

She answered yes — the two of them had had 'the talk' a few months before — but the truth was, she had no idea what to do, and it feels that same way now, the same lack of control, the sense of the body's fundamental unmanageability, its alienisms, the way it imposes. It's a reminder that she's a captive twice over; when you're alone almost all the time, the fact that you're a being living in a body is easy enough to forget. We first know our bodies by looking at others and by the way others look at us, and absent this reminder, the mind gathers an uncanny strength, growing more expansive until you can be forgiven for disregarding the body altogether, induced by solitude into all sorts of crackpot tangents. Like believing part of her exists as something separate from the physical world. Like her thoughts might of themselves influence events. Like whatever she is, it's something more than an electrochemical battery, the most complex object known to exist in the universe but, after all, merely a mass of proteins and tangled dendrites and blood.

That the cycle is seed, growth, blossoming, harvest, and decay, her period serves to remind. A progression unvarying and tragically inconvenient. Even now, in this place, her body would seek to reproduce itself.

Annas is in her cell with the door closed before she fully awakes. He's quicker this time, more determined, with no hesitation. She becomes aware as his besandaled foot presses down on the small of her back to keep her from rolling over, the barrel of his rifle resting on the nape of her neck. The words she first spoke to her mother eight years ago now come out just as involuntarily as they did back then, an exclamation of fact, no shame about it, but a warning, an excuse for him not to.

'I got my period.'

The mouth-breathing fool, he doesn't understand, his English rudimentary, the idiom lost on him, and her own words fail as he kneels and straddles her and cups a palm on the back of her skull, pressing her face into the pallet, groping her roughly with the other hand, spreading her legs. He whispers in her ear.

'Ugly woman, bad woman. You like this. Yes, you like this.'

He's mistaken her slickness for lubrication. He's left the lantern by the door, and he, hunched over her, is blocking the light with his shadow. His cock presses against her through half-unbuttoned trousers. Before he can penetrate her, he has to shift position to better support himself and he catches the black sheen on his fingers in the lantern light. Too excited, he isn't thinking straight; puzzled by the color, he lifts his hand and sniffs his finger. A beat passes, with smell comes understanding, and he cries out, a pained noise like he's been bitten, pushing himself to his feet. Once he's off her he doesn't seem to know what to do next, lurching around the cell like a house fire has broken out and he needs something to fight it with. He says a word in Arabic that can only be a curse. Buttons up his trousers the rest of the way and wipes his hand under the arm of his shirt. Before leaving the cell he shoots her a look of disgust that surpasses anything she's ever known.

* * *

Her condition, once discovered, sends the entire place into an uproar: she might as well have come down with leprosy. It begins when the old guard Mohammed arrives to change out her waste pail and notices the bloody strips that she's torn off her pallet and used over-night as pads. He recoils from the pail as if a snake were inside, then leaves the cell; her careful routine is lost in the revulsion of her captors. Before they'll bring her food or water or decide what to do about the pail, which Mohammed and everyone else absolutely refuses to touch or even to look at for very long — first thing — they confiscate her copy of the Qur'an. Hafs, the unlucky one who gave it to her, is designated to take it back. He appears in her cell looking puffy-eyed and sheepish, apparently roused from sleep specifically for this task. Ordinarily he would be happy to draw duty here, to have any sanctioned excuse to spend time with her; she has a feeling it is, by far, the highlight of his day, teaching her how to

237

recite in Arabic verses from the Qur'an, alternatively asking her about America, practicing his English, but there's none of that now. She has become a pariah, unclean, unfit even to touch the paper upon which scripture is printed.

He has her move against the wall before he'll enter farther to place a square of balding velvet in the middle of the floor. He goes back to the doorway and beckons her to come forward and wrap her Qur'an in the cloth. She does this and once again moves off a safe distance. Only then will he fetch the book, accomplishing the handoff as if disposing of a biohazard.

'Is bad for you to have now,' he says, hefting it. 'I bring again soon. After.'

'Fine. What I want to know is, when am I gonna get some more water? I'm really thirsty, okay? And I'll also need some pads. Sanitary pads.'

'What is sanitary?'

'Maxi pads or tampons. Feminine hygiene products, you know, for when you're on your period.'

'Yes, okay,' he says, tugging nervously at his ear. 'Is no problem. I find in bazaar.'

'Good. Thank you.'

He lifts his brow like he's partially relieved, heading out.

'Hafs, wait a second. How's McGinnis doing?'

He stops in his tracks. At first she chalks up his startled reaction to generalized anxiety at sharing the same room with a menstruating woman.

'You all took him out of his cell, right? To fix his arm.'

His eyes narrow, a sideways glare. 'How do you know this?'

'Just 'cause I heard his door opening and closing a bunch, but then it stopped all of a sudden,' she says, mind racing toward an explanation for her knowledge of McGinnis's situation that doesn't involve communicating with him through the pipe. 'I saw his arm when we made that video with all of us. It looked like he'd cut it or something pretty bad. I figured you all had moved him to do something about it. So I'm right?'

She hopes he'll buy the lie, cursing herself for asking about McGinnis in the first place, and apologizing silently to her sergeant for possibly, inadvertently, diming him out; Walid specifically warned them against trying to talk to each other. Why couldn't she have left well enough alone? Plenty of problems as it is. Must be slipping, getting reckless, but she has to know.

Hafs tilts his head, frowning, playing with his ear again. 'Yes,' he says. 'His arm was cut.'

'Is he okay now?'

'Is no problem.'

She has come to recognize this phrase as a manifestation of delusion, his refusal to acknowledge the horrific things happening all around him. If she needs further confirmation, there's the way he avoids her imploring look as he moves toward the door. Something is very wrong with McGinnis. That much is certain. She tries a final time to get it out of him.

'He's going to be okay, though, right?'

'Mohammed, he is bringing the food and water. Later, I bring the insanitary pad.'

★　★　★

239

Blindfolded with a red ski mask turned around backward she's removed from her cell at gunpoint with at least two guards trailing in the hallway but it could be more; it's difficult to judge their numbers by footfalls. Hafs is in front, heading up the procession. He leads her with voice commands and one of her hands clasped on his bony adolescent shoulder.

'Here are stairs. Careful.'

She takes mincing steps until the toes of her sandals meet the edge of the bottommost step, and she ascends. She's made this climb before, but they're not going to shoot a video now. In the hand that's not on Hafs's shoulder, she carries her waste pail. Her blankets are rolled, tied in a loop, and slung across her back. The guards are taking her outside, relocating her to a storage shed hastily prepared for her as a kind of quarantine. This is how they've resolved the dilemma of how to empty her pail. Put her outside. Make her do the dirty work herself.

★　★　★

When she acclimates to the sun enough to inspect her new cell, the shed, she finds it's been emptied of its contents, if there ever were any. Two walls are brick; two are corrugated zinc, as are the doors. The thatched roof has fallen in places, letting in sunlight and the weather, and the guards have cut jagged holes in the doors, looped a chain through these, and padlocked the chain on the outside. The holes are big enough to look out of, and so is the gap between the door and the ground, if she lies flat with her cheek to the dirt.

She does this for a long time. Her first view of where she's being held, the environs. The terrain seems unlike any she encountered on the march up from Kuwait or during her short stint at Palace Row. It's clear she's somewhere in the countryside but this is much lusher country than southern Iraq or the hardscrabble outskirts of Baghdad, this gapped view of hers, with palm trees shading the corner of a concrete structure that she takes for her recent prison. Other than this industrial-looking building, however, and the trucks parked near it under a camouflage tarpaulin blind, there's no sign of human habitation, only an overgrowth of dun and green and the wet stink of mildew.

She comes to hate that smell. Hard as it is for her to believe, before the day is out, she comes to wish she were back underground. Not that it wasn't just as damp there, water condensing on the walls and the broken fluorescent ballast and dripping a fine rusty mist that, she now sees, turned her skin carroty orange, but as the morning passes into afternoon, the temperature in the shed climbs until the zinc walls are too hot to touch for more than a second. A guard posted outside, a short white man whom she's seen before but whose name she doesn't know, looks in on her once in a while, scolding her in some Eastern European language every time he catches her with the hijab off and the abaya pulled down around her waist, exposing the dress beneath, which is all she can do for relief

241

from the heat. He won't have it. By gesture he makes clear he wants her fully covered at all times. She quickly gives up trying to curry favor with him and instead concentrates on locating the most comfortable spot in which to rest. Her wool pallet is just a little hotter than the hot dirt floor and so she abandons it and lies in the dirt like an overheated dog. Much too hot to walk or do any other form of exercise. She falls in and out of sleep, drooling imbecilic in the dirt. The stifling oppressiveness begins to subside only late in the evening. After which time the chain rasps through the doors and she's given a fresh pitcher of water and a cold glob of rice in a plastic sack. The white guard and the old one named Mohammed wait as she consumes it. Then she's blindfolded with the ski mask and taken at gunpoint and made to empty her waste pail with used pads in a pit dug in a field behind the shed. That task complete, they lock her in for the night. She can't believe they would house her out here rather than in the more secure underground cell, that they would take this risk over simply living under the same roof as a menstruating woman. None of it makes sense to her. She's never been one to abide the compulsion of taboo. More like one to break it.

★   ★   ★

She finishes the pitcher of warm water sometime in the night. The guard won't leave his post to bring more. Thirst makes her sleepless. After the heat subsided, the sand flies came, biting her on the back when she lay on her stomach, and her stomach when she lay on her back. The sand flies are invisible, their bites small, hard, and intolerably itchy. A pestilence. The night drags on like a chore. Later she's brought out of her thirsty haze and given a start when she realizes there's something circling the shed in the blackness. She can hear it breathing, its snout snuffling curiously along the bottom seam of the zinc wall. She rests against the mud bricks, listening to it smell her through the wall, and before long it's joined by another, and then another like it. They pace and snuffle in the dirt. The sound is eerie, but she's not very afraid. They're dogs, probably; no way they could get to her in here. But the gap beneath the door is big enough to admit vermin, and sometime near dawn she observes a mouse darting under and into the shed to claim a single grain of rice that she dropped while eating dinner. There's enough moonlight admitted through the holes in the roof that she can see the mouse as a blurry shape in grayscale, fur and bone. The creature sits back on its hind legs and feeds itself the rice. She kicks lazily at it. It scampers off. She isn't afraid of it but doesn't relish the thought of mice crawling over her while she sleeps — no telling what diseases they may carry, rabies and God knows what, a death sentence out here. Then there are the snakes that hunt mice. A half dozen vipers native to Iraq, all venomous, some deadly, like the saw-scaled viper — one bite and you'll bleed from all your orifices like an Ebola victim; the old hands in Kuwait told tales of camel spiders and snakes. She can abide mice or spiders but not snakes and she resolves to be absolutely impeccable with her food from here on, not to let a single morsel fall.

She gets her best sleep after dawn when the air is coolest. The sand-fly bites torment her dreams. In the morning she waits for the changing of the guard and to be fed and watered and in the meantime examines the sign left in the dirt by the mouse. Its tracks look just like a tiny bear's.

⋆　⋆　⋆

'Bush, Cheney, Rumsfeld! Bush, Cheney, Rumsfeld!'

She watches ruefully under the door gap, observing Walid in the middle distance near the prison building. He's disturbed her from rare sleep. He's the one doing the shouting, calling out loudly and multiple times in several directions, calling these names she knows so well, calling them like he's summoning the upper echelon of her chain of command and these men might actually be hiding somewhere within earshot. He does it a final time, 'Bush, Cheney, Rumsfeld!' and dumps a bucket of what look like chicken entrails on the ground; almost instantly, the mess is descended upon by black horseflies, and shortly thereafter, three large dogs come loping into view. Walid watches them feed but doesn't deign to pet them. Cassandra supposes they must be the same three that visited her last night. The hounds Bush, Cheney, and Rumsfeld. One mystery solved.

By late morning the heat has once again grown intolerable. The men keep indoors, out of the open, where satellites may be watching. From overhead, unless someone were paying very close attention, the place would look abandoned, like a crumbling way station succumbing to nature in the middle of nowhere, Iraq.

Not much happens until the afternoon, when there's a brief but intense excitement. The distant thumping of helicopter rotors, a pair of Chinooks by the sound of them, transport birds with a distinctively loud report. The guard moves under cover as a precaution but the helicopters pass somewhere out of sight, never actually coming into view, the beating of their rotors fading away to wind noise and despair.

Her one triumph that day comes when she observes the guard praying. He's still on shift, which must be edging past the twenty-four-hour mark. Confused by the heat, she wonders if this is how long the shifts have always lasted but she's only now noticing it because only now does she have the sun, God damn the sun, by which to judge time, or whether, as she believes true, the shifts have typically lasted closer to twelve hours and this one is much longer than usual. Which means something is up. She puzzles over the possibilities, what's the deal with McGinnis, watching absentmindedly through the door gap as the guard unfurls his prayer mat in the dirt and begins prostrating himself. It takes a minute for the significance of what she's seeing to hit her. When it does, she has to stop herself from laughing with the pleasure of unexpected knowledge. He's showing her the direction to Mecca. He might be strict but isn't too bright. She now possesses a kernel of knowledge where before there was none. She knows which way to start running if she gets free.

★ ★ ★

Near sundown the Eastern European guard is finally relieved. Even before the new man speaks to her, she knows it's Annas by the sight of his ankles, hairy and knotty and at her eye level — she's seen them twice before from about this same vantage and wouldn't mistake them. Near the door he and the other guard talk a few minutes in Arabic before the one ambles off and Annas remains. He doesn't waste any time, pounding on the corrugated door like he's pestering an animal.

'Ugly woman. Bad woman.'

She doesn't answer, unwilling to give him the benefit of reveling in any fear in her voice, and not trusting herself right now to master it.

'You here?' He rattles the chain against the door. For a second she thinks he might be removing the padlock and coming in to finish what he started the other night, menstrual blood be damned, but he's not. He's only jerking her chain. Literally.

'I know your friend,' he says, voice quieter, less openly vicious, but all the more disturbing for that. 'Very bad for them. Talk with me. I tell you things you need.'

That he's cruel, she never had any doubt, but there's a shrewdness to his cruelty that she underestimated. Of all the ploys he could've chosen to get her talking, this one probably affords the greatest chance of success. She could resist threats, the promise of special treatment, but from her isolation it's hard to refuse knowledge, a tantalizing bait even if it's bogus, something cooked up just to screw with her, as she tells herself it must be. Which is how she keeps from asking what he knows about Crump and McGinnis.

'Okay,' he says vindictively, when after a while it becomes apparent that she's not going to play his game. She's taken aback as his mouth appears in one of the door holes, finger held over his lips in a vow of silence. 'Shh. I am like this.' He smiles menacingly before moving off from the door like he's lost interest. 'Ugly woman, stupid woman. You are dead yesterday and tomorrow.'

★ ★ ★

She holds out a long time, considering. Another night without sleep, tormented by the temperature and the flies and the possibility that Annas could decide to enter the shed at any time. In the midnight hour, Bush, Cheney, and Rumsfeld return to investigate the perimeter before growing bored with her scent and moving on to patrol elsewhere. There are no more mice, but a nighthawk alights on the thatched roof, on the edge of one of the weather-beaten holes where she can see its severe avian silhouette against the moon before it takes wing and is gone. A few hours pass. She runs out of water again. She refuses to ask Annas for more. She scratches new bites on top of the old. She's filthy, lying in the dirt, the earth still hot from the day, the air humid, heavy. It's too much to bear. She says, 'Fuck it,' says this out loud while rising to cross the two and a half paces — exactly — to the shed door, pounding on it loud enough to startle him, she hopes, which is the least she can do if she's going to cave, to do it aggressively, fearlessly, and in a manner calculated to surprise.

'Hey, asshole. I want to know, okay? I'll talk to you. Just tell me what you know that's so fucking special.'

★   ★   ★

It's horrifying, what they do to Crump. She watches under the gap as a cadre of the guards frog-march him out of the prison into the adjacent plot of land across from the shed, near where their trucks are parked under cover. Crump blinks his eye rapidly and appears pale and disoriented at the brightness of the sun. The black banner with Arabic script hangs behind him on the prison wall. She watched them put it there earlier that morning and still didn't believe.

But Annas wasn't lying. Hafs faces Crump at a distance of a few meters, holding the video camera stiffly at his chest like a shield. Crump is bound and made to kneel in front of Walid, who stands behind him and makes a short pronouncement in Arabic. He finishes speaking to the camera and unsheathes a large knife and palms Crump's forehead, pressing head against his own thigh to give himself access to the throat. She cries out to see the blade go in, cries out once and then watches the rest of it silently.

At a certain point Hafs stops filming. He looks shaken and doesn't linger long near the body or laugh or boast over it as some of the other guards do. The dogs come nosing around, snuffling at the blood-soaked earth, but Walid shoos them away. Crump's decapitated body is slung by two men between them like an animal carcass and hoisted into the bed of one of the pickup trucks and driven off. It would be bad enough to have seen that happen to any person, but for it to be someone she knew, a friend, someone she had argued with, had watched in innocent sleep, to see him butchered like that, the look on his face, his legs kicking against the bindings. To watch that. To know the exact same thing may be in store for her soon. Cassandra stumbles toward the rear of the shed but falls short of the pail, dizzy, in shock, her limbs suddenly heavy and cold. She retches bile, splattering the mud-brick wall.

She's seen people killed, Aguirre right on top of her, and until now has been able to keep her stomach, but there's something especially hor-rific about a beheading. The ultimate mutilation. Only later does she recover enough to think about anything else. Like Hafs taping it. What that means. What will happen with that video, Crump existing everywhere and nowhere at once, memorialized at his worst and finest. They

249

never broke him. He went as bravely as is possible, never cowering, maintaining his scowl until the last moment, the moment the knife went in. No matter; they still took something like his soul. To set the manner of remembrance is the highest form of ownership.

She didn't want to accept it. She didn't want to believe Annas when he told her it would happen this way.

'We kill him soon, *inshallah*. Soon, the morning. You watch. You see. The other you not see. Now, you see.'

She thought he was bluffing to get a rise out of her, but now that it's happened, and in front of her eyes, she's also forced to believe what he told her about McGinnis.

Both men are gone. Her whole crew, dead. She's completely alone.

13

Sleed: The Lack of Life

```
Iraq (Camp Marlboro; Fallujah):
22 days after
```

The cigarette factory's official name was Camp Hope. That was too stupid to use so we all called it Camp Marlboro. It hadn't made any cigarettes in a long time. Higher transferred us there from Palace Row, couple weeks after the traffic circle. We moved into a bay on the factory floor, dusty and littered with scrap metal, empty water bottles, old pallets, and picked-over care packages that no one'd bothered to toss into the burn pit. One of the first things we did was rig up the big-screen and satellite dish we'd packed in a conex and brought with us. We found some ratty old couches in the foreman's office upstairs and dragged them down to the bay to complete our entertainment center, as we took to calling it. When we weren't on mission or guard we spent our time flipping between CNN International, Al Jazeera, Sky News, Al Arabiya, hungry for any word of the POWs. Their story was pretty much the biggest thing going. It was strange to watch the reports and know we were wrapped up in the middle of it, and not exactly playing the part of heroes. The whole world watching, and

251

no one but us knew the truth.

Given everything that'd happened, you might think I wouldn't have been able to watch the news. You might think I would've been sick with guilt on a minute-to-minute basis, but I don't remember it being that way. When you're in the thick of it, you don't have enough time. Stress, anger, sorrow, sure, yeah, but guilt is mostly a luxury afforded by enough space and quiet to think. It's like an itch that starts small but keeps getting worse until you've scratched it into a bloody hole. It's also like water. Some guys are stones but others, we're sponges who soak and soak, absorbing the bad until we're full up. The difference between the hard man and the soft, the guilty and the guiltless, is not a steady thing like his blood type or eye color. It changes over time according to what a person believes in, the stories he tells himself about himself. There's a certain way of doing it where the good guys become bad and the bad good, and there's another way that I wish I could do where there are no categories.

★　★　★

Things started to fall apart when that beheading tape came out. The one of Private Crump. With all the horrible things that have happened in the years since, it's hard to remember the way it was before that tape. Back then, a lot of guys still thought of themselves less like dead-eyed killers and more like the Peace Corps with rifles, like we'd really been sent there to build up that country and help those people. After the tape, that fantasy was over. More of us were calling the Iraqis hajjis, hating them secretly or openly, and caring more about making it out of there alive than doing anything to improve the place. There was even talk about suicide pacts. Groups of twos and threes, whole squads of us who'd agreed that if we were about to get captured by jihadis, someone would pull the pin on a grenade and take everybody out, friend and foe alike. Anything seemed better than winding up on one of those tapes.

Not even Al Jazeera would show the whole thing, but you could buy a copy in the bazaar. A dollar for a DVD in a plastic sleeve. Even little kids were selling them. A guy from First Platoon bought one and it got passed around the company until pretty much everyone had seen it, and even the hardest motherfucker couldn't play it off like he was just as gung ho afterward. Shit gave me nightmares, which were already becoming a problem after Galvan shot up that truck near Triangletown. But the dreams weren't about what I'd seen, the man and his wife, the two kids, the sick-looking girl and the little boy with the messed-up arm. I thought of them all the time but they never made it into my dreams. No blood and gore, no dead bodies snapping back to life, like the ones that bother guilty people in the movies. Instead, I started having this dream where I was onstage under bright lights. There was a huge audience out there, most of them dressed in tuxedos and fancy gowns, and everybody was waiting for me to say something, to deliver a final line they wanted to hear, so they could get up and go home, but I had no idea what I was supposed to say.

★ ★ ★

The war had turned for the worse — everyone knew that — but we didn't know just how bad it would get. Like going over a big hump on a roller coaster, the feeling of everything hanging in midair and about to fall — that's how it was. No one, not even Higher, knew if our deployment would last a few more weeks or forever. Rumors spread like the flu, and possible redeployment dates for our unit were tossed around, but when those dates came and went, and nothing happened, we were like a cult that'd expected the world to end on a certain day, but it didn't. The world is always still there in the morning, and you can only take so much disappointment. After a while most of us stopped obsessing about when we'd go home, fooling ourselves into believing home didn't exist, the entire idea of it was a lie, or worse, this place was home.

The weather got hotter until it was like a furnace baking any good feeling out of us. Made you listless and stupid till you couldn't get a thought across. I found it tough most mornings to summon the small amount of willpower needed to stumble outside and smoke the day's first cigarette. Those of us nicotine freaks in the platoon worked on Blornsbaum until he reversed his policy and allowed us to smoke inside the bay on our cots. We stripped down to our shorts, lay there sweating, and didn't move unless someone with rank ordered us to. The nights were just as bad. We sweated through our dreams and woke with bloodshot eyes and headaches from dehydration, sneezing away the plaster-fine dust that was everywhere, no one really knew where it came from, but it hung in the air like spilled talcum powder and settled on us all night long.

You went to bed dusty and woke up dusty. You went to bed hot and woke up hot. Morale was down the tubes, but on our crew, Galvan seemed to tolerate things better than most. There was something about him, I guess you could call it his coolness, a kind of steely ease he had, like a well-built machine with tight tolerances. He could work longer than the rest of us in the motor pool before he had to quit, which was no small thing. It wasn't even full-on summer yet, but the sun was like a nuclear bomb bleaching our desert camo almost white, the cotton stiff with a crust of old dried sweat. You could practically take off your pants and stand them up on their own, they were that crusty, and we were too, hands and necks salty, sunburned, constantly flaking off pieces of dead skin. The heat was like nothing I'd ever felt before, and that's coming from a kid raised in the Dirty Dirty. Hearing the guys in the platoon bitch about it, Blornsbaum would say something like, 'You think this is bad, well, some folks have it a lot worse. You start feeling sorry for yourselves, just think about *them*.'

Galvan, on the other hand, cool old Galvan,

he didn't bother with moralizing. He'd get at us with a kind of evil baby talk.

'Oh, it's hot?' he would say, making his voice high-pitched and too sweet. 'Is I-wack too hot for you? Is it too hot for my precious wittle boy?'

That usually ended the grumbling pretty quick. 'Fuck you' was about the only comeback to it.

★ ★ ★

The good thing about the heat was that it meant we didn't have to patrol much during the middle of the day. There was no need to. Life in Anbar Province slowed to a crawl. All living creatures, from people down to the goats and sheep and wild dogs and even the biting horseflies, found a piece of shade and would not budge. Few households in our sector had air-conditioning, the electrical grid only worked a couple hours at a time, the shops closed from midafternoon until dusk, and the Iraqis took a long siesta. They came out again at sunset, maybe to eat a roasted chicken and drink a few cups of chai tea in an open-air restaurant, before heading back to their roofs, to bed down together as families, preferring the roofs because the insides of their homes were intolerable.

When we did go out on patrol, one of the few tasks we enjoyed was passing out candy to the local kids. Galvan would toss handfuls from the turret like he was throwing favors in the world's most dangerous Mardi Gras parade. We stockpiled the candy from our MREs and guys wrote home requesting more in care packages. Fitzpatrick's mom sent him a five-gallon bucket of Dubble Bubble. It tripped me out to see that at mail call. We had the logistical supply chain in place to move that heavy-ass bucket of gum, which no one in his right mind could argue was essential or even important to our mission, ship it from the United States to the opposite side of the world, seven thousand miles in less than two weeks, but somehow, we couldn't figure a way to wrap up the war and get out. It didn't seem like we were going to anytime soon. Halliburton was busy at the Row, cleaning up the rubble, building out the palaces with offices for the generals, the CIA spooks, and the State Department honchos who'd moved in to replace us. We heard stories about how good they had it there at the newly renamed 'Green Zone.' We heard they served rib-eye steak and king crab every Friday, and they had a big PX that sold American cigarettes, and a mobile Burger King trailer, and movie nights and salsa dances on the weekends — I shit you not, really, they did. From time to time I'd think of the Row and what we'd done in the water palace. When I was feeling really rotten, I'd wonder what'd been inside those safes, the price of our souls unclaimed. I couldn't decide whether I wished it was a million bucks or nothing.

★　★　★

There was still no sign of Wigheard. Most of our missions were straight patrols and had nothing to do with her but sometimes we'd get tasked to pull cordon security for the Rangers or SEALs or whoever was going to raid a place where some informant had claimed she was being held. Higher got tips about her constantly, but after a while, with none of them panning out, you had the feeling the Iraqis had wised up to using her as a pawn in their internal beefs. Like, one sheikh who hated another would rat out his enemy to us, claiming dude was a terrorist holding Wigheard.

This time, SEAL Team Six was going to hit a mosque in a neighborhood with a rough reputation. Our task in the mission was to secure a particular street corner near the mosque and not let anyone through. We expected contact even if we didn't find her. When you roll into a hostile city with a battalion's worth, you are bound for mayhem any way you cut it.

In a long column like a bristling steel centipede, Crusader Battalion crossed the bridge into Fallujah. Only one tank at a time could enter the bridge, a two-lane truss with supporting beams connecting to the sides and top. It was like driving into a long cage. Forty-foot drop to the river. On more peaceful days I'd seen Iraqi men and boys taking elaborate dives off the upper trestles to prove their manhood.

We made the other side, and the platoon at the lead of the column reported a fire. I swung the turret over the front to check it out.

'Get back on your sector,' Galvan said. 'You're looking right where hajji wants you to.' He twisted the handle on his hatch and cracked the cupola. The smell of burning rubber came streaming in. 'Tires,' he said. 'They're burning fucking tires.'

The enemy had made a fiery wall across the road to slow us down and mess with our thermals. We could've rolled right through, but Higher thought the obstacle might be booby-trapped. I felt scared and also a little like it was Christmas morning. I knew it was just the chemicals in my brain making it feel okay to die. Somewhere out there were thousands of people who hated my guts and wanted me shot to pieces and dragged through the streets, or with my head sawed off. That shit was real. My mouth had long since gone dry.

The fighting started with many things happening at once. Colonel Easton got on the radio and ordered the lead tanks to open fire on the tire obstacle with high-explosive rounds. The report of the cannons came from the ground up, like a dangerously close thunderclap. With the obstacle cleared, our column crawled forward again, creaking steel track snuffing shreds of burning rubber. That was all I could smell. In the thermals I scanned a line of buildings at the edge of the city. There was a hot flash on a roof, and a bright-green dart hissing and cracking through the air. 'RPG!' Galvan yelled, and more flashes came from the uneven line of rooftops, some of them dimmer than the rocket, blinking like flashlights switching on and off, small-arms fire. Someone on company net was reporting contact northwest. All at about the same time.

In dim green light my face was reflected in the

LCD like the ghost of a better world. I placed the reticle on the roof where they were shooting at us and let off a burst. Squeezed the trigger and the coax shuddered beside me in the servo mount. It took one long second for the rounds to arc through the air and smack the building. They hit short, the points of impact like dirt clods thrown and bursting against the wall. I'd missed badly, forgetting to laze to the target. I pressed a little red button on the paddle to activate the laser range finder, the firing computer came up with a solution, and the hydraulics jolted the gun to a forty-five-degree angle, a dicey shot, half a mile, the edge of the max range for the coax, like lobbing the ball from half court, spraying and praying, a twist of my wrists moving the reticle and the gun, the turret, me, Galvan, and Patterson, who'd been subbed onto the crew to load for us that day, since we were short-manned. Fitzpatrick was down below in the driver's hull and only moved when the tracks did.

I covered the roof with burning tracers that chipped and burst concrete and raised a white haze that made it impossible to see what I'd just destroyed.

'Gunner, heat, troops!' Galvan said.

I switched the fire selector knob to HEAT. Patterson hit a lever to arm the gun and hollered, 'Up!' He shrank to the side of the turret behind the radios so the recoiling breach wouldn't crush him.

'Fire!'

'On the way!'

Boom.

The big round flew faster and flatter than the small arms. The top corner of the building disappeared in flame and a lingering cloud of pulverized cement. The sound of the cannon firing just off my shoulder was like the smacking of a machine press that weighed two tons and was being worked by an angry giant as we rode on top of it. A sharp, violent *kuh-chunk*. Enough to rattle every organ in my body.

'Target, target!'

The roofline fell quiet. Our column pressed forward into the city, driving on both sides of a divided road. On either flank there were store-fronts shuttered with steel accordion curtains. The buildings' upper floors, five and six stories tall, were subdivided into apartments, laundry hanging on lines strung between balconies, colorful dresses and starched shirts, burqas twisting in-the wind like black flags. I was most worried about what was going on above us, since there was no way to get a good sight picture on the balconies. They were too close — the gun wouldn't elevate enough, the tank designed to fight at distances of miles, not meters — so I settled for watching the streets. Normally they would've been packed with traffic, everything from donkey carts to semi trucks, but now were empty. Not one person anywhere. The lack of life in such a dense city was the most frightening thing, like we were on display, like seeing the world after the end.

An attack helicopter banked overhead and dropped a salvo of rockets that shook the next block over. The smoke grew denser, twisting the

261

light brown. Our tank passed an alleyway and someone on my blind side launched a rocket that hit our turret with a loud *bang* like a sledge-hammer against the armor, and we cursed and flinched in our stations, but Fitzpatrick kept rolling, gassing the throttle, knowing that you can never lose the momentum in a tank fight or you'll get stuck and die. The smell of burning metal drifted into the turret, but we were all still alive, which meant the rocket had failed to penetrate.

'Get the gun over the side,' Galvan said. 'They might try us again from that next one.'

I traversed the gun perpendicular to our line of march and we passed the next alley, where a bearded man wearing black sweatpants and a green silk sash draped around his chest stepped from behind a parked car and hefted a rocket tube onto his shoulder, kneeling for a solid base to launch it from, when he saw our gun pointed directly at him, too late to scramble for cover, though he tried. The coax flung tracers down the alley at twice the speed of sound, and I remember seeing a burning round like a small hurtling star disappearing through the center of him. He sat down hard, dropping the rocket, catching himself with his palms. A stunned expression crossed his face like he never thought this would happen to him.

'Oww-woo-woo-woo! Mother-fuck yeah!' Galvan whooped and crowed, reaching forward from his station, clutching my shoulder like a proud father. The way he sounded, we might as well have just scored a touchdown or been shotgunning beers

262

as killed a man who was trying to kill us. People always want to know what it feels like to do that, and when it's happening, the answer is simple, and usually disappointing. Like fear and adrenaline and not much else, like winning at Russian roulette and having the taste of gunmetal forever on your tongue because even if you win, you lose. The man with the green sash in Fallujah was the first and only person I ever killed that I'm sure about and meant to. The rest were accidents. Except you can't really call them that. They're not accidents.

Our line of tanks crawled forward, stretching over ten blocks. We turned a corner and sighted the remains of a burning fueler. Diesel smoke billowed from it like drops of black ink spreading through water. A platoon from Lancer Battalion had gotten it bad. They had Bradleys on scene and were fighting back, puffs of white vapor streaking out from their machine gun ports. You could almost see the flit of the bullets if you trained your eye. We neared their position and crossed a major intersection about half a klick away. That was when we got it. I was thrown from my scat, head slamming against the turret ceiling, the tank hanging weightless for a moment before crashing back to the street. I was poleax-stunned, vibration shooting through me. Sound as pain. An overload of sensation that left behind no memory of itself.

My neck hurt and the soles of my feet throbbed. I could see nothing through my sights. The bomb buried in the road had sent up a plume of dust and we were in the middle of it. I clicked the control paddles for the hydraulics but got no response.

'Fucking god,' Galvan said. 'Holy shit that was crazy.'

'My back,' Fitzpatrick groaned from down below in the driver's hull, where he'd been nearest the blast.

'You bleeding?' Galvan said. 'Can you move your feet?'

'Yeah.'

'Bleeding?'

'No, I can move.'

On the other side of the turret, Patterson clutched his thigh.

'Lemme see.' Galvan took Patterson's wrist and pried his hand away from the leg. No blood. Concussive wound from the blast wave. He turned to me. 'You all right, Sleed?'

'I think so,' I said, my feet still throbbing, going numb, but only the soles. A strange pain I'd never felt before.

'Try and start it.'

Fitzpatrick said he had already but the engine wouldn't fire up.

'You have hydraulics?'

'Negative.'

Colonel Easton came on the radio. 'Blue Two, Crusader Six. What's your status? Over.'

Galvan keyed the net. 'Six, Two. No critical wounded. May be a couple routine. I'm gonna need a tow. Over.'

'Roger that. Goddamn. We thought we'd lost you men.'

Galvan dropped the hand mic. 'Get your vests

on,' he said. 'Everybody. We're gonna have to dismount to help the mechanics when they bring up the Hercules.'

I reached below my seat where I kept my gear, struggling to shoulder my body armor in the cramped space. We waited for word about the mechanics. A couple minutes passed. The lieutenant came over the net.

'Two, One.'

'Two,' Galvan said.

'Battalion's saying it's gonna be twenty mikes, minimum, on a Hercules.'

'I ain't sitting here no twenty minutes.'

'Roger,' the lieutenant said. 'Crusader is saying we should self-recover.'

'Let's do it,' Galvan said. 'Back up to my six. When you're set, I'll dismount with my guys to hook up to you.'

He spun in the cupola, watching the vision blocks to see what was happening outside. The lieutenant maneuvered his tank into position directly behind us while other tanks in the column overwatched either direction of the cross street. Whoever had detonated the bomb was out there somewhere.

The lieutenant said he was set.

Galvan flicked his head at the loader's hatch.

'Pop it,' he ordered.

The last thing any tanker wants to do in battle is to dismount, but Patterson obeyed and opened the hatch. It was the lesser of two evils. Better to get out and take care of the problem ourselves than give the enemy enough time to mass a coordinated attack.

Galvan and I grabbed our carbines. He swung open his hatch and hoisted himself through, and I shimmied past the tank commander's station and pulled myself into the light with the very clear and distinct thought that if I was going to die in Iraq, today would be the day. Into the blinding sun. Fitzpatrick had scrambled from the driver's hull to the top of the turret and was digging through the sponson box for his rifle. My feet were still feeling numb and I was so jittery with adrenaline, I rolled my ankle leaping down to the front slope. I caught myself, hunched over, and limped down the side of the hull like moving from bow to stern on a small boat with narrow gangways. I saw where the RPG from earlier had exploded against our turret, a bright-silver splat mark like someone had thrown a snowball of liquid metal. A machine gun fired, close, one of ours, gunshots echoing off the buildings rising around us. A chopper zoomed low overhead, blowing rotor wash that kicked up the dust on the street, the sound of the blades and the tanks and gunfire coming from every side and from above like a tornado or the rush in your ears of a panic attack.

'Come on!' Galvan called from across the tank, where he and Patterson were struggling to free one of the tow cables from its mount.

I told myself to do whatever he said, concentrate on what was right in front of me. I worked with Fitzpatrick to free our cable, thick braided steel covered in tar to keep it from rusting, eight feet long, two hook fasteners on its ends like the eyes of giant needles. We jerked it free, dropped it to the street, and climbed down.

The bomb had exploded under our right track, carving a crater two feet deep in the pavement and earth below. It'd blown off the tank's front skirt which weighed a metric ton, tossing it across the median like scrap metal, shearing the first three road wheels from their spindles. The wheels were nowhere in sight. Worst of all, the tank's track had broken and a section lay unspooled. Even if we'd been able to restart the engine, we wouldn't have gone anywhere.

Little puffs of dust rose from the pavement in the intersection and I stared at them, puzzled, but then realized they were bullets skipping off concrete. I couldn't hear them whining. It was too loud to hear any one thing. I took a knee and fired my carbine down the street in the direction I thought they'd come from, but I didn't really know what I was shooting at, not using the aperture sight on the weapon, just squeezing the trigger over and over.

Galvan grabbed me by the nape of my tactical vest. 'Forget that! Help me with this fucking cable!'

★   ★   ★

It was the heaviest shit I ever got into. Later, back at the staging area, Galvan said he'd seen a bullet fly right over my head while we were dragging the tow cables across the street.

'Damn,' I said. 'Really?'

'I don't know what the fuck it was,' he said.

'Bullet, chunk of concrete, shrapnel, whatever. Looked like it came about this far from you. Lucky fuck.'

He knocked on my Kevlar.

'Damn.'

After all that, we weren't even done for the day. The mission was still on. We took a break to get some water, upload ammo, and trade out our damaged tank for one from First Platoon with two crew members who had combat fatigue. One guy was crying so hard he was hyperventilating. We took their tank and left them behind, heading back into the shit for another couple hours while the SEALs searched the mosque top to bottom, even with some kind of portable X-ray machine, hunting for secret compartments but not finding a trace of her.

'I sure hope she's worth it,' Galvan said when it was all over and done with and we were rolling back to Camp Marlboro.

'I know I'm not.'

'No argument there. How many people we gonna have to kill, anyway, just to save one fucking life?'

PART IV

But the women, and the little ones, and the livestock, and all that is in the city, even all the spoil thereof, shalt thou take unto thyself, and thou shalt eat the spoil of thine enemies, which the Lord thy God hath given thee.

— Deuteronomy 20:14

14

Abu al-Hool: The Time of Scorching Dryness

Iraq (water treatment plant; Fallujah):
53 days after

All I wanted was my leave. It seemed like an easy enough request for the doctor to grant, but over the years I've found it best not to plan according to what is easiest. So, one morning not long after Michael Crump's execution, I retrieved the vest I'd fashioned. I laid it out, inspecting my handiwork, touching a voltmeter to the wires I then connected to the detonator, nervous, working with the blasting cap and battery, inserting the nine-volt, priming the device; I am a passable bomb maker but no expert.

The moment had come for me and my old comrade Walid. A test of intentions, wills, nerves. I put on the vest and over it my shalwar, the bright-white garment loose enough to obscure the bulky outline beneath. I palmed the trigger and said a prayer for my soul. Then I went to see him.

'There you are.' He glanced up from his reading and waved me into his room like an overwrought maitre d'hôtel. 'Come in. We have a lot to discuss.'

'We do,' I said coolly.

He closed the book he'd been studying and appraised me closer. 'Are you feeling all right?'

'I'm afraid not.'

'I noticed you weren't there when the sentence was carried out.'

'No, I wasn't,' I said.

'Are you ill?'

'No.'

'An existential malady, then. I can't say that surprises me. I assume you believe there's something I can do about it?'

'Yes. I want you to release me. Give me my leave today. If we were ever true brothers, let me have that much.'

'Leave? For how long?'

'Indefinitely.'

'Ah, you!' he cried, as if with reverent affection. 'Do you remember what Field Commander Jawad said about you when you first met?'

'He said I was green as a new shoot and eager to kill Russians. He said I had the look of one who would die quickly.'

'What a compliment, coming from a man like that.'

'But he was wrong. God knows I've been willing, but I'm still alive. All these years, I am still alive. Why is that, do you think? What about me did he misjudge?'

'It may've been your fortitude,' Dr. Walid said, his mood abruptly turning.

I ignored the gibe. 'Will you give me what I want?'

'You swore an oath.'

'I know. I'm asking you to relieve me of it.'

'What if I won't? What if I take this for backsliding apostasy?'

There. That was all he needed to say for me to know that in his eyes, I was already a dead man. The time had come to show him I did not plan to go gently.

'If the sheep wander astray,' I said, 'they'll have been led by an ill goat. In which case it's best to cull the whole flock.' I opened my hand and revealed the detonator, placing my thumb delicately on the trigger. He maintained his facade, cultivating an amused look like he was observing some heretofore unnoticed foible about me, a quirk or mannerism that struck him as delightful, but I could tell by the way he kept glancing at my hand that he wasn't truly prepared to die. A man who's afraid is most attentive to the weapon. By the same token, a man who's prepared looks inward or, occasionally, if he's more defiant than most, on the face of his enemy.

''I wish I could raid and be slain, and then raid and be slain, and then raid and be slain,'' he said, quoting the Messenger of God, peace be upon him.

'I take it by that, your mind is made up?'

A tense moment, this. Neither of us spoke; we hardly moved.

'Put it away,' he said after a while. 'There is no need. You're released of any obligation to me or this brotherhood. But there's one final task I have to ask of you. My God. It's what I wanted to talk to you about before you started in with this nonsense. One last errand, then you go. Come on, brother. Put it away.'

★ ★ ★

Not many people are capable of going to their deaths with dignity, and I am no exception. Trying for thanatological decorum but falling well short, I sweated and fidgeted behind the wheel of a rusted-out Volkswagen Golf. Abu Annas and I had departed the water plant after the *zuhr* prayer; on the seat between us was a satchel containing four thousand American dollars from our treasury. The doctor's last request, the price of my freedom, was for me to act as courier and deliver the money to Abu Ali the Cripple, in Fallujah. He had claimed it was a payment for arms and other supplies, but I thought it just as likely a pretense to give me a false sense of security; why trust a man you intend to kill with so much?

'I've just finished telling him about the Fallujah drop-off,' Walid had said, filling in Abu Annas as he entered my room carrying a suit of clothes, gray slacks and a button-up shirt. He'd changed into something similar and had cut his beard to appear more like an ordinary Iraqi, less like a soldier.

'Put these on,' he said, tossing me the clothes. 'That shalwar marks you too easily as a foreigner.'

'No, it doesn't,' I said, still wearing the martyrdom vest and wishing to keep them

274

guessing about it. 'The shalwar is common enough here. If we're ready, let's go. I'd like to make it before nightfall.'

Abu Annas scowled at Dr. Walid, but the doctor wasn't going to press me on this. It was a peculiar and deadly dance the two of us were making. The vest was real but effectively a tool for bluffing with. Neither of us was eager for a final showdown then and there, but rather, we wanted enough distance from the other to act with greater precision, less risk. Even with my power much diminished, I remained an alternate source of authority to which the men might return if they grew to mistrust his command. Mindful of the depths of his jealousies, I had, until that morning, given him little reason to plot against me; but at the same time, I had known that once I did make my move, I had to act decisively, or he would use any chance to cut down a perceived threat before it grew unmanageable. The one-way courier mission suited us both. Abu Annas, however, did not look happy to be caught in the middle of it.

★ ★ ★

The Golf's suspension was shot, janking and jolting us down the road. Abu Annas had asked me to drive, claiming his eyes were bothering him. I took it for a ruse to keep my hands occupied and visible. I thought there was a good chance the doctor wanted me dead on the road to the city; that he'd assigned this man to be my escort increased my suspicions. There were some

275

in the brotherhood who still had love for me and who would think twice before cutting my throat on anyone's orders. Abu Annas was not one of them.

I wondered again how he planned to kill me. Knife or pistol, or maybe he meant to travel with me all the way to our destination, to put me more at ease, to park the car and walk up to the flat of Abu Ali the Cripple, where together, enjoying better odds, they'd dispatch me.

I kept my hands loosely on the wheel, mindful not to tense up so that I'd be able to react in time to parry his attack, whenever it came. Grueling to be so attentive; the weather fair but my back damp against the seat. We passed through the marsh in the area where the river bends sluggishly and broadly, almost doubling back on itself. Here it overflows its banks in places, creating a morass of wetlands, untended canals, overgrown rice fields, a few of which were still in cultivation. Neither of us said much, listening to a cassette tape he'd brought, a mix of *nasheeds* popular with the Palestinian resistance. The songs heartened me, and I thought again how I might've mis-judged the doctor's intentions. We'd been together through so much: I remember vividly the time in Afghanistan when we were young men and the bombs fell from Soviet jets, whistling through the air and exploding so near, they threw us from our feet in the cave and collapsed a section of the roof, sending a wooden support beam slicing downward to brain Abu Mahfouz the Libyan, martyring him before he knew what had

276

happened, and even then Dr. Walid never cowered or pressed himself flat to the earth but rather ran out of the cave mouth and into the open air where shrapnel flew thick as leaves in a whirlwind. A joyful lion, he cried with his face to the sky, thanking God for the death he was finally to receive after two long years in the jihad. The rest of us marveled at his purity. After that day, many who lived through the bombardment swore that he was made of a special substance that, like copper, grows stronger the harder it is hammered upon.

The marsh ended. We followed the river through farmland, approaching the city; we'd agreed it was best to circle around and enter Fallujah by the north road. The Americans had been reinforcing their positions in the south and east. Abu Annas shifted uncomfortably in his seat and adjusted his crotch.

'Pull over in that grove, would you, brother. I've got to get some relief.'

'All right.'

This was it, I felt certain. When I stopped the car, he'd do it. Too dangerous to do it with us moving.

I pressed down on the accelerator. The Golf s engine strained hoarsely, the car rattling and jouncing over the ruts in the canal road.

'Whoa — I don't have to piss that bad.'

I laughed and said, 'Relax, brother, relax,' but neither did I let up on the accelerator, flooring it, and in the final few seconds before I jerked the wheel, sending us off the road, hurtling chaotically into the palms, the stately trees planted in a tight-knit checkerboard pattern, he realized very well what I was up to and fought me for control of the wheel; we grappled in the front seat as the Golf's jouncing became weightlessness, the car clearing a dry ditch and bottoming out, zooming and fishtailing through a gap in the first row of trees before smashing head-on into the second.

★ ★ ★

When I came to, the Golf was lodged against a palm, engine still running but with a pinging rattle, flames darting out from under the hood. My face throbbed. I poked around with my tongue and couldn't find my front teeth. I saw one on the dashboard and focused on it oddly, the tooth with its bloody stump amid pieces of windshield glass shattered into crystalline pellets. I looked to the passenger's side: Abu Annas was unconscious, with a nasty gash in his forehead. He had not been wearing his belt, whereas, quite deliberately, I had.. Black smoke began to pour from the car's front end, choking me. I tried my door but it was stuck. I pulled myself through the window and gasped when I hit the ground; my ankle refused to bear weight. I hadn't felt it was broken before then. I hopped around to the other side, wanting to be sure of myself, of what I'd just done, leaning through the passenger window, patting him down for a weapon and not finding one, but the fire cut short my search, making it too cursory to be definitive. It's possible he meant to kill me with his bare hands.

It's possible he had a pistol hidden under the seat or that Abu Ali was waiting with one in his flat. It's also possible, I must admit, that I murdered him out of paranoia.

I took the satchel and left him to die in the burning car. I made for the canal road. An excruciating kilometer later, it intersected the Fallujah highway, and a barley farmer and his son taking their crop to market stopped their truck out of alarmed pity at the sight of me — bedraggled, battered, bloody — limping along the shoulder. They offered a ride the rest of the way.

* * *

In the hubbub of the bazaar I found a street boy who was willing, for a fee, to acquire a few items that would make my next hours bearable. While he searched the market stalls with my hastily scrawled shopping list in hand, I found an out-of-the-way bench on which to rest, elevating my leg. I groaned to see the ankle had already swollen to nearly the size of a grapefruit.

I tried to take my mind off the pain by deliberating over Dr. Walid's most likely course of action. By evening he would've certainly heard that Abu Annas and I hadn't kept our appointment with Abu Ali. After that, it would be only a matter of time before the remains of the car were discovered and the hunt for me was on. I could try to flee. I had the benefit of a head start, but with a revoked passport and four thousand dollars — which would go a long way in Iraq but not so very far outside it — I could not see myself escaping the doctor's reach for long. There would be a fatwa, a bounty, faxes sent to every node in his network of contacts within the movement. The other emirs would take his side, of course. He was one of them. I was a traitor and a murderer.

I thought of returning to Pakistan and my wife, but that was out of the question. Even assuming she would take me in, her home would be one of the most obvious places for them to look. I mulled over other options, but the more I considered a life on the run, the less it appealed. A life spent looking over my shoulder. I had already lived it, always expecting death to come from the enemy when, as it turned out, old friends were at least as dangerous.

That afternoon in Fallujah I knew I had reached the end of something. The time for running was over. It was time to take a stand.

★   ★   ★

The boy returned from the bazaar with a pair of crutches, a stack of fashion magazines, some electrical tape, a new shalwar, and a bottle of Valium. I had asked for morphine, but the boy said he could find none, telling me that Valium was always easy enough to come by, and now the war had turned it into a staple. He claimed his own mother was a regular customer, her nervous condition making it otherwise impossible for her to tolerate the American air strikes.

I went into my satchel, paid him for his labor,

and after we hashed out a few last arrangements, he went on his way. Using rolled magazines and electrical tape, I constructed a crude brace for my ankle, then hobbled on the crutches to a juice stand where I bought a cup and swallowed two of the pills. I went to the toilet and took off my clothing and the martyrdom vest, removing the battery and placing it, along with the vest and money, in the satchel, covering the contraband with the old bloody shalwar. I washed my face and did what I could to clean up. I changed into the fresh clothes, took two twenty-dollar bills and put them in my pocket, and rested a minute before making my way to the street, my black eyes and crutches attracting a few questioning glances, but the curiosity of the passersby was mostly casual. Here, the maimed and wounded were common.

I flagged down a cab and climbed into the rear seat, the upholstery shredded like the driver had been ferrying loads of wild cats. The man was an African who spoke Arabic only adequately. When he asked, 'Where to?' I noticed his teeth, stained brown with khat: a Somali, I guessed. Odd to find one in Iraq, but not unheard of.

'The American base across the highway,' I told him, having never seen the place but knowing of it through Walid; the doctor had ways of staying informed. 'The one east of the city. Can you get me there?'

The Somali clucked and whistled and looked surprised, as if he'd pegged me for many things, none a collaborator.

'That is extra charge,' he said. 'Very risky.'

I went into my pocket for twenty dollars. 'Here, all I have.'

'Nice. Okay, we go.'

We drove out of the city. I rested my forehead against the window and drowsily watched the progression of slapdash little villages, farms and canals, children tending livestock, rummaging through mounds of rubbish dumped on the side of the road, hunting a few dinars' worth of scrap metal. The Valium began to take effect; Iraq never looked so beautiful. It was the palm groves, I think, the neat rows of them, the way they appeared from the moving car, each tree shifting in parallax with those in front and behind, creating the illusion of infinite depth, as if you could walk forever through the groves.

'Hey, so tell me, man. What happen to you?'

I was annoyed the cabbie wanted to make conversation, and a tactless one at that. When I used to do this same work, I always had sense enough to let my fares dictate the mood.

'Car crash,' I said.

'Whoa. You are lucky.'

'I would've thought the opposite.'

'I mean you are lucky to be alive.'

'I know what you meant.'

He turned and gave me a look before returning his concentration to the road.

'You should be more careful. Like the way you are going to the Americans. Very dangerous now. You work for them?'

'No,' I said.

'But you are not afraid the mujahideen will think so?'

'I'm not afraid at all.'

The Somali whistled again at my bravado, which was actually a kind of resignation. Why be afraid? All things must die. The palm trees of Iraq, which I found so beautiful, they were dying, all of them. Thousands of years of civilization had robbed the soil of its ability to sustain life, the once-Fertile Crescent leached of nutrients, sown with salt. Slowly but surely what man touches passes into desert.

'Me, I'm careful,' the cabbie said. 'The mujahideen take your head just for talking to the Americans.'

I decided, rather than succumb to silent annoyance, to have a little fun with him. I rested a hand on his seat back and leaned forward congenially.

'You want to know why I'm not afraid? I'll tell you. It's because I *am* a mujahid. You've heard of the ones who captured that American girl? That brotherhood wouldn't even *exist* without me. And neither will you, if you keep up your stupid yammering. Just drive, and don't worry so much about me.'

I was being reckless, but cabbies hear and see so much in any given day, he probably took me for a lunatic. I caught a look at myself reflected in the mirror and had to admit, I did appear addled: face swollen like a losing boxer, bloodshot eyes betraying no fear at all, not of man or death or the Americans, and a gaunt desperation to me, like I might without warning or motive scramble the rest of the way out of the backseat and bite off his ear, wrench the steering wheel out of his control, and send the car careening off the road just as I had with Abu Annas.

His hands flexed on the knobbed wheel like he'd intuited my train of thought.

'Are you a good Muslim?' I said, gentler now. 'Good with God?'

'Who knows,' he said. 'I make the prayers.'

'Then you have nothing to be afraid of. If we're with God, death cannot touch us. Or don't you believe that?'

It was as much a provocation to myself as to him, and it went unanswered by either of us. We drove the rest of the way without talking. He slowed when we sighted the base, concrete blast walls erected around it like a palisade. I went into my pocket for another twenty dollars. 'I may not be so poor as I thought. This one is for your time if you wait here. And another, when I get back, for the return fare to Fallujah.'

He agreed to the deal. I got out of the cab and took my crutches but not the satchel, which, having no better option — and being more worried about losing the vest than the cash — I'd placed on the floor-board and shoved behind his seat in hopes he wouldn't notice it. I approached the base. It was obvious the Americans hadn't built their garrison themselves but had repurposed it. I saw a faded sign painted in orange and red on the tallest building behind the blast walls. It advertised a defunct brand of Iraqi cigarettes; buoyed by the Valium and my audaciousness in coming here, I chuckled to think the place had maintained its essential function — manufacturing dependency, death, vice — even while changing ownership so dramatically.

Two Iraqi police officers stood guard. I told them the reason for my visit and was patted down and let through the first gate. Inside an American base for the first time, I was struck by its mundanity: there was nothing so remarkable about this supposedly elite force. Aside from its strange location in the old cigarette factory, it looked like similar-sized Russian installations I'd observed in Chechnya. Drab, utilitarian, everything careworn and a little faded, men with the expression of yoked beasts performing manual labors of both the colossal and tedious varieties.

At a second checkpoint, a team of guards searched me more thoroughly. I feigned to speak no English, and the soldier in charge asked me through one of the Iraqis how I'd been injured. Although I'd told the cabbie the truth, this time I did not. The American spent some time on the radio with his supervisor before blindfolding me and leading me deeper into the base, my arm around one of his men for support, a second soldier carrying my crutches. Eventually I found myself in a bare room with a desk and chairs, where the blindfold was removed.

A man who introduced himself as Captain Brugone arrived to conduct my debriefing. Our discussion was facilitated by a young Iraqi in Western dress who never did give his name. I assume he was, until recently, a student at Baghdad University, although that's conjecture. I've heard that those fluent in English and who're at all sympathetic to the occupation — and some who aren't — have found work as translators. It's now one of the best-paying jobs in Iraq, unless one is lucky enough to sit on the Puppet Council or otherwise find himself poised to skim the fat off a government ministry.

'Is there anything I can do to make you more comfortable?' Brugone asked, his translator relaying the courtesy, and all of our following exchanges.

'No, thank you. As long as I can keep my leg up, it's all right.'

'After we're done talking, I'd like to have one of my medics take a look at that.'

'I would be in your debt.'

With pleasantries out of the way, Brugone launched into the formal part of the interrogation. I was fingerprinted and photographed. He scribbled on a yellow legal pad as I gave my name (false) and occupation (farmer). He asked where I was born; I claimed al-Sadhan, a village outside the city. Throughout the course of these introductory questions and answers, the translator regarded me circumspectly, so shrewdly and warily, I grew convinced he knew, or at least strongly suspected, I wasn't born anywhere near Fallujah. I'd tried to disguise my accent but am no great actor and now, doubting my abilities, was sure he could tell I was lying through my teeth.

I prepared for him to challenge me, but to my relief, as the interrogation progressed, the translator did not raise objections over my testimony. He simply did his job, not interjecting his own opinions: he might've been instructed not to while the interview was ongoing, or maybe he simply didn't care enough to complicate it. If he were to raise a cloud of doubt over me, it would only make the session longer and more involved, more work for him.

'Show me on the map where this happened,' Brugone said, interrupting my story of how, while tending rice fields on my family's land, I'd seen a group of armed men traveling into the marsh on several occasions.

I studied his map and pointed to a place not far from the water treatment plant, where the events I had reported could have reasonably happened. Brugone circled it with his pen.

'There,' I said. 'Like I told you, I saw them on the canal road. I kept working, minding my business. I'm just a farmer and didn't think they would care about me. But this time they spotted me and came over. They began asking questions. What was I doing there? Why was I always watching them? I told the truth — I was just working — but they accused me of lying and beat me. You can see what they did, but nothing would make me confess to being a spy. Eventually they stopped and said that if I ever told anyone what I'd seen, they'd come back and kill me and my wife and children, even my children's children. At first, I said nothing. Not even to my wife when she asked how I'd been hurt. But I began to think. Why should I be afraid to walk my own land, just because some foreigners want to fight the Americans?'

'You say they were foreigners. What made you think that?'

'Well, by their voices,' I said, stumbling some. I made eye contact with the translator and thought I detected a glimmer of ironic recognition; surely he could tell, by my own voice, that my falsehood was now eating its tail. 'A few sounded like they may have been Syrian. It was a mix of people. About a dozen.'

I hoped I had not just made a fatal misstep, but once again the Iraqi student translated my report, and once again he said nothing about any suspicions he may have harbored. His silence seemed to stretch beyond mere carelessness. I began to imagine he was secretly working for some brotherhood or militia, informing on the informants, a double agent collecting paychecks from both sides; clearly, the smartest man in the room.

'Was there anything else that stood out about these guys?' Brugone asked. 'Their vehicles? Weapons?'

'They were driving two Kia trucks. They had mortars, but I couldn't tell you what kind. Kalashnikovs, rockets — oh — this is important. I almost forgot. I heard one say they were part of the Martyr Khattab Brigade. He told me that when he threatened my family.'

'Huh,' Brugone grunted, making more notes on his pad. I hoped the bit about the Khattab Brigade would throw him off the scent of Walid and the girl, which he hadn't seemed to detect, anyway. I wanted no chance of my being detained or of the doctor being captured alive. When I'd first conceived of the plan, I'd toyed with the idea of telling the Americans more but had soon realized mentioning their names would make me one of the most sought-after men in Iraq. Many people would've wanted to interrogate me, some more competent than this Brugone, who, for an American, was surprisingly unparanoid.

'I'll pass it along,' he continued. 'It's damn good intel. These insurgent groups come and go, but it's Iraqis like you that get caught in the middle. And you're the ones who'll make the difference in this war. I know it wasn't easy for you to come here today, but we appreciate it. *Shukran*. I mean it, *shukran*.'

'But I haven't told you the best part,' I said, motioning for the map. 'I have an idea where they're staying, though I doubt they'll be there for long. It's this place here.' I tapped on a spot indicating the old water plant. 'Watch it with your helicopters and your planes, and surely you will rain fire down on your enemies.'

15

Cassandra: The Profession

```
Iraq (water treatment plant):
48 days after
```

Brought back from the shed, her period over, she's clean enough for them to live with again. After four days with sunlight the adjustment to the underground cell is just as bad as it was the first time. Every so often they bring her a fresh pitcher of water, and rice, olives, sometimes chicken or canned tuna. Every so often they remove her waste pail and return with another, and in the hallway they chant and sing verses from the Qur'an to pass the time, and the light near the door is on, but mostly it's off, and she paces in the dark and dreams of home, and it's all like it was before, nothing has changed, but at the same time, everything is different.

To be the only captive left alive. No tapping on the drain. No possibility of any human contact except with the enemy. No connection to the window, the world, or even time itself: lying on the pallet, Cassandra rolls to her side. She has not felt like exercising since returning to her cell, and lets out a low groan. When McGinnis was still around to talk to — to compare herself to — it was easier to be the plucky one, the salty one, the one who refused despair. Both to raise his spirits and to keep them from infecting her. But to be the only one still alive is to maintain a front only for oneself. The only one still alive is next to die. And eventually, Annas is going to come back. This time, whenever he does, she promises herself she won't be asleep.

★ ★ ★

Hafs is on shift. He leaves his rifle propped against the wall in the usual place near the cell door. This is the first she's seen him since the shed; she thinks of him filming what they did to Crump and has the urge to make a grab for the weapon and blow his brains out. But that would be suicide; even if she managed it, she'd be too greatly outnumbered and outgunned to escape, with no idea about where the other guards are posted. She hasn't come this far to throw it all away, Rambo-style, on a one-in-a-million gamble. Plus, with McGinnis gone, Hafs now qualifies as the closest thing she has to an ally. Definitely the most important person in her life. Even so, she'll kill him if it means improving her chances.

'Hello, sister,' he says. 'I brought this for you.'

He returns the Qur'an that he took away after she got her period, kissing the book and touching it to his forehead.

Like nothing has changed, they get to work. But her mind will not stay focused, even as she understands this exchange of languages is important, potentially life-or-death.

'Hafs. Stop for a minute. I need to know

something. What happened to McGinnis?'

'He is gone. We are here, okay? This talk is not good.'

'Did he die while they were operating on him, or did they kill him?'

'I cannot say. I am only new soldier. Many heads are above my head.'

'You're just following orders? You know that's bullshit. I saw you, you know that? You filming Crump.'

He looks down at the notebook in his lap. He takes a long breath, steadying himself. '*Inshallah*, everything is okay for you, sister. Please. We must practice.'

'No. No more. If you won't tell me anything else, I'm done. No more English lessons.'

The market is up this year.

I have an account with your bank.

The unemployment rate was highest during the depression.

Before the shed, in what seems in retrospect almost like an untroubled age of her captivity, she gave him a dozen more like that, 'business phrases,' per his request, printed on coarse brown paper with extra-wide rule, the kind of notebook kids use to practice the alphabet. Hafs approaches his studies with utmost seriousness. He says that after the jihad, he wants to go to college and study economics.

★ ★ ★

In the darkness, without McGinnis or Hafs to talk to, she begins speaking to Crump. She's not

so far gone as to believe these are actual conver-
sations; nor are they completely fantastical. They're
liminal. Trick of the mind deprived, like the blue
lights she sees hovering in her cell. Like the
future. The past. Crump's voice, loud and clear,
intruding.

Death is always right around the corner.
Ain't negative or positive, just is. Look
at this way. Not many people get to
choose how.
Yeah, you're right about that. I didn't.
Come on. There's only two ways out, Wigheard.
You really need me to tell you?
Did you see what they did to me? Fuck. Just like
I was a fucking animal.

★   ★   ★

The light on the wall turns on. The hum of its
electricity sounds louder than before, but that
may be her imagination, the volume of all things
increasing. Real enough is another meal, this
time rice, olives, tuna, a thermos of lukewarm
tea. Hafs brought it. She's on speaking terms
with him today. It was a choice between that or
silence. The army must be searching for her, and
anything she can do to buy time and curry favor
with Hafs is worth it; there may be a final limit,
but she hasn't yet reached it, and whenever she
thinks she has, Crump surfaces, reminding her of
the alternative.
'Ashadu illallaha ashadu an Muhammed
urrasullallah,' she says to Hafs.
'L'ah,' he says, patiently correcting her.

'*Ashadu an la illaha illalaha oh ashadu an Muhammed urrasullalah.*'

He's reviewing the Shahada with her, though she hasn't yet professed the faith. If a person speaks these words and truly believes them, she becomes a Muslim. *I testify there is no God but God, and I testify Mohammed is His prophet.* She knows — though no one has come right out and said it — that they want to tape her saying this.

'The Shahada is very important,' Hafs said before they began practicing it. 'When a person is dying, it should be the last thing they say. If they do, they go to paradise, easy.'

'What? — Why'd you say that? Is something about to happen?'

'No, no. I did not mean that.'

'Are you sure?'

'Yes. Is no problem.'

'What's going on, Hafs? You seem different.'

'Maybe. It's nothing. A friend, he is gone today. Not dead. He is gone from here.'

'Oh.' She nodded, suspicions allayed enough to go on with the lesson. By the end of the hour, she's fighting to keep her eyes open. She's done her best to avoid sleep, can't bear the thought of Annas catching her unawares again, but sooner or later, willpower won't be enough, and she will crash for a very long time.

They practice a little while longer. Hafs looks at his watch, the notebook, her. It's never going to feel like the right moment to do it, but time's running out, sleep will come, and she works up the courage to tell him. It's a gamble that could backfire and bring even more pain down on her, but in this case, the odds are worth it.

'Hafs. I need to tell you something. It's Annas. He — he's come to me a few times. He did things that are haram.' She stops there, hoping she won't have to spell it out. 'Do you understand what I'm telling you?'

'Yes, maybe,' he says, brow knitted, mortified by even the hint of sex. He's never once in their many hours of conversation brought up anything remotely sexual. A childish prudishness. God and sex, she thinks. The whole thing with them and God and sex isn't really about religion at all. It's about power, plain and simple. Just another expression of their lack of it.

'What you want me to do about this ?' he says, further digesting what she's told him, and frustrated, like she's unfairly burdened him with too much responsibility.

'Make him stop. Please, whatever you can think of. Maybe talk to the emir about it.'

Hafs grimaces.

'Please. You're the only one who can help me.'

She hates begging him, but what she's saying is the truth; she's reliant on this boy, the enemy — not for salvation, which has grown to seem nearly out of reach, a self-indulgent dream, but simply for her basic needs, the lessening of pain.

'Is possible,' he finally says.

That isn't good enough. She knows what *possible* means, and it's literal. 'Promise me.'

He frowns and checks his wristwatch again, staring at it too long, like it holds the answer. He rises, collects his notebook of phrases, and the

AK-47, propped against the wall.

'Okay. I will talk to him. Is no problem, sister.'

★ ★ ★

If this thing happens, that thing will happen.

If this thing happened, that thing would happen.

If this thing had happened, that thing would have happened.

If this thing had happened, that thing would happen (but this thing didn't happen, so that thing isn't happening).

The conditional tense. Cassandra doesn't remember to call it that but knows more than enough to teach it, is halfheartedly explicating examples from Hafs's notebook when his walkabout radio crackles to life. Which in itself is not unusual, and she starts to pick up where she left off, but Hafs holds up a finger for silence. She listens to the transmission that follows but is unable to pick out any words, even those few she's learned so far; they're coming too fast.

'Sorry,' he says, an intensely preoccupied look on his face. 'I must go.'

'Okay.'

The creaking door. A beat, two, before she realizes. Can't be. He's left it. A stroke of unbelievable fortune, good or bad: in his haste, he's forgotten it there, his rifle against the wall near the door in the same place he's been keeping it, but never like this, with nothing stopping her from crossing the cell and picking it up. She sits Indian-style on her pallet exactly where he left her, heart accelerating from the unexpectedness of this turn of events, the now-or-never quality to this decision that's befallen her like a head-on collision or winning the lottery. For a second she wonders if it could be a loyalty test; say she picks it up, finds it loaded, the door open, steps into the passage to make her escape and is cut down by a waiting gunman — test failed. The scenario seems far-fetched and she discounts it. You're valuable to them, she thinks. Why waste her that way, no video or anything? And, despite her misgivings, she does trust Hafs to some extent. Not totally, but he is her best and only option, her trust strengthened by her strong suspicion that he's a little in love with her, an infatuation she hasn't actively encouraged, but neither has she dissuaded him of it; in any case, they've become too familiar. He's let his guard down in every sense of the word. The proof is right there, against the wall, demanding some reaction. Check to see if it's loaded. Plainly there's a magazine in there, but could be empty, just for show, like the time when they were waiting to shoot the video and he pulled back the charging handle to reveal the rifle was nothing more than a prop.

If he also forgot to lock the door, she could be in business. She gets up and goes to it. Shut tight. Which means she'd either have to attempt, with thirty rounds or less, to shoot through and disable the lock, or wait until one of the guards opened it and then ambush him. Would probably be Hafs. Would probably not be long before he discovered it missing and returned. If he was smart he wouldn't come alone — he'd tell the others, unless he was too embarrassed, but what a risk to save face. Regardless, she might get off a few rounds. Take out one or two of them before they tossed in a grenade. Very little chance of exploiting this situation to escape. But it's the best she's been presented with. Won't happen again. Not like this.

She picks up the rifle, eases back the bolt and sees the chamber unloaded but the magazine full. She does not immediately chamber a round. All the other times she handled weapons, whether as a girl back home or in the military, they exerted a kind of talismanic force that made her feel more powerful, more in control of her own fate, but this time, the gun does not work that way. Almost the opposite. Her cell has never felt so small. And the AK feels like just what it is: a crude object of steel and wood.

One other possibility occurs. A second way to leave this cell for good. Rack a round, seat the flash suppressor in the soft flesh between her lower jawbone, and pull the trigger. Skull in the ceiling. High-power rifle like this would be instantaneous.

Death is always right around the corner.

Not many people get to choose how.

Only two ways out.

* * *

There are quick footsteps in the hallway. They pause outside her door. Sounds like he's alone. He hasn't come back with five other guards and a grenade. Until this moment she's had to put her life in his hands by necessity, but when she hears his lone footsteps she knows that he's entrusted her with his life as well. The pact is unspoken but real. She doesn't know whether it means he might simply warn her of what Walid is planning or, hope beyond hope, help her escape somehow, help her to survive if the army busts down the door one day, but whatever it signifies, the understanding between them shifts the odds a fraction in her favor. Maybe she won't *have* to choose how to die, in a hail of bullets or with one unleashed by her own hand. Maybe Crump was wrong. She puts the gun down.

'Hafs?'

'Yes. It's me.' He's nervous. Very on edge.

'Okay,' she says. 'I think you forgot something kind of important in here.'

★ ★ ★

The generator kicks on. She has light and shortly thereafter hears someone working the lock on her door; she assumes the worst every time. Expecting Annas, despite Hafs's promise to intervene, but it's Walid — a rare visit from the emir. He enters the cell smiling affably, eyes bright and intelligent; this is the same man who killed her friends in cold blood.

'How are you?' he asks in a tone of charming complicity, as though they might go for drinks and reminisce about the good old days.

She shrubs, looking away.

'The boy's told me what you told him.'

299

'Yeah,' she says.

'It is . . . unfortunate.'

'Maybe you'd call it that. I'd call it evil.'

'No,' he says, paternally concerned. 'Your government is evil. What Abu did to you is merely unfortunate. But there's no need to worry about him bothering you anymore. He won't be back on your cell.'

'How can you know that for sure?'

'Because I do. You won't be seeing him anymore. You have my word.'

Silence follows. The drip of condensation from the fluorescent ballast. She has to ask.

'What happened to Sergeant McGinnis?'

'Who says anything did?'

'I know he was sick. I know you were helping him. I know he's gone.'

'Did that boy tell you this?'

'No. It doesn't matter how I know.'

'Yes, it does. It matters to me a great deal. Tell me, or I'll have to assume it's him and deal with him accordingly.'

'Annas was the one who told me. If you want to be angry at anyone, be angry at him, not Hafs. Hafs had nothing to do with it.'

Walid perceives her discomfiture and also an involuntary tic of her eyes because he motions for her to get up and jerks her pallet aside to see what she might be hiding. He notices the grated drain underneath and peers into it and speaks into it in Arabic, gauging the echo. He turns to her with a look of smug self-possession.

'Clever,' he says. 'But that's over. And now you want to know what happened to him.' It's more a

300

statement than a question.

'Yes.'

'Very well then. What you heard is true. He had an infection, gangrenous. But we didn't have to go looking for a suitable antibiotic. We had one all along, you know. Only we wanted to test his faith, this so-called conversion of his.'

'He converted ?'

'He kept that from you, did he? Ha. Yes, he'd said the Shahada. But that's easy to do, especially with one's life at stake. Don't misunderstand me — we were pleased with it, but at the same time, we had to test him. We withheld the medicine, letting him believe we were searching for it. Then one day we came to him and said, 'We found Keflex for you.' You can imagine how overjoyed he was. But in order to receive it, he'd have to prove his faithfulness.'

'How?'

'By carrying out an execution.'

'Crump.'

'Correct. If he would've gone through with it, he'd be alive right now. Unfortunately he chose the path of unbelief and death. Do you see I'm telling you the truth?'

'Yes.'

'Good. Think about what I've said. And prepare yourself; we're leaving this place soon, all of us. I'll send someone for you in about an hour. Tell me, Cassandra Wigheard. Are you ready to make the profession?'

16

Abu al-Hool: The Time of Separation

Iraq (Fallujah): 54 days after

It's been twenty-four hours since I paid a visit to the Americans, and I am still here in Fallujah, brooding over these soot-smeared windows from which I regard the city: the room I rented last night reminds me of a place where I lived while a student in Cairo, the building's fit and finish no better than a tenement's — I could've afforded something nicer, even as a student, but preferred slumming it, using the money I saved from Father's monthly checks to buy bottles of Johnnie Walker Red and as many grams of bango as I could get my hands on. My roommate named our flat the Fishbowl, a reference both to how much we drank and to the fact that at all hours of the day and night, a rotating cast of puffed-up young people congregated there to see and be seen.

Burned out, born-again, newly sober, I declared my intention to join the jihad. None of my friends could believe I'd go through with it. They thought I was being dramatic. They told me the journey to Afghanistan would be too hard.

Never was anyone more wrong. The getting in was easy. It's the getting out that kills.

The electricity cycles off, and the fan I've placed near my bedding whirs to a stop. The air in the room grows still. I heave myself into a sitting position and push the window open wide, letting in a puff of night breeze but also the smell of the dump site below. The building's superintendent apologized for the odor when he showed me the room, explaining that some of the mujahideen had taken to killing the trash-men. Just a few, but the rest quit in fear. It seems a dastardly tactic, though effective, making life as miserable as possible for the common people so they'll view the occupation as a failure.

I look out the window over the low-slung roofs of this small, simple, rustic city. The chatter of conversation rises from the street: the café on the building's first floor, one of the few businesses open on this block, is doing a brisk trade despite the dark times. The streetlights are in disrepair, and the café's proprietor has strung Chinese lanterns over his section of the sidewalk. Their bulbs, screened by rice paper, cast an orange glow like candlelight on the walls. A shepherd leads his flock down the alley. The lanterns, the livestock, the lack of cars on the road due to the American curfew, together recall olden times; the illusion is persistent but also transparent. We're not in the caliphate but crumbling modernity. A generator chugs in the alley out back, adding hints of scorched oil to the cacophony of scent: roasted coffee, the tang of sewage, baking bread, chicken turning on a spit, fat dripped into the fire, the pleasant and noxious, unfiltered and honest stuff of human life.

★ ★ ★

In the morning I awake to the sounds of turbine engines and steel track running through the sprockets of American tanks. I bolt up and check the window but my view does not allow sight of them, though, judging by the noise, they're heading west on the highway from the old cigarette factory, the base on the city's outskirts. Moments later, two attack helicopters soar overhead, and these I can see, though briefly, and they too are westbound.

This could be it, I think, filled with both dread and excitement but with slim possibility of resolution. I expect there will be no way of knowing for certain if my plan has succeeded, not until days, perhaps weeks after. And I don't wish to stay here that long.

The tanks rumble out of earshot — all these machines, a thousand tons of steel — simply to kill one man. Because, after all, there is only one of them I really want dead. The Americans have a sufficient euphemism for the rest: *collateral damage*. It's not that one intends to kill innocents but that one is aware they may die and proceeds anyway. I reproach myself for the waste in that, the cold-bloodedness of it, and if I could turn back the clock, I might well have behaved differently in Dr. Walid's room when, under the weight of the vest, I asked for my leave. Finger on the detonator, I might have gotten it over with then and there, but I was desperate and not yet ready to die. I was vain enough to want to *taste* the poison-green fruit, revenge.

I tell myself it was not all selfishness. Walid must be removed from power for other reasons. Over time a man like that will do the resistance more harm than good. But this is poor consolation: the truth is, he does not even compare with the worst of them. Even at the water plant, rumors reached us of torture houses springing up in the city, and they, we knew, were intended to accommodate Iraqi prisoners, not Americans. Abu Musab al-Zarqawi, that sheikh of the slaughterers, has wasted no time in his quest to consolidate power. His methods make Walid's seem benign, if not quaint. Jihad has changed. None of us, even the doctor, realized how much. He wanted to create a spectacle and achieved one beyond what I imagine were his wildest dreams. But in the process, he ceded — I won't call it the moral high ground, but a certain timeless astringency that's essential to keeping a movement like ours from devouring itself.

I don't know if it's possible to stop that happening. I don't know much, presently; I look in the mirror and see a stranger whose hands will soon be stained with his brothers' blood. Many of them do not deserve this. I have agonized the most over Abu Hafs: it has been like failing my son all over again. With the Valium from the bazaar I have managed to keep myself numb enough to avoid thinking too much about Hassan or the Yemeni, but when they do intrude on my thoughts, I concentrate on the differences between their situations. I can't bear to think I am repeating the same mistakes over and again, that the years have taught me nothing or, worse, that I *have* learned something vital but am unable to apply the lesson.

There are differences, I am sure. I gave my son no quarter, but to Abu Hafs I extended the olive branch. I offered the cub a way out. Only, he refused it, and for that he may perish; the girl, too — though it affords me no great pleasure, I prefer the irony of what she may receive by my doing over the straightforward horror Walid had in store for her.

But then, I may be wrong in all this. There is only one justice in this world, and it does not proceed from man. Of those who reckon lives against lives, who permit themselves to take life in the name of justice, only the fool believes he always decides rightly. I'm no fool. I'm more like the blind man who claims it's impossible for anyone to see.

★   ★   ★

I've never spoken at length about what happened with Hassan. Never told the complete story, not to a soul, not even his mother. I couldn't bring myself to tell Mariam exactly what her boy had done or why I hadn't been with him when he passed. She and I had already started to grow apart before his death, but that tragedy, and my refusal to answer her questions about it, was the final wedge to cleave us.

I can't know exactly how Hassan behaved in

his last moments, but I was told he fought bravely. He was no ordinary boy, that's for sure. The first quality many people noticed about him was his exceeding piety: he was much more pious at his age than I ever was. I'd been brought up in a household where we were permitted to watch American television shows; I loved the westerns, *Bonanza* being my favorite. Hassan, however, was raised very differently, and, unlike some of my children, he never seriously rebelled against our family's strictures. As he came of age he immersed himself in studying the Recitation. His lips were constantly, almost imperceptibly, moving in silent prayer. It was the kind of thing you might not see at first, but spend any amount of time around him, and you'd pick up on it. A teenage boy, always praying. That was how pious he was.

He'd followed me to Chechnya against his mother's wishes. There's another story in that, but I won't digress any further. Suffice to say, the campaign was his first. We were encamped within walking distance of an aul built on a forested hillside not far from the Georgian border. Down the road, barely visible on the rare day with no mist, was a Russian army position: a bunker, a few tanks, a platoon of infantry. They were regulars, not Spetsnaz, and their commander a bloated alcoholic whom I'd glassed several times.

On both national and local scales, the war was locked in an evil stasis. It'd been months since either side had engaged in a frontal assault. The odd skirmish, but no attempt to rout the other from his stronghold; a mutual, unspoken détente had set in. Several factors could explain why. The brothers were low on ammunition and men. It was nearing winter, the weather miserable for living in the field, and, more saliently, many of the Russian commanders shied away from prosecuting the war, preferring to remain in their bunkers where it was safer, and from that position of comfort to enrich themselves through extortion, wheedling, double-dealing, outright highway robbery, and all manner of schemes perpetrated on the Chechen people. It was not unheard of for Russian officers to sell the brothers arms and other military supplies on the black market, thus doing their part to prolong a war whose continuance was vital to their own economic self-interest.

Midway between our aul and their position was a small farming village of wattle huts still heated in the ancient way, by burning *kizyak*, a mixture of dried sheep dung and wheat chaff. The village was set off the road, down the side of a dell, and a traveler would always smell the *kizyak* smoke and hear the lowing of cattle before he actually saw it. Meager, pitiful, but somehow warm and homey, like something out of medieval Europe, how I imagine it must've looked — the brothers occasionally stopped there to buy fresh milk and other food. Prices were lower than in the towns. The people were honest and didn't overcharge simply because we were foreigners, many of us Arabs and therefore assumed to be rich. Things went along that way; winter set in. During an expedition to the village we became snowbound and were hosted by Aquil, a man with whom we often bargained. That night my son set his heart on one of Aquil's daughters, Ayeesha, middle child of three sisters.

From what I could tell, she lived a cloistered and virtuous life, which most likely endeared her to my son with his grave piety. The night we spent in her home, I noticed the way he admired her as she tended to the cooking while the men conducted business; that was all, just a passing moment, forgotten the next day, but some time later it came to mind, and I was only half surprised when Hassan mentioned her to me. He was tentative, stumbling in his request, but I put him at ease with my blessing.

On our next trip he worked up the courage to talk to Ayeesha's father. The old man seemed agreeable and introduced the two. Their courtship lasted several days, during which time they walked together in the afternoons, taking in the crisp mountain air under the supervision of her mother and aunts. In the end, the match was found suitable to all parties, and they were betrothed, a date set for the wedding a week later. As is the case with their burials, the marriages of mujahideen are often expedited affairs. If one should fall in battle, there's no need to wash his body; in the case of his wedding, there's no need for an overly long or formal engagement. It's understood that time is of the essence. War foreshortens human affairs. Delays, even sacred ones, are best avoided.

Even though my son was quite young to take a wife, I'd advocated for the marriage in no small degree because I'd thought it would provide a pacifying influence. To my knowledge, his piety had extended to chastity, and secretly I hoped his burgeoning romantic interest might displace the jihad once and for all. Part of me was proud he'd insisted on coming, but another part would be glad to see him gone. It wasn't that I believed the cause unworthy or martyrdom hollow and ignoble — very much the opposite — but there are human impulses more basic than the religious ones, the same self-serving impulses that martyrdom seeks to overcome, and the simple fact was that, as a father, I wanted to see Hassan choose life over death. The reverse would be mournful indeed.

However, my thoughts on his marriage were all wrong. Rather than drawing him out of the war, becoming a husband invested him more fully in it. Now he had Chechen in-laws.

★   ★   ★

That winter, I was called away from the aul by Emir Khattab, who was then at the head of all the brothers in the Caucasus. Khattab summoned me to a *shura* of field commanders from around the country. A council of this magnitude was unusual and seemed to forebode momentous events. I said as much to the brothers before I set out for the *shura*, to be held deep in the mountains.

'Dr. Walid will act as emir while I'm away. It'll only be a few days, but let's see if we can't finish shoring up the tunnel in the meantime. One more thing. Under no circumstances are any of you to provoke the Russians. That's straight from the council. No offensive operations until further notice. Big plans are in the works. We don't want to muck them up.'

The brothers told me not to worry and wished me well. My son especially was in high spirits. Since marrying Ayeesha he'd blossomed rapidly into manhood; seldom had I seen him happier or more confident. Why God so often chooses to lay low the high and pure and noble while allowing the basest iniquities to go unpunished, I couldn't tell you. In my absence at the *shura*, something terrible happened. Three Russian soldiers, drunk to wickedness on vodka, left their post and went on a spree. Like us, they knew about the village in the dell, and their eyes, like my son's, had been snared by Aquil's daughters. They arrived at their farm and as a pretense asked to buy some food. When they were rebuffed, they drove their UAZ through a neighboring pasture, tearing up the field and machine-gunning the better part of Aquil's herd. This was a man who'd never opened a bank account, who dealt rarely with paper money but who was considered rich by the standards of his place and time. That day, in one fell swoop, he lost most of a great fortune.

Ignorant of all this, I was making the return trip from the *shura*. The day was clear and cold. I drove the mountain road in an old panel van, creaking and swaying unnervingly on the curves. Emir Khattab's news hadn't been good: at any moment, the Russians were expected to unleash a major offensive to retake Grozny. Despite it, I was in a fine mood. I'd made good time and expected to rejoin my men sooner than I'd thought.

On the winding road to the aul I was met with a gruesome sight. I drove closer, and my hopes were dashed that it was some kind of prank, the work of local boys, a scarecrow emplaced to startle passing motorists. I stopped the van and got out. By the side of the road hung a corpse, Russian, by the look of his bright-blond hair and blue eyes. He had been crucified on the sagging lower boughs of a pine. A crude sign hammered to the tree read, *The fate of all criminals and invaders*.

The sign was written in Arabic, and immediately I suspected the brothers had done this. Rage took me; they'd violated my order to lie low while I was away. I cut down the body and dragged it into the forest so it was no longer visible from the road, where the van was still idling, the driver's door hanging open. I climbed back in and hurried on to the aul. For the first time, the thought entered my mind that my son could've had a part in this.

★   ★   ★

Dr. Walid and I hoisted our rucks and hiked into the forest, the light falling through the pines, our breath crystallizing in the freezing air, little clouds of it hanging over the steep rocky trail as we passed. Even with the weather, after a few kilometers I worked up enough body heat to make my field jacket uncomfortably warm, and we stopped so that I could take it off. We'd climbed above tree line and were nearing a pass. The brothers had fled the aul, fearing reprisal, relocating camp to the cut on the other side. Dr. Walid was leading me there.

I was still reeling from the news he'd delivered: seeing what the Russians had done to Aquil's cattle, my son had conspired with his father-in-law and some of the other villagers to take revenge. Under Hassan's direction, they'd set an ambush on the road, killing five and taking one prisoner, the man I'd found crucified. For a ragtag force, it was a spectacular victory. It was also an act of insubordination in direct defiance of my authority, and my emotions, normally so controlled, now oscillated wildly between grief, disbelief, and anger. I felt light-headed, my skin clammy, as if I'd been struck with a bout of mountain sickness.

We arrived in camp, and no one was pleased to see me. The men were right to be afraid of how I'd react. Before even dropping my gear, I ordered them assembled, questioning them, and specifically Hassan, to learn the particulars of his outrage.

'I didn't do it as your soldier,' he said, making no effort to deny responsibility. 'This was a family matter. It's between me, Aquil, and the Russian.'

'You may be married to a Chechen, but you're here as a mujahid. You don't get to pick and choose when you belong to this brotherhood. If you want to be a farmer, go farm.'

'Those farmers and I killed six of the dogs without taking one casualty. Can you say that about any attack you've led?'

He had never spoken so harshly to me in his entire life. It took a moment for me to regain my composure. 'You were given a clear order. You chose to disobey it. There are consequences for that.'

'You should be celebrating my victory. I think you enjoy shaming me like this. You know what I think? I think, Father, you're jealous of your own son.'

'Today, you're not even my son. Today you're a scoundrel and a scapegrace.' Even then it occurred to me to wonder if he was right, not that I envied him — it wasn't that simple — but maybe I was being too harsh with the boy precisely because he was my flesh and blood. Sometimes we hold our families too highly and are therefore more disappointed than we should be when they reveal themselves as only human. I should've listened to this voice of mercy but believed it was more important to demonstrate my impartial adherence to the law. As emir I'd punish any of my men who went against my orders, including my own firstborn. For me to do otherwise would be disqualifying.

Hassan and I faced off. The men lingered at the margins, no one speaking, watching us in the embarrassed yet enthralled way of those who unexpectedly find themselves spectators to what should be an intimate confrontation. I thought to dismiss them and continue with Hassan in private, but that would have only undercut my

314

authority further, making it seem like I was trying to downgrade a soldier's mutiny into a domestic squabble.

Seeing things escalating, Walid stepped forward to placate me. Perhaps he worried that I would blame him, the one who'd been placed in command during my absence, for the lapse in discipline. Perhaps his motives were more sinister and shrewd, and he knew patronizing me in that moment would tip the scales.

'My emir, you're exhausted from the trip. Maybe you should — '

'No,' I said calmly, not looking at him, still focused on my son's defiant face. 'I am not tired at all. What I am is disgusted. He admitted he disobeyed me. You all heard it, and you can see he shows no remorse. So, here is my judgment. He will no longer serve me as a mujahid. You are banished, boy: leave Chechnya and return to your mother. In time I might reconsider and send for you, but only if I feel you've truly repented and made great strides to purify your heart. Until then, be gone.'

'You can send me away,' he said. 'But I won't go home. My place is here at the front, fighting to protect these people. I'll show you I'm no boy. You'll see what kind of a man I am.'

We said no farewells. He made quick work to tear down his tent, pack his gear, and set off down the trail. As he hiked up to the ridge, I'd already begun to reconsider, hoping he might turn back and throw himself on my mercy. I might've let him stay if he'd begged, but neither did I call out and plead with him not to go, to

315

tell him I'd spoken too severely, both of us prideful beyond repair. I thought of my own father and how we'd parted with cross words. Before I left the second time for Afghanistan, he told me I was wasting my life, and in turn I told him he was a corrupt money-grubber who never cared about anything enough to fight for it.

The trouble with angry words is you never know if they'll be your last. Hassan disappeared from view in the upper forest, and I saw him no more. He was killed a week later in the Siege of Grozny; I'm told it was defending a trench outside the city. Those who were with him near the end say he never thought to retreat or surrender, even when it was very clear the battle was hopeless. They say his dying words were the Shahada. I tell myself he's the lucky one, resting beneath that ice-hard field. I never found the exact spot where they buried him, though I heard generally where he fell and how he fought when the Spetsnaz broke through the rebel lines. You were a lion, my son, who teaches me every day how to die.

★　★　★

In the late afternoon there is a knock on my door, which alarms me until I remember I am in fact expecting someone, the errand boy who helped me the other day in the bazaar. He arrives carrying a heavy-looking duffel bag.

'Sorry it took longer than I told you,' he says after I let him in. 'I didn't forget.'

'I didn't think you had. Here, one moment.'

316

Leaning on a crutch, I go to retrieve what I owe him while he lays out the contents of his bag: a Kalashnikov, seven magazines with ammunition, four hand grenades, and a chest rig to carry it all.

'Bulgarian,' he says, passing me the rifle and pointing out the manufacturer's stamp. 'My guy says they're rare to find but much better than the Iraqi knockoffs, or even the Chinese-made.'

'I'm grateful for it.' I inspect the weapon, then set it down. I hand over the satchel containing the four thousand dollars I stole from Walid less what I've paid for the room and other short-term expenses. 'The other half of what I owe you, plus gratuity. I'd offer some chai, but my kerosene tank is empty, and there're none to be had anywhere, for any price.'

The boy opens the satchel and is astonished. He looks at me in disbelief. 'This is much more than we agreed on.'

'Yes,' I say, trying to sound lighthearted. 'Very much more. Take it, I insist. Go get your mother and leave this place. Start again somewhere else.'

He smiles skeptically, as if there must be some catch. But I offer none, only forbidding silence, and his smile slowly fades to a look of concern.

'What are you going to do?'

I say nothing; the armament he has laid out before me is answer enough.

'But why?' he asks. 'You can hardly even walk.'

'Hardly is good enough.'

'*Sayyidi*, with respect, I don't understand. This isn't your town. It's not even your country. Look around you — there's nothing left to fight for. Come on, I can show you a road out of here that the Americans don't watch. Come with me.'

'You're striking cold iron,' I say. 'My mind is made up. Here, there, it doesn't matter. I'm not fighting for a place. Not the way you mean. Not money, power, or anything of this earth. I do it only for God.'

As I speak these words it's like another person is speaking through me, like I'm reciting a creed that I've uttered many times, but until this moment the words have been just that, an idea espoused but fallen short of embodiment. Only now do I know it as my life's truth.

The errand boy looks uncomfortable. He is obviously not a person who believes in the unseen, in making dramatic last stands, or in redeeming oneself in the eyes of the dead. I know he thinks the living matter infinitely more, that only a fanatic would squander his life like this.

'For God, then,' he says, clutching the satchel, looking at the door as if already to make his escape.

* * *

I limp around the room lighting candles so that I can see to prepare my kit. The Kalashnikov, the grenades, the vest. Soon I'll go on and join the caravan: Field Commander Jawad, Emir Khattab, my son — my dear Hassan — and all the others too numerous to name who've meant something to me in this life, who've taught me the vital lessons, who've walked beside me on this path.

How strange to think it ends here. I'd never even heard of Fallujah until I was well into my twenties and I met a mujahid in Peshawar who claimed it as his hometown. Iraq was not then a country I thought of much. As a young man, Afghanistan and the Caucasus were the places that commanded my imagination more. How guarded are our fates, how unknown, and strange.

Even now I hear the night's fighting beginning. An explosion, a few heartbeats of silence, then the gunfire like clipped shouting across the alleyways. However feebly, I'm ready to go into the streets and take part. I've lived past my time and put this off much too long — long enough to know the hardest fight is the fight against your own anger. Compared with that, this will be easy. This I'll do without anger. I'll do it with something like longing in my heart.

17

Cassandra: Mother of Ammara

Iraq (undisclosed): 55 days after

Climbing into the scuffed metal bed of the pickup, Cassandra felt sure she was about to die. With each passing minute that she hasn't, the panic dissipates a little more, the brain unwilling to allow itself to persist too long in that level of distress. They're under way on a canal road graded like a rail line above the surrounding fields, the clouds huge, silvery and oppressive; crushed by the weight of sky, her lungs feel constricted, though no bindings shackle her in the truck bed, very exposed; they're the tallest thing around except for a frizzy line of palms on the horizon toward which they travel. The road wind keeps blowing the abaya into her face, ruining the shot. Walid is annoyed.

'Again,' he says, hunched against the tailgate near Hafs, who's filming her with the handheld. She balances herself as they lurch over ruts in the road, readjusting her shoulders against the rear window to hold down the abaya, starting from the beginning.

'*Bismillah ir rahman ir rahim* . . . '

In the name of God, most compassionate, most merciful . . . She's said the line enough times in the last few minutes, it begins to work. The calming force of repetition — passing time, this is just a moment in time and it will pass, things will be different — and it's true she's not quite so agoraphobic as she first was when they brought her out of the cell, upstairs, outside, into the light — intolerable — the guards loading gear into the trucks, packing everything up. Momentous change before her eyes, the lack of a blindfold — that they're letting her see this — alarming her even more, none of the guards seeming excited to leave, grim faces and a feeling of desperation in the air. She stayed close to Hafs and listened in to every conversation she could, overhearing 'Hool' said a few times in scorn, not knowing what to make of it. Walid was everywhere at once, a manic edge to the way he checked on the preparations and exhorted the men to work faster.

'What's he saying?' she whispered to Hafs. 'Tell me the truth — I don't care how bad it is.'

'He is talking about the sword. The sword will not stop killing the heads of these — I do not know the English for this. People who say bad words for God.'

'Blasphemers?'

'Yes, I think.'

When the guards finished loading the trucks, they mounted up, and she with them. Just before she climbed into the bed, Walid brought her a bulletproof vest similar to those worn by several of the men. She inspected it in a soldierly way, feeling the ballistic panels; it was Vietnam-era U.S. surplus — fucking go figure.

'Am I actually going to need this?' she asked.
'Put it on.'

In a convoy of six trucks they drove down the canal road through an inundated rice field. As her prison receded from view she realized she was terrified to leave it. The presence of the camera and the vest are now the only clues as to what's about to happen. Better the devil you know.

They hit pavement, the highway, but follow it only briefly. The truck she and Walid are riding in slows, pulling onto the shoulder. The other five trucks keep on the highway while hers turns off, following a hard-pack trail along another canal.

This separation, the lone truck, seems to have been prearranged. Part of Walid's plan, whatever it is. The camera trained on her is worse than a gun to the head.

★   ★   ★

Hafs keeps the tape rolling. She tries the Basmala another time, gets it right, and without her abaya blowing around to obscure her face. Walid approves. She moves on to the next part of his statement. This is in English. Much easier to speak. Harder to say. He tells her to do it louder, over the engine noise.

'I'm Umm Ammara. Today I join the fight against the American occupiers of this country.'

A psychologist would call her affect flat. Acceptable to Walid and at the same time it might convey to the people she cares about that this person speaking isn't really her. That she's left already. As if there were any doubt about that, or her terror, which she suppresses in her voice as best as she can.

You are still alive.

They pass through a date-palm grove and come upon more rice fields, these fallow a long time. Beyond is no discernible attempt at cultivation, only a shaggy overgrowth of trees and brush, and the rich, earthy smell of a river that can't be far. Headed lower, through marsh in some places, the truck eases over a muddy track. Before long they come to a stand of cypress that enfolds them under a tight canopy. Drooping feathered boughs lay tiger-stripe patterns of light and dark on the road, such as it is, which ends here. The driver — the guard who refused to talk to her in the shed — parks the truck and kills the engine.

'Don't try,' Walid says. 'Running would be pointless, and we didn't come here to hurt you.'

This does nothing to alleviate her fears; she doesn't believe him for a minute. 'Then what are we doing here?'

'You'll see soon.'

They clamber down from the bed, and Cassandra and the others follow Walid as he moves out on foot. No one speaks. The driver walks behind her, rear security, last in the column. They are going to cut off my head, she thinks. Something has gone wrong, and they've had to leave the prison and get rid of me on the way, and they are going to grab me from behind and cut off my head. Her legs feel wooden and unstable as she trudges through the stand of cypress, surrounded by low ground like a natural moat on three sides. The way Walid is leading them, they have to cross the marsh at a narrow but deep point, clinging to stands of reeds; once, she makes a wrong step and goes in the water hip-deep, the abaya heavy and clinging as Hafs extends a hand to pull her up.

They make the far side and slightly higher ground. She wrings out the hem of the abaya while the others wait, and Hafs goes up ahead so that he can film them, an establishing shot as they walk toward him in single file, beating a path through a bright-green field of rye. Walid takes them into some scraggly cedar along the edge of the field. He studies the terrain to get his bearings, then heads deeper into the scrub. At the base of one of the trees he finds what he's looking for: an ammo cache, a large metal chest half-buried, covered in camo netting and dropped cedar needles, which he sweeps away with his hands. He opens the chest, assesses its contents, then nods at the European guard, who in a feat of strength lifts out an 82-millimeter mortar tube, shouldering it across his back like a steel yoke.

'Umm Ammara,' Walid says, hefting a rucksack from the chest and offering it to her. 'You'll carry this.'

He renamed her in the statement to memorize that morning. Printed on card stock, like the others. When they took her out of the cell and she saw Hafs with the camera, it was like hearing the first words of a death sentence. The only thing missing was the knife, which she's been waiting for ever since. But with this mortar cache, it seems like the statement — *Today, I join the fight* — was literally true. Walid wants to film her attacking her own people.

★ ★ ★

She worries the shoulder straps on the rucksack as they march back into the rye field. Fifty meters from the tree line, Walid tells them to stop. On a patch of flat ground the European guard heaves the mortar tube off his shoulder and begins to emplace it, unfolding the bipod and staking out the baseplate for support. He fiddles with the locking sleeves, getting the alignment just right. Cassandra squats in the grass, up past her knees, watching him work, thinking for a moment about that night at the traffic circle, coming under fire, maybe from this exact same weapon. Two months ago, maybe not even that long. Back then, she would've fought to the death. Almost did. No matter what happens she'll never be that person again. She remembers how strange it felt: someone she'd never even seen was actually trying to kill her. Nothing about that situation seems strange anymore. It was just one particular kind of murder, and she's become conversant with many others.

You better focus, she tells herself, use your head; what do you know about that thing? She guesses at the mortar's maximum range. Can't be more than four or five klicks. Which means a friendly position is close. She even knows the exact direction to run in order to find it. The same direction the weapon is pointed: there lies safety. They'd shoot you in the back if you tried. Maybe that'd be better.

But you're not there yet. Slow down, think this through. Something about it feels wrong. Why would they be out here, just the four of them, if they were about to attack an American position? Walid would expect a counterattack, and they're not equipped to deal with one. Doesn't make sense.

Unless, she thinks, he's not expecting a counterattack. Because the whole performance is a sham and they're not about to launch mortars at anyone. She'd never be the wiser; shooting at nothing, sending a few rounds harmlessly into the swamp, would make a lot more sense than an actual engagement. Same reward for them — they get their video — at much less risk. That's got to be it. This is all for show. Which means she can go through with it. There are limits, but this can be forgiven. It can't be real.

When beckoned, she brings forward the rucksack. It contains mortar rounds, dense and substantial, rolling against one another like canned goods.

'You'll be the gunner,' Walid says. 'Do you know how to work it?'

'No.'

'See this switch?'

'Yes.'

'This means it's set to Drop Fire. Here. Kneel on this side. I'll be like this. I'll say the *takbir*, then you. Then I pass you the rounds. Don't let any part of your body hang over the tube, drop the round in, then get low. Watch yourself; it'll be much more than a rifle. Abu Hafs, set up over there. We'll rehearse it once before we fire.'

★ ★ ★

Round in hand she kneels, hesitating a moment before proclaiming the *takbir* herself: *God is greater*. She feeds the mortar into the tube with a dead-limbed trembling clumsiness and lets go, dropping — it's beyond her control now, a concussion like a gut punch juddering everything.

'Another!' Walid says, passing her a round. '*Allahu akbar!*'

'Wait, wait! I hit the button!' Hafs cries.

They look to him, fiddling with the camera. A distant explosion. *Thump*. Goddamn, I hope no one's downrange. She's holding the round just handed to her by Walid, who curses and jogs over to confer with Hafs, the two of them huddling to watch what they've gotten on the LCD, and she can't hear exactly what they're saying, but Walid appears to calm down. Hafs gets set to film again. The driver lurks cagily a ways off, near the tree line, alert, scanning the sky, interested only in tactical soundness, not the theater of terror. Alone near the mortar she's separated from the others by twenty yards or more when from the direction of the canal road there's a faint rumbling like a distant freight train approaching. She knows that sound. Tanks on the move, and fast. The others have also heard it, eyes on the horizon — for a moment, nothing, then a dust cloud rising in the east.

'Down!' Walid orders. He's already on his belly in the tall grass. Hafs is, too. The other guard is nowhere to be seen, having disappeared into the scrub at the first sign of trouble.

'Get down!' Walid barks at her again. 'Push over the tube!'

The hot tube standing upright in the grass, muzzle poking a foot or two over the tops of the seed heads, is a glaring target that she's still kneeling by. The dust cloud in the east has become two tanks emerging on the high ground on the other side of the swamp. A momentary rush of hope — the impossible, a rescue; the tanks roll to a stop, maybe a klick away, their turrets moving robotically, scanning for the enemy. Their gun tubes are pointing in the wrong direction, as if they've been clued in to the mortar shot, the general area, a grid square, but don't know exactly where it came from.

Then it hits her. Why tanks, why here, now. No matter how much she wants it to be otherwise, she knows she's right. The setup is totally wrong for a rescue. It would be SEALs fast-roping from Black Hawks in the middle of the night, not tanks in this field, and especially not moments after they've fired a mortar. These tanks aren't hunting for her. They're out hunting, period. Her bad luck to be in the way.

'Push it over right now or I'll kill you!'

The tanks still haven't seen them. You are still alive. She looks at the mortar round in her hand and knows what she has to do next, suddenly remembering a piece of knowledge from basic: run unpredictable zigzags if you have to cross open ground with someone shooting at you — One, two, three, ready, rush. She drops the round down the tube and without even waiting for the concussion takes off at a sprint through the field, the brush catching in her robes as she ducks low to avoid the hell she is deliberately calling down on them. A burst of machine gun fire snaps overhead like five whips cracking in rapid consecution, missing by what sounds like inches. With no idea who just took a shot at her — Walid, the tanks, both — she bears down through the scrub and can hear the armor maneuvering again in the distance and now something new from the air, approaching rotor noise, birds flying low, fast, just above the power lines, but she knows better than to believe they're coming to save her.

They crest the horizon, two Apache attack helicopters. She unhoods the abaya and stands and waves her arms in big arcs so they'll be sure to see her. It's the best she can do. You can't surrender to a helicopter. These flyboys won't notice her dirty, blond hair, won't register the lightness of her skin. To them she's just another green humanoid blob in their infrared vision, a hajji running panicked from a hot mortar tube, a black widow out with the boys, dead meat in their reticle. A kilometer. Half a kilometer. Approaching that fast. The lead helicopter opens up with its chain gun, a hammering roar like it's tearing the fabric of the sky itself, high-explosive rounds strafing the field, the area around the mortar, continuing into the scrub, missing her but not by enough, and she's down from the blast, the now-familiar burn of shrapnel.

She rolls onto her elbows, knees, frantically stripping off the vest and then the abaya like they're soaked in boiling oil. Still with the simple long dress on underneath, her sandals lost after the chain gun salvo, feet and legs filthy, cut up from the brush. Sweating, heart racing like she's just run miles. Tunnel vision. The world through a keyhole slot. She searches for the Apaches and finds them circling the horizon, rotors a blur nearly perpendicular, banking hard, coming around for another pass, their sleek wasplike underbellies and electronic noses aslant, racks of Hellfire missiles hanging on their wings, and she lurches to her feet and sets off at a fast limp deeper into the scrub toward another stand of cypress, the best cover around. Her only hope is to make those trees, find someplace to hide until she can get close enough to a friendly for them to recognize her.

'Cassandra! Cassandra!'

It's Hafs. He's calling to her loudly but not aggressively. She turns and sees him closing on her through the brush. But she's not going anywhere with him or any of the others, not anymore. The rotor noise changes in tone.

Death is always right around the corner.

Not many people get to choose how.

She braces to take him down. He's surprised by the reaction; they clinch, pummeling, fighting over his rifle. He's strong but an inch shorter, a few pounds lighter, and, along with the element

330

of surprise, all the pacing and push-ups alone in the dark are rewarded; she frees an arm and throws an elbow into his face; he staggers, bleeding; she takes hold of his rifle and jerks it free from his grip, screaming a great war cry, pointing it center mass as he turns to her, reeling, just now realizing she's about to shoot him, the helicopters racing over the trees, and there appears before them a bright-orange light like a second sun.

★ ★ ★

She's down, this time for good. Superpressurized air, rounds whipping overhead, the iron tang of gore in her sinuses, some invisible force tearing through her hand like a claw-foot hammer; this new and sharp, spreading, *thwacking* pain setting her into reflexive motion, she drags herself by the elbows, pushing with toes and knees toward Hafs until she makes it alongside him.

He's losing his breath, arching his back in the grass. She reaches out to touch him, and he becomes aware of her presence. She says she's sorry. Can't catch her breath, and it comes out a whisper, her last words. Sorry for what, no telling. The fact they both have to die like this.

He looks at her with no recognition at all before turning his gaze away. Hands wet with her own blood; getting harder to see; not that the light has changed but she's sinking farther behind her eyes, the ringing in her ears — *wah, wah, wah* — like the feeling after a euphoric dose of nitrous.

Human touch persists longer than any other sense, but consciousness exceeds even that. Something smells fresh and good, like a lemon just after you cut it. Hafs has changed under her touch, diaphragm no longer rising. *Peace* is the wrong word. *Stillness* is best. *You are still alive.*

She slips deeper into a barely describable state. Time slows as her facility to perceive it diminishes, like this will last forever, the nature of those last few moments stretching slower and slower, approaching eternity but never quite reaching it because eternity exists only in relation to its inconceivability, covering half the distance to it, then half that distance, halve a half, quarter a millisecond, shaving time infinitesimally thin, like slivers off a yardstick that is your remaining life. You never really reach the moment. That's the truth. You just get closer until.

18

Sleed: Spoil

The mission was on a tip from a farmer. Bunch of us, on the ground and in the air, heading to this old water treatment plant when a drone that was spotting for us caught the heat signature from a mortar. We took a detour and let them have it. When there was no more movement in the thermals, we fanned out to search for bodies, leaving a guard on the tanks because it was too wet to drive them any closer to the river without getting mired. We crossed a ditch where black mud pulled at our boots, into a field of tall green grass, where we found a blood trail that led the rest of the way. It was a woman. That was the first thing wrong. They had to use DNA to make the ID for sure, but Blornsbaum was the one to notice the hair. Hard to see with all the dust and blood, but there it was, strands of blond in the field. That was when we knew. She was lying right next to this teenager, like side to side, one facing the other. We found a Yemeni passport on him and a camera back in the grass. I picked it up. It was still recording.

Acknowledgements

To family, above all. To the teachers who encouraged efforts toward this book: Speer Morgan, Michael Adams, Steven Harrigan, Anthony Giardina, Trudy Lewis, Peter LaSalle, Jim Magnuson, Nathan Oates, and Marly Swick. To Marcy Nicklas, for believing I was a writer, early on. To Philipp Meyer, big-hearted champion. To the Michener Center, one of the best things I ever stumbled into. To Ben Falby, Kevin Powers, Claudia Ballard, Phil Klay, Aaron Gwyn, Julia Delacroix, Alexandra Becker, Ben Roberts, Matthew and Melissa Stuart, Lucas Kline, and Brian Hockin, for taking the time over the years to read and comment on my attempts at novels.

To Peter Straus, Laurence Laluyaux, Stephen Edwards, Matthew Turner, Tristan Kendrick, Zoë Nelson, and Katharina Volckmer at Rogers, Coleridge & White; to Lee Boudreaux and Carina Guiterman at Lee Boudreaux Books, and their colleagues Terry Adams, Sabrina Callahan, Nicole Dewey, Michael Noon, and Craig Young at Little, Brown; to Michal Shavit, Ana Fletcher, Clare Bullock, and Aidan O'Neill at Jonathan Cape; to Olivier Cohen at L'Olivier; to Marcus Gärtner at Rowohlt; to Luigi Brioschi at Guanda; to Jessica Nash at Atlas Contact; and to everyone else who believed in this book and worked on its behalf, I owe a debt of gratitude.

Additionally, I would like to thank the

following authors and film-makers, and to recommend their works that I drew on while composing this story:

Ingrid Betancourt, *Even Silence Has an End*; Lisa Bowden & Shannon Cain, editors of *Powder*, Rick Bragg, *I Am a Soldier, Too*; Aukai Collins, *My Jihad*; Kirby Dick, *The Invisible War*; Dexter Filkins, *The Forever War*; Jim Frederick, *Black Hearts*; Mike German, *Thinking Like a Terrorist*; Roy Hallums, *Buried Alive*; Sebastian Junger, War; Brian Keenan, *An Evil Cradling*; Sara Corbett and Amanda Lindhout, *A House in the Sky*; Hussein Maxos, *The Arabic Idioms*; Loretta Napoleoni, *Insurgent Iraq*; Omar Nasiri, *Inside the Jihad*; Riverbend, *Baghdad Burning*; Meg McLagan and Daria Sommers, *Lioness*; Helen Thorpe, *Soldier Girls*; Brian Turner, Patrick Hicks, 'A Conversation with Brian Turner', *The Missouri Review*; Jere Van Dyk, *Captive*; Terry Waite, *Taken on Trust*; and Lawrence Wright, *The Looming Tower*.

To the dead, and to those people of all nations whose lives have been diminished by war. You are not forgotten.

BVR

We do hope that you have enjoyed reading this large print book.

Did you know that all of our titles are available for purchase?

We publish a wide range of high quality large print books including:
Romances, Mysteries, Classics
General Fiction
Non Fiction and Westerns

Special interest titles available in large print are:
The Little Oxford Dictionary
Music Book
Song Book
Hymn Book
Service Book

Also available from us courtesy of Oxford University Press:
Young Readers' Dictionary
(large print edition)
Young Readers' Thesaurus
(large print edition)

For further information or a free brochure, please contact us at:
Ulverscroft Large Print Books Ltd.,
The Green, Bradgate Road, Anstey,
Leicester, LE7 7FU, England.
Tel: (00 44) 0116 236 4325
Fax: (00 44) 0116 234 0205